Cruel Scars

JANE BLYTHE

Acknowledgments

I'd like to thank everyone who played a part in bringing this story to life. Particularly my mom who is always there to share her thoughts and opinions with me. My wonderful cover designer Letitia who did an amazing job with this stunning cover. My fabulous editor Lisa for all the hard work she puts into polishing my work. My awesome team, Sophie, Robyn, and Clayr, without your help I'd never be able to run my street team. And my fantastic street team members who help share my books with every share, comment, and like!

And of course a big thank you to all of you, my readers! Without you I wouldn't be living my dreams of sharing the stories in my head with the world!

CHAPTER

One

This had better work.

Patrick "Trick" Kramer was tired of watching his family fall apart.

Enough was enough.

It was time to end this once and for all.

He just prayed that whatever they found here in this tiny town in the middle of Nebraska gave them the answers they so desperately needed.

Trick had never been in a cornfield before. He'd grown up in Los Angeles in a middle-class family in the middle of the city. His dad walked out on them when he was a toddler, but he'd lived with his mom, an accountant, and his stepdad, the chief financial officer for a large company. They were definitely not the kind of family to go off camping, let alone to a middle-of-nowhere farm. Still, he'd seen enough horror movies to know nothing good ever came from slinking through a cornfield in the middle of the night.

Even with the snow and the brown stalks of corn, not quite as tall as they would be at the peak of their growing season, it was creepy enough.

Maybe it was the remoteness.

They were miles from the nearest town, and that town consisted only of a small street of shops and a couple of dozen houses. The rest of the area was rural, consisting of several farms. Not the kind of farms that fed thousands but the kind of small farms that were mostly just a small holding to take care of the owners.

He and his team moved quietly as they approached the little farmhouse. It was in excellent condition, looked like it had recently been given a fresh coat of paint, and stood out in the bright winter night, a crisp white with red trim. The barn sitting just a little way off to the left of it was painted the opposite, red with white trim, and similarly looked like it had recently been repainted.

A couple of vehicles and a tractor stood off to the right of the farmhouse, and an old, rusted swing set was in the backyard. Someone had started building a treehouse in a huge oak tree behind the house at some point, but it looked like they had either stopped partway through or had fallen apart, some of the wood taken and used elsewhere.

While the buildings were all in great condition, the fence surrounding this part of the farm was dilapidated, broken almost to the point of being unable to be repaired in places. The wooden gate at the end of the driveway sat open, and a few letters had fallen out of the letterbox, strewn around on the cold, wet, soggy ground.

While some of the snow had started to get mushy, it didn't look like anyone had walked outside the house and through it since the last snowfall, which according to the intel they had gathered before coming out here, was over a week ago.

Not good news.

Not for him and the rest of Bravo Team, and not for whoever lived there.

The house's inhabitant was supposed to be a woman they had rescued in their last mission on Delta Force before they joined Prey Security. A mission that had gotten so far out of control that they had all been forced to leave their careers behind after targets were painted on all of their backs because they'd gotten too close to bringing down a notorious human trafficker.

Leonid Baranov was more monster than man. A Russian oligarch who used his money to purchase mostly women, but some men as well, and keep them in one of his houses of horrors, torturing them in unimaginable ways.

Only four victims had ever survived their ordeals with Baranov. A man who had escaped on his own, dedicated his life to bringing down the monster. Six months ago, the man had reached out and had set up a meeting with them, but by the time they showed up at the place, he had been tortured and murdered. The other three survivors were all females and had been rescued by him and his team five years ago. One had committed suicide not long after being reunited with her family, one had been given a new identity and disappeared, and the third had wound up marrying Axel "Axe" Lindon, a member of Trick's team.

They all loved Beth like a little sister, and the woman's story was something out of a nightmare. She had never known a normal life, yet against all the odds, she had bonded with him and his team, Axe in particular. The two were married now, and when Beth disappeared around eighteen months ago, it had almost destroyed Axe. Then to get her back only for her to have no memory of him was the worst blow possible.

There wasn't anything any one of the men on Bravo Team wouldn't do to get answers for Axe and Beth. They were family, and they all hated seeing how hard it was for Axe to have his wife back and yet have a vast chasm between them he couldn't seem to cross no matter how hard he tried.

Answers were why they were here.

With Beth abducted and the only surviving male victim tortured and murdered, they had to believe that Baranov had decided to clean house, take out the surviving victims, then possibly come after Bravo Team as well. Just because they worked for the world-renowned Prey Security now and not as part of Delta Force, they were still a team, and they were a more formidable opponent with the money and power of Prey behind them.

So they *would* get the answers they sought.

And they *would* take down Leonid Baranov.

There was no way the man was getting his hands on Beth again, and if they could save Sarah Sanders as well, they would.

"No movement on the west side," Gabriel "Tank" Dawson's voice came through the comms.

"None on the east side either," Sebastian "Rock" Rockman added.

"Let's move in," Axe commanded. Although he had been their team leader when they were on Delta, and when they had joined Prey as Bravo Team, Axe had stepped down when Beth went missing over a year ago. Even after she was back, he'd allowed Tank to lead the team, wanting to be there for Beth, but the bigger the distance between the two had grown the more Axe had returned to the team.

Like the well-oiled machine they were, having been together for a decade, they moved in on the farmhouse. It was two stories tall, with dormer windows in the attic, meaning there was at least one room on the third floor, and given this was a farm property there was probably a basement as well. Four levels to clear, and Trick didn't have a good feeling about what they were going to find inside.

Even though they were converging on the house from different sides, he could feel the tension in the air. Seemed like he wasn't the only one who felt like something was wrong.

It was the snow.

It was too clean, too undisturbed.

Who lived on a farm but didn't go outside in over a week?

No one.

Didn't have to be a farm boy to know that.

Animals needed tending even if you were sick, so there was no way Sarah—now known as Adele MacDonald—would stay inside her house for so many days in a row.

Unless she didn't have a choice.

Three doors were visible as they approached, and they quickly paired off into teams. Axe and Mason "Scorpion" Markson took the front door, Tank and Rock took the basement door, and he went with Rafe "Panther" Neal through the back door.

It was unlocked, but he was pretty sure people in the country were known for leaving their doors unlocked, part of that whole community aspect that made people feel safe. With Panther at his back and his weapon in his hands, he stepped into the kitchen.

Immediately he smelled it.

Blood.

The coppery scent was strong, and he knew whoever the blood belonged to had lost too much to have survived their injuries.

Guess that explained why no one had been outside the house in days.

Even though he was sure whoever had committed the murder was long since gone, they still needed to clear the house. Room to room they went, clearing the kitchen, the dining room, a living room, den, four upstairs bedrooms, two bathrooms, a large, airy attic, and the basement before he and the rest of his teammates met back up in the kitchen.

"No body," he said, stating the obvious as was his way.

"It has to be Sarah's blood," Axe said.

"Agreed. Who else could it belong to?" Tank asked the rhetorical question.

Because he enjoyed puzzles, games, and tricks, he couldn't help but think there was indeed another answer to that question. "Guess Sarah could have killed whoever came after her."

"Wouldn't she contact someone if that had happened?" Rock asked.

Trick shrugged. "If she was scared and didn't know who to trust, maybe she thought it was a better idea just to run. If Baranov did get to her and had her killed, why wouldn't they leave the body behind? Not like they're trying to hide evidence of a crime, look at all the blood." It was smeared all over the kitchen floor and splattered on the walls and furniture, even some on the ceiling. "Sooner or later, someone would have reported Adele MacDonald as missing and come looking for her. When they found all this blood, guaranteed they'd call the cops. If they took the body, it would have made sense to clean up the blood as well. Unless."

"Unless what?" Panther asked.

"Unless they wanted *us* to find the crime scene. What are the chances that we find the male victim just after he's been murdered then we finally get a lead on Sarah's new identity only to find a pool of blood instead of the woman herself? It feels like someone is toying with us."

~

January 20th
    12:40 P.M.

Sun, sand, warmth, clear blue skies, and the soft crashing of the waves against the shore. Could life get any better?

Stephanie Fuller thought not.

This vacation had been a long time coming and was absolutely needed. It had been a really rough year. Her brother, who served in the military, had been killed in action, then her mom had died of a broken heart just a couple of months later. Since her dad split when she and her brother were little, no one could help her carry the load.

It was just her.

Alone.

Grieving and trying to deal with all the stuff that went with death. Life insurance policies, funerals, and clearing out houses, it was a lot when all you wanted to do was curl up in a ball and cry because it hurt so much to lose the two most important people in your life so close together.

Add to that a stressful job and a jerk of an ex who had cheated on her because she was, quote, "too emotional and needy," and this vacation had been a necessity, not a luxury.

Time to regroup, heal, cry a little—which Steph did not think made her needy like her ex had claimed, after all, she was grieving the only family she had—and enjoy the gorgeous beach.

This had to be a little like what Heaven would be.

Peace.

Quiet.

Even with the happy families playing out in the waves, swimming and surfing, the kids chasing balls and frisbees, and building sandcastles, it was still very peaceful here. The giggles and squeals of delight somehow didn't seem like noise, they were just part of the landscape, part of the vibe.

Running her toes through the sand, Stephanie closed her book, tilted her head back to get the full feel of the sun on her skin, and took in a deep breath of fresh sea air. It was hard to believe that half of her weeklong vacation was already gone. It had gone too quickly, and she wasn't looking forward to having to go back to real life in a few short days.

But if she wanted to be able to pay the bills and maybe save for another vacation in the not-too-distant future, then she had to go back to work. It wasn't so bad running a small gym that catered almost entirely to families. Come down with the kids, spend family time together, keep active, that was her goal and it seemed to be working. It had only been two years, and she was already looking at opening a second gym, maybe a third. Of course, it was exciting, but she'd never wanted a chain, and the whole thing was overwhelming and totally stressful.

Still, she shouldn't complain. She was lucky her small business was doing so well, and the only upside to her brother and mother's deaths were that she could take the money she inherited—not that it was a considerable amount, but it was a nice little chunk—pay off her mortgage and sink the rest into her business.

Silver linings.

Gotta keep looking for those silver linings on the clouds or you'd drown in all the rain.

When her stomach gave a loud and insistent rumble, she knew it was time to head back to her hotel room and grab something for lunch. Then after that, she might take a nap, maybe a swim in the hotel's pool, and then be back on the beach in time to watch the sunset.

That was her little ritual while she was away. Every time she sat on the warm sand and watched as the sun sank in a huge golden ball, it reminded her that even though it brought darkness with it, it always rose again.

Right now, her life might be dark and filled with grief, but one day it would be bright again.

She hoped.

She prayed.

Gathering her belongings, she shoved her book, her water bottle, and the rest of her packet of chips into her bag and then stood. Feet shoved into flip-flops, she slung the strap of her bag over her shoulder and righted her sunhat. With her wild mop of brown curls, it was definitely a struggle getting a hat to fit on her head. Between the humidity and all the swimming she'd been doing, her hair seemed to have doubled in size, and was so wild it was a wonder she could do anything with it. Picking up her towel, Stephanie shook it off, then folded it over her arm as she headed off the beach.

No sooner had she reached the road than a man on a motorbike pulled up beside her. He pulled off his helmet and shot her a somewhat smarmy smile. Although he was handsome, with thick dark hair, long-lashed dark eyes, and a cut body, at least from what she could see with his white T-shirt and jeans, she didn't get a good vibe from him.

Always trust your gut.

How many times had her big brother told her that when she was younger? There were six years between them, and he'd always relished being the older brother, giving her advice like he was decades older, and watching out for her.

As a kid, she'd thought it was annoying, he had to have scared off at least a dozen prospective boyfriends over the years. Now she'd give anything to have him by her side, telling this guy to leave her alone.

"Hop on, I'll give you a ride," he said.

Trust your gut. This time the words echoed inside her head in her brother's voice. It had been six months since she'd seen him before he died ten months ago, but she heard it as crystal clear as if he was standing beside her on the sidewalk. Her gut said to pass on this guy. "No, thank you though." To soften her words, she gave a polite smile and began walking.

To her annoyance, he sidled up beside her again. "Aww, come on."

"No thank you," she repeated firmly. It sucked when guys didn't take no for an answer. It wasn't like she was the only girl around, likely there would be some other woman who would be only too happy to take him up on what he was clearly offering. It just wouldn't be her. Sex was important to her, it meant something, she only had it with a man she knew and was involved with. Her life might have fallen apart this last year, but not so much that she was going to sleep with some random guy who approached her on the street.

The man's fake smile faded, and something else took its place.
Something darker.
Something dangerous.
A prickle of uneasiness struck her.
Something wasn't right.

If something wasn't right, she needed to get out of there and back to her hotel. There was a chance the guy would follow her, but the hotel was large, and it would be almost impossible for him to find her once she got inside. Maybe she'd mention at reception that a man had been harassing her, make sure they knew if someone was asking about her that they weren't someone she knew or was interested in and shouldn't be given her room number.

It wasn't far to go to the hotel, and Stephanie picked up her pace. There were people around, if she needed to, she could scream, and someone would come. Surely the guy wouldn't try anything stupid when there were so many witnesses around them.

Right?

Wrong.

What she'd thought was just an overly pushy guy who, at worst, might try to rape her if she agreed to go anywhere with him had turned into every young woman's worst nightmare. Alone in Mexico, she had no family to search for her when she disappeared off the face of the earth, no one to help, no one to care, no one to stop what was going to happen next.

A van pulled up before them, just a couple of yards away, this guy wasn't working alone, he was part of a team, which meant he had to be a human trafficker. Stephanie sucked in a breath, prepared to scream for all she was worth and fight with everything she had to give, but the next thing she knew, something cold and hard was pressed up against her spine.

A hard hand clamped around her bicep. "Should have done this the easy way," the man hissed in her ear a second before the back of the van opened and she was shoved inside.

"You can't do this to me," she shouted, praying someone overheard. Just because there were people around didn't mean anyone would step in and help her. "Help!"

Stephanie couldn't see if anyone turned at her screams because the guy followed her into the back of the van, slamming the door shut behind them. They weren't alone in there, another two men were there, and even though she kicked and scratched and screamed for all she was worth she was outnumbered.

Pain exploded in her head, and the world disappeared.

CHAPTER

Two

January 20th
   6:08 P.M.

Trick felt like he needed to make a joke, do something to break the oppressive silence in the vehicle, but for once in his life, he couldn't come up with anything to say or do.

Making jokes, keeping things light, magic tricks, that was the man he had become after he'd learned the hard way that taking out his anger and dealing with his problems by using his fists only wound up hurting him in the long run.

Lesson learned.

The hard way, sure, but at least he'd learned it.

Then discipline and self-control came through his years in the military. Serving on Delta Force had been a great honor, and then to be offered a job at Prey Security after their careers were tanked thanks to Leonid Baranov was like the icing on the cake. Trick made sure he never took for granted the things he had achieved because his life could so easily have gone in a completely different direction.

To keep a lid on that old anger, he used humor and magic. When his teammates, or a victim they were rescuing, needed something lighter to focus on so the darkness didn't consume them, he was always there and prepared to give that little flicker of light in the dark.

Always.

Except now.

As they returned from their failed mission, knowing that now the only surviving victim of Baranov's house of horror was their own Beth, he had no light in him to share.

How long would it be before Baranov made another attempt at snatching her away from them? And how would they survive losing her?

Axe wouldn't.

That much Trick knew for sure, which was why he was struggling to think of anything he could say or do to lighten anyone's mood.

When Rock pulled down the driveway of the compound, coming to a stop outside the main building, the first thing he noticed was that everyone was waiting for them. Beth was there, standing slightly off to the side on her own. Tillie, Ariel, and Jessica were all waiting for their men, and Andy was bouncing about Mrs. Pfeffer, the older woman who watched the eight-year-old when his father was off on an op.

Family.

His family, yes, sure. But these were the people, the men he considered his brothers and loved more than anything else in the world.

As they all piled out of the vehicle, he watched Andy jump into Panther's arms while Tillie ran to Tank, kissing her new fiancé like even a few hours away from him was too much. There was no hesitation as Ariel went straight to Rock, wrapped her arms around him, and kissed him, and even though they had been together only a little over a month, Jessica went right to Scorpion, grabbed his shoulders, and pulled him down so she could kiss him.

Even Beth walked tentatively toward Axe, reached out, and gave his hand a quick squeeze. It wasn't much, but the way Axe lit up at the contact, even though Beth snatched her hand back quickly and took a step away from him, was like his whole world was a better place just by having his wife in it.

For the first time ... ever ... Trick felt a twinge in his chest.

There was no one there to greet him, no one who cared about him the way these women and this little boy cared about the men he considered his brothers. He had no biological siblings, and his relationship with his mother was strained at best, the one with his father non-existent. For so long, it had just been him and these men, and watching them fall one by one had been a lot of fun. Trick had never resented them finding their other halves or felt lonely or left out.

Until now.

For some reason, the twinge in his chest grew to an ache where he had to lift a hand and rub over the spot to attempt to ease it.

Or erase it completely.

He wasn't jealous of his friends falling in love, he wanted them to be happy, and he'd never wanted more than fun and casual with any of the women who entered his life. Nothing had changed, he still didn't want anything permanent, and he wasn't into the whole marriage commitment for life idea. Kids also weren't on his agenda, although he adored hanging with Panther's little boy. Andy was a great kid, but he was perfectly content to just be Uncle Trick, the fun guy who taught the boy magic tricks.

So, if he didn't want more, why did he suddenly feel ... strange?

Shaking it off, Trick assumed it must just be because so much had happened to his teammates over the last eighteen months, and he didn't like the idea of danger hovering over the heads of the people he loved. If Baranov was determined to get his hands on Beth again, then not only was she not safe, but none of them were. It wasn't just him and his teammates who lived on the compound now. Tillie and Ariel did, too, and it was only a matter of time before Jessica moved out of the penthouse Scorpion had given her to join them there. Add in Andy and Mrs. Pfeffer, who was there more than she wasn't, and there were a lot of people who could wind up being collateral damage if Baranov tried anything.

That had to be it.

Still, he couldn't deny his sudden urge to get away from all the happy couples. A night out, that's what he needed. Given everything that had been going on, he hadn't had the chance to get out on his own much. Actually, he was kind of surprised he had an ache in his chest when he should have it in his pants. How long had it been since he had a woman in his bed?

Well, not his bed. There was no way he would compromise the safety of the people he loved by bringing a stranger out there to their secure compound. Usually, he rented a room in a hotel and took his women there, better than going to their places and risking giving them the impression he was after more than fun, casual, hot sex.

Nothing wrong with fun, casual, hot sex. He lived for it. At least he had.

But in this moment, it felt ... hollow.

"I'm going to get out of here for the night," he announced to the group, who were making their way inside the large communal building.

"Oh, we thought we'd all have dinner together," Jessica said, looking disappointed.

"We cooked," Tillie added.

"I baked cookies for dessert," Andy piped up, looking pleased as punch with himself.

"Some other time, yeah?" he said, looking around at the people he loved. People that he suddenly found himself needing space from.

"Everything okay, man?" Panther asked.

"Course." Painting on the brightest smile he could muster, he waved then headed off to his cabin to change, all too aware of the eleven sets of eyes watching him go.

The chilly air helped clear his mind, and by the time he reached his place, took a quick shower, and changed into jeans and a shirt, he was more than ready to head into the city and find a hookup. Getting back into his old routine, that was what he needed. It used to be he'd head into the city at least once a week if they weren't on or planning an op. When had that changed?

Had to be around the time Ariel went missing. They'd been so focused on finding Rock's woman, and still looking into Beth's disappearance, that the appeal of looking for a casual hookup hadn't seemed anywhere near as important as being there for his team.

Now they were all doing great, moving on with their lives, and while Beth's situation had to be attended to, it wasn't like anyone needed him around anymore.

Because he didn't want to think, he turned the radio up as loud as it would go as he drove into the city. It wasn't a conscious decision to head to his favorite bar. The place was nice, with good music, good food, and a good atmosphere, and the women who usually frequented it were there looking for the same thing he was. A good time with no strings attached.

When he parked his car, the lot was already mostly full even though it wasn't all that late. Perfect. He could hang out for a while, find a suitable hookup, spend some fun time with her at a hotel, and then be back to spend the rest of the night in his own bed. Often, he spent the whole night with the woman he took home with him and had a couple of rounds of hot sex, but tonight, he wanted one and done and get out of there.

Trick was aware that sort of thinking could make people describe him as sleazy. But there was nothing wrong with wanting just sex, no commitment. At least he was honest and upfront about it. He made sure the woman had a good time, got off at least once, and he was always careful to make sure there were no baby Trick's running around out there.

As he was walking toward the bar's front door, he heard what sounded like muffled screams coming from the alley beside the building.

No way he could walk by without checking it out.

Wishing he had a weapon on him, Trick approached the alley. He could see movement in the shadows and heard another muffled scream that he swore had come from a woman.

"Hey!" he yelled as he ran toward what looked like three people involved in a scuffle, making the worst mistake a soldier could make.

He didn't pay attention to his surroundings or stop to take stock of the situation before rushing in.

The mistake might wind up costing him his life.

Pain exploded in his head, and the world disappeared.

∼

January 20th
    10:35 P.M.

. . .

A rush of bile burning her throat woke her up.

Stephanie's stomach cramped as she threw up, somehow managing to turn her head at the last second so the meager contents of her stomach wound up on the floor and not all over herself.

Ugh.

Her head pounded with a vicious headache. She didn't get headaches. The last one she'd had was when she was in a minor car accident during her senior year of high school. She'd hit her head but thankfully been lucky enough to avoid a concussion. Still, she'd been out of school for a few days and almost missed prom.

Was that what had happened now?

Frantically, Stephanie searched her memories, seeking the reason why her head throbbed and her stomach felt like she had the flu.

Maybe that was the problem?

She was sick.

Terror mounted inside her when she realized she didn't know why she felt so bad. She couldn't remember.

No, stop it, don't panic.

Her attempt to calm herself did little to actually work because she couldn't summon up a single reason why something was wrong with her. Not one. The last thing she remembered was ... arriving in Mexico on vacation.

That was it.

After that, everything was a blank. She had no idea what day it was, what time it was, where she was, or why she felt so bad. She could have been in Mexico for a minute, a day, or a week. Heck, for all she knew, maybe she was already back home, and something had happened to her there.

What's wrong with me?

Another rush of bile had her rolling onto her side as it burned up her throat and out her mouth. It was only then she realized wherever she was, it wasn't some nice comfortable—okay, that might be stretching it a tiny bit—hospital bed. Wherever she was it was cold and hard and damp.

It felt like she was lying on ... concrete.

But that ... couldn't be right.

Could it?

Why would she be lying on concrete?

Remember, please.

The plea didn't work. It was like her memory had just checked out. Leaving her alone and vulnerable because she just didn't know where she was or why she was there.

Knowing that she needed answers, Stephanie rolled over onto her stomach. Planting her palms on the scratchy concrete, she summoned what little strength she seemed to have left and somehow managed to push herself up onto her hands and knees.

That little bit of strength wasn't much, and she swayed as she stayed here, on all fours, praying the headache would clear enough that she could think. She had to figure this out, Stephanie knew that much even trapped as she was in this dazed state.

It was important.

Why she was there ... wherever there was ... she had to figure out if she wanted to ... survive.

Was that true?

Was her very survival at stake?

Somehow finding strength she hadn't known she had, Stephanie staggered to her feet as her eyes popped open.

Or did they?

It was dark. Dark enough that when she lifted a trembling hand and held it right in front of her face, all she could see was a vague shadowy outline.

Panic clawed at her insides, mixing with the nausea and churning inside her stomach. Sure she was about to throw up again, Stephanie pressed a hand to her stomach in a desperate attempt to keep what was left in there.

That was the moment she realized she was naked.

Her hand didn't touch ... whatever it was she'd been wearing when she was brought to this cold, dark room ... it touched bare skin.

"No, no, no, no, no," she wailed as she swayed again, this time not finding enough strength to keep her on her feet. She landed hard on her knees, pain shooting up from the joints and through her legs. Stomach cramping, she dry heaved since there was nothing left in there, over and over again until the pain in her abdomen matched the agony in her head.

What was going on?

Why was she naked and hurt in a damp and dark room?

Where was the room?

How did she get there?

Who brought her there?

Shaking so badly she couldn't even remain on her knees, Stephanie curled up on her side, pulling her knees to her chest and wrapping her arms around herself in an attempt to physically hold herself together.

"P-please, is anyone there?" she called into the darkness. "W-where am I? Why d-did you b-bring me here?"

There was no answer to her stammered questions.

There was no sound at all.

Well, nothing other than the sound of her own ragged breathing.

Naked, cold, and hurting, there was no comfort to be found anywhere. All she could do was cry and huddle in a ball, praying that something happened to get her out of there.

She still had no idea how she'd ended up there, her memories ended when she walked into her hotel room in Mexico and didn't seem inclined to return. This was obviously not the hotel she'd spent way too much money on. Five stars, three pools, and a block from the beach, it was supposed to be the perfect way to start healing from her brother and mom's deaths. Instead ...

Instead, it had turned into a nightmare.

Even as awful as she felt, and with no memories to back it up, Stephanie could figure out at least part of what had happened to her.

It was obvious she'd been kidnapped. There was no other explanation for why she'd woken up in a cold, dark room, all alone, naked, and with a killer headache that hinted at the fact she'd been hit over the head. Concussion. It had to be. It would explain both the headache and the nausea, and why she didn't remember what had happened. Those memories had been wiped away, probably permanently, by a blow to her head.

But why would anyone kidnap her?

Well, she guessed besides the obvious. She was a young, twenty-six-year-old woman, reasonably attractive, she guessed, with her large brown eyes and wild mess of brown curls, and she was alone in Mexico. A target for sure, even if she was positive she wouldn't have put herself in any sort of dangerous situation.

She never did.

Play it safe, that was her motto. She wasn't a risk taker, she didn't have a crazy job that put her in danger, and she didn't even really like to go out much and hang out at bars or clubs because she was always aware that something could happen to her.

Why didn't she think anything would happen to her in Mexico?

It never even entered her mind.

All she'd been thinking was that she needed some time to herself to start healing from her losses, and a beach in Mexico had seemed like a good way to go about getting it.

Never in her wildest dreams did she think she would be abducted and ... possibly raped. Just because she didn't feel any pain down there didn't mean anything. If she'd been raped, they could have done it without being too rough, especially if she was unconscious. And even if they hadn't touched her there yet, it didn't mean that they wouldn't. Why else would they go to all the trouble of snatching her and bringing her there if they didn't plan on hurting her?

Or maybe they planned on selling her.

Human trafficking was a thing, she knew that even though it felt so far removed from the safe little life she lived.

Only her life wasn't so safe anymore.

The opposite, in fact.

She wasn't safe, whatever the reason she'd been brought there, whether to be raped by her abductor or sold to someone else, it didn't really matter, her future wasn't looking bright. In fact, it was as dark as the room she was trapped in.

A surge of surreal energy flowed through her veins, and she stumbled to her feet.

Maybe she wasn't trapped.

She hadn't even thought to check to see if there was a way for her to escape.

Eyes adjusted slightly to the dark, she staggered around, arms out in front of her so she didn't crash into anything she couldn't see. Concrete walls met her trembling hands as she searched around, they were so solid, so impenetrable that her heart sunk a little more each time her palms ran across the rough concrete.

There had to be a door somewhere, right now, it was her only chance to get out of there, her only hope of finding a way to escape.

But when her hands touched metal bars, that hope dried up.

Shriveled like a grape in the sun.

Her fingers curled around the cold metal, and she yanked on it with all her might.

It didn't budge.

She wasn't getting out of there.

A scream died on her lips as she dropped to the ground, curling herself back into a ball as she sobbed. After months of missing her mom and her brother, it seemed she was going to be joining them sooner than she could ever have expected.

CHAPTER

Three

January 21ˢᵗ
11:52 A.M.

Trick's head pounded.

Hard as he tried to snap his mind awake, it didn't seem to want to cooperate.

What was going on?

Lifting his head proved to be a whole lot harder than it ought to be. It felt like the inside of his skull had been filled with rocks, making it heavy and almost impossible to move. Pain spread from between his temples down his neck, and every muscle in his body felt cramped like he'd been shoved inside a space too small for his large frame for too long, and his body had locked up on him.

Not good.

Somehow, he managed to ignore the pain and shove it aside, boxing it away because even hurting and groggy, he seemed to know on some instinctual level that he didn't have time for it right now.

Blinking open his eyes, he found himself encased in darkness. A few shadows danced about as his vision swam, and he couldn't make out anything that would help him figure out where he was.

Not knowing where he was wasn't okay.

Something was wrong, and he had to pull it together and figure out what it was.

Pushing up onto his knees, he flung out a hand and braced it against the first solid thing he found. It felt hard and rough like concrete, and Trick didn't like the implications of that. Still, he used it as leverage to get himself to his feet.

Answers.

He needed answers.

Once he had them, he could figure out a solution to whatever problem he seemed to have gotten stuck in.

When he tried to move, he found he couldn't. A tug on his ankle prevented him from going more than a step or so. Yanking his leg as hard as he could didn't seem to help, and exhausted, he had to admit defeat.

Sinking back down to sit on the floor, Trick reached for his ankle, horrified when not only did his fingers touch metal, but they also touched bare skin.

This wasn't good.

Wasn't good at all.

He had no memory of where he was or what had happened to him.

The last thing he remembered was ...

He couldn't even recall.

It was all a blur.

Focus.

Gathering all his mental energy, he focused on the last thing he could recall. Blood. On the floor, the metallic stench was so strong in the air that it made you want to gag. The farmhouse in Nebraska. Empty, no signs of the only other surviving victim of Leonid Baranov's houses of horror. Sarah Sanders was dead, and they'd returned home to break the news to Beth and the rest of their Bravo Team family.

That was the last thing he could consciously recall. How he went from going home with the rest of his team to winding up in this dark, cold space with a killer headache and no memories he had zero idea.

"Hey," he croaked, calling out to anyone who might be within range. "Hello. Is anyone there?"

There was no answer.

Once again, he tried to move.

Couldn't.

Anger pulsed through his body along with the pain and heavy weight of exhaustion. Something was wrong, someone had brought him here, stripped him naked, and cuffed him. To do that, the person must have gotten the drop on him somehow, which meant he had no one to blame for his current circumstances except himself.

Yanking on the cuff secured around his ankle with every drop of energy still left in his weak body achieved nothing but draining away those last reserves of strength, and the blackness overtook him, and he faded away.

When he awoke, he was chilled to the bone.

It took less time this time around to figure out why.

Trick's eyes popped open only to be met with darkness and shadows, but his head hurt a little less, and he was able to figure out that he was in some sort of dank room that felt like an underground dungeon.

Now that his mind was clearing, he was able to start putting things together. He was naked and cuffed to a wall in a windowless room. All rooms had a way in so this one had to be no different. Restrained as he was, he might not be able to get to the door, but he most certainly wasn't going to just give up.

Someone might have gotten the drop on him, but he was smart and trained. His body was a honed weapon even if he wasn't operating at one hundred percent, and whoever had taken him was going to regret it.

Big time.

Since he couldn't move much, and it was too dark to see very well, Trick focused on his other senses. Along with the heavy odor of dampness that hung in the air there was something else. Blood. Not as much as had been at the farmhouse where they'd hoped to find Sarah Sanders. No one had died in this room, at least not recently, but there was enough blood that it was a noticeable smell.

Lifting his hand, he touched it to the epicenter of pain in the back of his head. His fingers touched something dried with a slight hint of stickiness. Whoever had abducted him must have somehow gotten the drop on him and hit him over the head to knock him out. It explained his headache and sluggishness, but there was more to it than that. Felt like after being knocked out, he'd been drugged. Probably so his abductor could take him there ... wherever there was.

There wasn't enough blood on his head though to account for the smell in the room, and mixed with the metallic scent of blood, there was the acidic stench of vomit. Only he hadn't thrown up. When he blocked out the sound of his own pulse echoing in his ears he could hear the sounds of someone else's breathing.

He wasn't alone.

Trick's entire body tensed. His memories might be hazy at best, he might have no idea where he was or what had been done to him, but some of his skills were so ingrained he didn't need to function at his best to perform them.

Someone else was in this room with him.

Was whoever was in the room with him responsible for his abduction?

Anger was able to push away some of the fogginess. It didn't help his memories return but it helped clear his head and allowed him to focus. While not all of his anger was directed at his abductors—a healthy portion could only rightly be aimed at himself—there was enough of it aimed at the person responsible for taking him there that all he needed was to get close enough to grab hold of them and he'd make them regret ever making a move on him.

While he might be a fairly cheerful guy these days, anger was an old friend he was well acquainted with, and he couldn't wait to unload it onto whoever dared to kidnap him.

Scanning the room, this time he found that his eyes had adjusted to the dark, and he was just able to make out a shadowy form hidden in the corner furthest from where he had been chained up.

Threat or fellow victim?

Only one way to find out.

"Hello?" Trick called out. "Who's there?"

There was no answer, but he could have sworn the shadowy figure flinched and tried to meld into the wall as though that would save them from his wrath.

"Who are you?" he demanded. Anger made his voice harsh, and he wished he could just go running over there, find out for himself who else was in this underground dungeon with him, but he couldn't thanks to the damn cuff on his ankle.

Again, there was no answer except for a small whimper.

He forced himself to calm down, if this was another victim then scaring them wasn't going to be productive. They would need to work together to get out of this hellhole, so alienating them wasn't smart.

Gentling his voice this time, he spoke again. "Sorry. I'm not angry with you. I'm angry with myself for allowing someone to take me out without me realizing it was going to happen. Is there someone over there?"

The shadow moved slowly as though still unsure whether it wanted to come any closer to him. "H-hello?" came the tentative voice, and Trick felt his heart sink. It was a woman. One who sounded every bit as confused and scared to find themselves there as he himself did. Was this woman going to have what it took to help him get them both out of there alive and in one piece?

All he could do was pray that she did.

This wasn't going to be easy. They were going to have to pull on every bit of strength and smarts they had to even stand a chance. While he at least had his training, years in Delta Force and then with Prey to draw on, he had no idea who this woman was or if she had any training that would help them.

"My name's Trick, who are you?"

"Stephanie."

That didn't tell him anything. He didn't know a Stephanie, didn't know if she was someone he could or should trust, didn't know if she was going to be an asset or a hindrance to him, and still didn't know a single thing about why someone had kidnapped him and brought him here.

It wasn't just anger that flowed through his veins, it was pure, unbridled, red hot fury.

∾

January 21st
    1:13 P.M.

"Where are we?" the man growled, sounding so dangerous that Stephanie immediately shrunk back into her corner of the dark, dank cell.

This man was terrifying, no doubt about it.

When the light had danced outside the metal bars of her cell, she'd thought that was it, that whoever had kidnapped her was here to rape, beat, sell, or kill her, whatever their reason was for taking her.

But they hadn't.

All they'd done was open the door, throw the man in, chain him up, and then lock it and walk away.

Stephanie had been torn between calling out to them to come back, she needed water to drink and something to eat, she wanted to know why she was here and who they were. But she was also terrified of these men and hadn't been able to make herself utter a single sound as she huddled in a corner and watched them.

It had taken her at least an hour—well she was guessing since she had no watch and there was no clock or way to mark time in there— before she gathered up enough courage to creep across the cell toward the man left behind. He'd been unconscious, and when she'd tentatively called out to him, he hadn't responded. Other than checking his pulse to make sure he was still alive she'd done nothing else.

What could she do?

She had no medical supplies, not even some water to offer him, and from the moment he woke up he'd been so angry. She'd sensed it, felt it filling their small dungeon and been too afraid to let him know she was there.

Now he knew though.

And it didn't seem like he was happy to have a cellmate.

"I-I don't know," she whispered. Who was this man who called himself Trick, and why had they put him in there with her?

Through the dark came the sound of a deep, long, slow breath, and when the man spoke again he sounded calmer, his voice gentle. At least he seemed to be able to keep his anger under control. Hopefully, he wouldn't wind up hurting her.

Or killing her.

"Sorry, I'm just angry that someone got the drop on me."

He'd said that already. It seemed like he was as confused and fuzzy-headed as she had been when she'd woken up. If they'd hit her over the head to knock her unconscious and given her a concussion when taking her, chances were they'd done the same thing to him. It would explain why he'd been unconscious when he arrived and why he'd passed back out again after waking that first time.

"That's not your fault," Trick continued. "Can you come closer so I can see you? They have me chained to the floor."

They hadn't cuffed her, thankfully. Maybe it was because they didn't think she was much of a threat, but this man ... he had threat written all over him.

Should she move closer?

If he was a danger to her, she was safe so long as she remained out of reach, but if he was another victim, brought here against his will like she had been—and why would they knock him out and chain him up if he wasn't—then maybe he could help her get out of there. Surely, together, they could figure something out.

Moving hesitantly, Stephanie edged out from the shadows, inching through the darkness until she could see the man. Until he could see her.

It was dark, but her eyes had adjusted enough that she could just make out his shadowy form. Like earlier when she'd approached him to make sure he was alive, she was struck by how big he was. Huge really. And his muscles were amazing. They were the kind of enormous that made her wonder if maybe there was a chance he could brute force his way out of there if they could just get that cuff off his ankle.

Fear and hope warred inside her. On the one hand, this man might just be big enough and strong enough to defeat the men who'd brought her there, but on the other ... what if he turned that strength on her?

"It's okay," he soothed as though sensing her terror and indecision.

"I know you're scared, but I need you to tell me everything you know if I'm going to get us out of here."

"I don't know anything," Stephanie said, fighting back tears. What chance did they really have of getting out? As much as she wanted to believe this big, muscled man could do the impossible, she was pretty sure it was just that. Impossible. "One minute I was arriving for a gorgeous Mexican vacation, the next I was ... here."

Here where she hadn't been fed in hours or days, where she was afraid to go to sleep for fear of what the men who brought her here would do to her, where she knew she was going to spend her final hours before suffering what was likely to be a horrible death.

"Okay, it's okay," he murmured again, his voice like a warm, soft caress, and she found she wanted to lean into it, soak up the strength and comfort it offered. Without even realizing it she crept a little bit closer. "What do you do, Stephanie?"

"I own a gym that encourages families to come and work out together, making exercising fun and something to enjoy instead of a chore." Certainly, nothing that would have gotten her abducted.

"I hate to ask this, but are you involved in anything illegal?"

Indignant, she shifted away from him again. "No. Of course not." Her life was the opposite of illegal. She was the kind of person who always drove the speed limit, never parked anywhere that wasn't a designated parking space, paid her taxes on time, and she'd never even used drugs as a teenager because it was against the rules. Stephanie was a rule follower to a fault.

"Sorry, had to ask. The only way I know how to get us out of here is to know what I'm dealing with." Trick sounded so confident, so unrattled by being abducted and caged, exactly like her brother used to sound. He was definitely angry where she was afraid, and she had to believe that he had some sort of skill that could be used to at least give them a chance.

"It's okay," she grudgingly agreed since he did, in fact, sound like he hadn't meant to hurt her feelings. After all, he didn't know her any better than she knew him. Stephanie certainly didn't have the skills to get herself out of there so she had no choice but to rely on the man who called himself Trick.

"What about your family?" Trick continued. "Any criminal connections? Cops? Military? Anything that might have made enemies?"

"No criminal connections. It's always just been me, my mom, and my big brother. My mom worked three jobs to pay the bills after my dad skipped out on us. She was the sweetest woman who wouldn't hurt a fly and was definitely not into anything illegal. Besides, she died a few months ago. Heart attack. My brother was in the military."

"Was?" Trick asked.

That familiar ache in her chest tightened as she thought of the brother she had idolized growing up. Absently, she rubbed at the spot above her heart, but it never helped. That pain was always there and felt like it was always going to be there. "He died almost a year ago. Killed in action. He was special forces, so I never knew where he was or what he was doing. I don't know how he died, they wouldn't give my mom and me any details, said it was classified." That had been the worst part. Not knowing anything about how her brother had died, it was like the wound of his loss couldn't scab over because they didn't have any concrete information to hold onto. He was just there, and then he was gone.

In the dark she could see him still, like what she'd said was something crazy.

Was he in the military, too? It would explain why he gave off the same calm and in-control vibes that her brother always did. Maybe he knew Chris? But she hadn't even said his name so how would Trick know who it was?

"Is your name Stephanie Fuller?" Trick asked, voice tight. Sounded like he was angry again.

"H-how did you know that?" Stephanie didn't like the tone of his voice. It scared her. Whatever he was thinking wasn't good. In fact, if his tone was anything to go by it was about as far away from good as you could get.

"Because I think I just figured out who took us and why we're here."

Trick didn't have to add anything to that. She wasn't stupid, she knew that what her brother did was dangerous, she just never thought that the dangers of his job would ever touch her.

Seemed she might have been wrong.

If whatever Trick thought was true, she had been kidnapped for a reason, and that reason was connected to her brother.

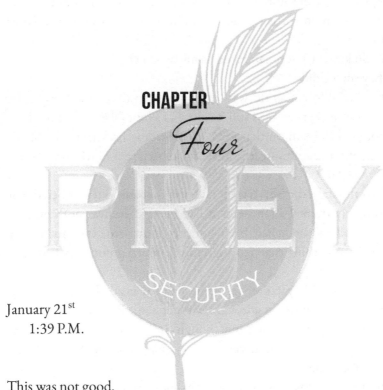

CHAPTER
Four

January 21st
1:39 P.M.

This was not good.

Not good at all.

For him or for Stephanie.

The room was dark, and Trick could only just make out the woman. She was small with wild curls that stuck up all around her head, and like him she was naked.

Vulnerable.

Tiny and fragile.

Protectiveness hit him like a brick, smacking him in the face.

Of course, Trick had the protective gene, he'd made a living out of protecting the innocent and his country.

But this was different.

This was a visceral reaction like his entire body drummed with need to do what he could to keep this woman safe.

Only he knew he couldn't.

It was impossible.

Stephanie getting hurt was already a foregone conclusion and had been since the moment her brother and his team went on that disaster of a mission.

"Y-you know what h-happened to my brother?"

Oh, yeah, he did.

The special forces world was small, and even though he was in the private sector now, they were still involved in a lot of what went on. Prey was supposed to be in on that mission, providing backup to the SEAL team, but at the last minute, the SEALs had been sent in without them.

Big mistake.

Unfortunately, the SEAL team had been so badly outnumbered that even as highly trained as those men had been, there was nothing they could do. All of them had been horribly murdered, but not before they'd done something that had angered the militia group they had been sent to target.

While a horrible picture was being painted inside his head of just how bad their situation was, it was clear Stephanie had no clue what he meant. She was going to find out though. In horrible, vivid detail that she would never be able to forget even if by some miracle they were able to survive this ordeal.

The mission was classified, no one—not even the families of the deceased—was supposed to know what had happened. But Stephanie was here now, dragged into it, and she deserved to know why her life was hanging in the balance.

"We were sent in after your brother's team got into trouble," he told her. "They were taking out a small militant army based in Liberia that was planning an attack on US soil. Only someone didn't want the attack stopped. They walked into a trap, the militia knew they were coming. Everyone was killed before we got there, I'm sorry, Stephanie." There was a whole lot more to it than that, but she didn't need to know that her brother and the other men on his SEAL team had been horribly tortured before finally being executed by having their throats slit.

Pressing her hands to her mouth, Stephanie swallowed a sob. It was obvious that she was trying to hold it together and he couldn't be prouder of her. It was good she was stronger than she looked because she was going to need to be to survive this.

As much as Trick wanted to reach out to her, do something to lighten the mood, hold her, soothe her, something, anything, he couldn't. Not because he didn't care or wouldn't do everything in his power to find a way for them to escape. But because he couldn't allow himself to get emotionally attached to this woman and feel her pain, because if he did, he might do something stupid.

Something that would wind up getting a whole lot of people killed.

Big picture.

That was what he had to keep in mind no matter how much it was going to hurt to do it.

Hurt so much he could hardly breathe, could hardly keep his composure in front of this woman who had done nothing wrong except for having the misfortune of being the sister of one of the men who had taken something the militia wanted back.

Unfortunately for Stephanie, she was still going to be kept in the dark. There were things that she just couldn't know, but not knowing them was going to make this all so much worse for her.

His heart ached in his chest for all this woman was about to endure, and she didn't have a clue what was coming.

"I can't tell you more than that because if you know they'll use it against you," he told her gently. Trick had told her all he could without adding to the danger she was already in.

"Use it against me? How? I don't understand."

No, she didn't. The poor woman sounded so damn confused that the pain in his chest increased, and he couldn't help but rub at the spot. Stephanie was about to get an up close and personal schooling in just how evil the world could be, and there was absolutely nothing he could do to stop it from happening.

And not because he was cuffed to the wall unable to move more than half a step in any direction. Even if he wasn't chained up, he couldn't stop the coming storm from picking them both up and tossing them about.

While he wasn't denying this was going to be worse for her than it was for him, it wasn't going to be easy for either of them. Knowing he was going to play a part in destroying this woman would kill him as surely as whatever their abductors finally did to him to end his life.

What he was going to have to do went against everything he stood for, against his moral code, against his job, against his heart, against everything he was as a person.

Yet he had no choice.

Protecting Stephanie wasn't going to do her any good in the long run, and it would result in thousands of deaths.

Still, there wasn't a single thing about this that he didn't hate with a vengeance.

"You're here so they can see if you know anything about that assault," he said. True, but not the only reason. Not even the main reason.

"But I don't," Stephanie said, helplessness dripping from her every word. He could only imagine what the poor woman must be thinking. Grabbed while on vacation, injured, and brought to this dank, dark dungeon, which he assumed was somewhere in Liberia, although they could be anywhere in the world. No idea why she'd been taken, only to learn that it was because of the brother she obviously loved and had been grieving.

Unfortunately, it was about to get a whole lot worse for her.

Knowing she had no idea what was going to happen to her and that he would have to be the one to break the news made nausea churn in his gut.

He didn't want to do this.

Yet he didn't have a choice.

"Sit down, Stephanie," he said, uncertain of how she was going to take the news. From the dried blood he could just make out on the side of her face, she likely had a head injury, the last thing he needed was for her to faint and hit her head again.

"Why?" The hint of defiance in her tone made him smile. Maybe she was strong enough to survive what was coming.

"Please," Trick said.

Somewhat tentatively, she took a step closer and lowered herself to the floor. She folded her legs to the side in what he was sure was an attempt at modesty and crossed her arms over her chest. As much as he wanted to tell her she was going to have to get over her need for modesty, no one here cared about her body, it was about to be used and abused in ways she couldn't even imagine.

Ways no person should have to endure.

"Thank you," he said when he could tell her eyes were on him. "Finding out if your brother told you anything about that mission isn't the only reason they took you."

"Wh-what is the other reason?" Although Stephanie's voice trembled a little, he respected that she was facing this head-on and wasn't curled up in a corner hysterical or catatonic.

"You're motivation," he told her gently.

"Motivation? What does that mean?"

"It means they have to know I was on the team that found the bodies. You're motivation for me. They know I was there, they know I have the information they want. Not everyone was dead when we arrived, your brother was fatally wounded, dying. But before he died, he told me something. Something they want to know. Something I won't tell them. No matter what. I can't. Lives depend on it. So even if they torture me, I won't give up that intel." Trick sighed and agitatedly dragged his fingers through his hair. He didn't like this. It was going to destroy him and there was no worse feeling in the world than knowing he had no other choice. Not that Stephanie would understand that. How could she? "Even if they torture you, I can't tell them what they want to know."

January 21st
2:00 P.M.

This couldn't be happening.

Stephanie couldn't believe this was real.

She didn't want to believe this was real.

How had her life devolved to this point?

When she lost her brother, then watched her mom fade and wither away into nothingness, and then got dumped by a man she had thought she would wind up marrying, she had thought her life couldn't get any worse.

How very wrong she had been.

Her stomach, empty though it was, swirled with nausea and she scrambled up onto her knees, turning her head to the side, away from Trick as she dry retched over and over again until her stomach cramped and her head throbbed.

When it finally eased enough for her to draw a proper breath, Stephanie sank onto the cold, hard, unforgiving concrete floor. Shivers rocked her body so hard her teeth were chattering.

Motivation.

Torture.

No mercy.

Cracking open her eyes, she looked at the shadowy form of the man she knew only as Trick. There was a stiffness to him like he was carved from marble rather than a flesh and blood man, a coldness, a hardness.

Unforgiving.

They didn't know each other, sure, but he had known her brother, and even if he hadn't, she was a human being. How could he just sit by and do nothing while she was going to be tortured?

Wasn't he human?

Anger gave her a burst of strength, much like it had done earlier when she was stupid enough to think there was a way out of this place, and she lunged at the man. There was no conscious thought to what she was doing, no plan, no idea of what she hoped to achieve, all Stephanie knew was this man was going to stand by and do nothing while she was the one who would be tortured.

It wasn't fair.

She hadn't done anything wrong.

Didn't deserve this.

How could he do this to her?

Beating her fists on his chest she howled out her frustration, hating that there was no one around who cared. The men who had somehow figured out who she was, cared only that she might be a useful tool to achieve their goals, and this man cared more about keeping his secrets than he did about protecting her.

"It's okay, darlin'," he murmured. "Let it out. I know this sucks, honey. I know it does."

His acquiescence to her meltdown, doing nothing to stop her hammering on his chest even though she knew if he wanted to, he could not only stop her but kill her, took the wind out of her sails. He wouldn't need a weapon to end her life, he was the weapon. His bare hands would do the job, and she knew how powerful and dangerous men like him, like her brother, could be.

Even though she had never once feared her brother, it didn't mean she wasn't aware of what he was capable of. What he had to do to make the world a safer place for her and their mom and everybody else.

She was so darn proud of Chris.

So proud.

There wasn't anything he wouldn't do to make the world a safer place for the people he loved.

Why would she expect Trick to be any different?

Cut from the same cloth, this man wasn't doing anything her brother wouldn't do if he had found himself trapped in a dungeon with a woman he didn't know and lives at stake. Chris would hate it, it would destroy him, but he would stand by and let the woman be hurt if it was the only way to protect her and their mom, and all the other innocents in the world.

Feeling stupid now about her meltdown and knowing that her own brother would do the same thing Trick was, Stephanie's cheeks heated in embarrassment and she stopped beating her fists against Trick's chest.

"I'm sorry, Stephanie," he said, his voice filled with so much guilt and regret it made her heart hurt. He might be going to let her be tortured, but he hated the idea of it. Somehow knowing that made her feel a little better about this horrific mess they had both found themselves in.

As much as she wanted to beg him to reconsider, to not let these men hurt her, how could she do that knowing innocent lives could be lost if Trick gave up the information he knew?

It wasn't what Chris would do if he had been there.

Wasn't what Chris would want her to do either.

Terrified as she was, she was going to have to find a way to be brave.

"Stephanie, if there was any other ..."

"It's okay," she said, cutting him off. "I know you don't want to do this. I think it's going to be as hard for you as it is for me. I understand, you don't have to feel bad." It was easier than she would have thought to say the words. The thing was, she even meant them. What was the point in making this worse on both of them by taking out her anger, fear, and helplessness on Trick? The people she was really angry at, the ones who were really to blame for what was going to happen to her, were the men who had kidnapped her and brought her there.

Trick muttered something which she was pretty sure was a curse of helplessness. Despite her reassurance that he didn't need to blame himself, Stephanie knew he would carry deep guilt over what she was to suffer in this dark, cold little room.

"They didn't chain you up," Trick said, or asked. She wasn't sure if it was a question, but she shook her head anyway.

"No, they didn't. Don't know why." Although, she assumed it was because they didn't deem her to be a threat. They knew that Trick was dangerous and was highly trained, but they knew she was just the sister or a fallen SEAL. She spent her days running classes for kids and adults, and personal training, not fighting bad guys. While she had some self-defense training, it wasn't like she stood a chance at fighting these men and succeeding.

"Do you know how long you've been here?"

Realizing that she was still sitting half in his lap, where she'd thrown herself when she decided attacking Trick and taking out her anger on him was a good use of her mental and physical energy, embarrassed she shifted so she sat beside him. When she went to move away from him, he'd been good about the meltdown, but she was sure he hadn't appreciated it, Trick stopped her.

When he wrapped an arm around her shoulder, settling her against his side, she went completely still. It wasn't that she was naked or that he was naked, too. Although she'd been embarrassed earlier, now she didn't have time or space for another emotion, so there was no embarrassment over this stranger seeing her naked body. It was that she didn't understand how he could want her near him when she'd just taken out her anger on him.

"Umm, I'm sorry about, you know ... hitting you," she murmured. She didn't use her fists to solve her problems, her mom had taught her that when she was a small child. Stephanie also knew better than to blame someone for her problems when she knew they weren't really responsible.

"Stephanie, you didn't do anything wrong. You had a little freakout, trust me, you're entitled. This isn't something that you can prepare for, it's not just scary its top-level terrifying." Since his arm was still around her shoulders, she felt the shudder that rippled through his big, toned body. "I'm the one who's sorry."

"I know."

"If I could change this I would."

"I know that, too." It was obvious that Trick was a good guy. He'd been kidnapped and brought here, too, he had to be scared even if he wasn't letting it show. Men like Trick, like her brother, they were strong, and brave, they didn't hesitate to risk their lives for others, but they were still human, they still felt the same emotions as everybody else, and he had to be worried about what was coming. Maybe he had a family waiting for him at home, one he thought he might never get to see again. At the least, he had a team, and she knew from Chris that for these guys, their team was their family.

The last thing he needed was her adding to his worries when he had enough already or her making herself more of a burden than she already was by making him worry that she was going to have another meltdown.

Be brave.

No matter what happened, she had to find a way to hold it together. How she was going to do that she had no idea, but she wasn't going to make things worse for Trick by begging and pleading with him when neither of them could change their situation.

Since Trick was warm and strong, hadn't held her meltdown against her, and seemed like a good guy, she slowly relaxed against his side. When his arm tightened around her shoulders, she didn't hesitate to snuggle closer, soaking up whatever strength she could.

"I wish there was something I could do," he said.

"In that case, I hope you have a plan of escape."

CHAPTER

Five

January 21st
2:12 P.M.

Of course I do!

The words wanted to burst out of him with as much reassurance and confidence as it took to convince Stephanie it was true, but the reality was, Trick didn't know how he was going to get himself or her out of there.

She was being so brave, trying her best to hold it together in a situation that no matter how much training you had, you could never completely be prepared for. Even with all his training, and the fact that he and his team had been held captive before, this was a lot for him to deal with. There was no team at his back and nobody knew where he was or who had taken him. While his team would start looking as soon as they realized he was missing, there were no guarantees they would find him.

Help wasn't coming.

Chained as he was, he wasn't going to be able to do much to get them out of there. Didn't mean he wouldn't bide his time and watch for an opportunity to strike, but there was no guarantee there would be any opportunities to take advantage of.

That Stephanie was doing her best not to make him feel bad for what he was going to do to her was so much more than he deserved.

"Your brother would be proud of you," he told her. While he hadn't known Chris Fuller all that well, the man was a SEAL, and he'd gone above and beyond to do what he could, even as he knew he wasn't going to survive, to stop the Liberian militia from carrying out their plans. His sister was staring unimaginable horrors in the face with so much strength and bravery it would make the SEAL proud.

"I ... I'm scared ... terrified," Stephanie whispered.

"Being brave or strong isn't about not being scared," he told her. "It's about being scared and facing those fears head-on. I'm proud of you."

Her head shifted, and he knew she was looking up at him even though he didn't turn his head to look down at her.

He couldn't.

Bringing his gaze to meet hers, knowing the role he was going to play in her suffering was beyond him at the moment.

Helplessness.

It swamped him, slowly smothering him. There was nothing he could do, but not being able to do anything to fix his situation, to protect Stephanie who was completely innocent, was the worst feeling in the world.

"I'll figure something out," he assured the woman snuggled against his side, tightening his hold on her as though that was enough to keep them both safe.

"Okay," she whispered. It was clear she didn't believe him, but he was grateful she was trying to understand and not falling apart on him. Not that he'd blame her if she did fall apart, he certainly didn't hold her little freakout against her.

Stephanie was absolutely entitled to another bout of hysterics, but he needed her to be brave.

Needed it if he was going to have any hope of holding it together himself.

This was going to be hell on them both.

Protecting people was who he was, who he had always been, being forced to sit by and do nothing to stop a woman from being tortured was going to be hell.

Pure hell.

Yet he didn't have a choice.

Neither did she.

Fate.

He'd never been a big believer in fate. He hadn't believed it when his dad walked out on him and his mom when he was a toddler, hadn't believed it when his mom married the strict stepfather from hell. Trick hadn't even believed it when he was lucky enough when he was fighting a couple of boys to be caught by a vet who had taken it upon himself to make sure a young Trick didn't wind up going down a path there would be no coming back from.

You made your own path in life.

That was what he had always believed.

Only this was one time he prayed that fate was going to play a hand in what happened to them, because he was afraid if it was up to him to forge a path out of there for himself and Stephanie, they wouldn't be getting out.

Trick wasn't sure how long they sat there, her curled up in his arms. It likely wasn't smart to be holding her, they could be being watched, and if they saw him doing anything that indicated that he cared about her in any way, they would know that hurting her was an effective method of making him want to talk.

Then again, they already knew that. It was why she was here.

Men like him didn't stand by and allow an innocent to be tortured.

Normally.

No matter how much he wanted to save Stephanie from the coming pain, thousands of lives depended on him not giving up what he'd learned from her brother.

The slight sound of footsteps approaching told him that it was time.

He wanted to say a million things to Stephanie, more apologies, words of encouragement, and promises that he would find a way to save them if she would just hold on. None of them seemed appropriate. Most of it wasn't true, except for how very sorry he was.

Even if he wanted to say something there was no time. The door to their cell was flung open and four men stormed inside their dungeon.

Every instinct he had screamed at him to fight them, protect the girl, but he was chained up, unarmed, and there was only one of him to their four. Still, his arms tightened around her, and he angled his body so he was between her and their captors.

"I won't beg for you to tell them what they want to know," Stephanie whispered seconds before she was violently yanked from his arms.

Too bad he hadn't met this woman under other circumstances, because the gift she had just given him meant more than any other gift he had ever received. Stephanie was brave, understanding, and compassionate, and by the end of this, if they survived, she would hate his guts for making her endure the horrific pain that was only seconds away.

As she was dragged toward a chair the men had brought in with them, her eyes never left his. The men had turned on a light when they entered the cell, bathing it in bright white that was much too light for his eyes after so long in the dark. Now that he could see her clearly, Trick was struck by how beautiful Stephanie was. Full, plump lips, a soft shade of pink, large, warm brown eyes framed by thick black lashes, and chestnut curls that hung just below her shoulders. Because she was naked there wasn't an inch of her he couldn't see, each soft curve, each long, toned limb, her flat stomach with the small emerald belly button ring, her perky set of breasts.

Attractive as she was, seeing her so vulnerable, so fragile, and knowing what was about to happen to her stoked a raging fire of protective energy inside him.

He'd kill each and every one of these men given half a chance.

A quarter of a chance.

Hell, give him point one percent of a chance and he'd be all over it. For daring to lay a hand on Stephanie these men deserved a long, slow, painful death, and he hoped he would be the one to deliver it to them.

Stephanie struggled as the men attempted to shove her into the chair, and one of them hauled back and slammed a fist into the side of her head. Seeing her stumble, fresh blood oozed from the wound on her head that had been split back open when one of the men hit her, the sight of the bright red against the snow-white pallor of her skin had him vibrating with rage.

This woman wasn't his, but in a way, she had become his when they both drew the short straws and wound up in this place. It was just the two of them, and while there wasn't much either of them could do, if they wanted even a chance of surviving, they had only one another to rely on.

Whatever it took, he was going to find a way to get Stephanie out or die trying.

Her whispered promise that she wouldn't beg him to save her, her understanding that while she was definitely going to take the brunt of the physical torture, he was going to take the brunt of the psychological torture, knowing he couldn't do anything for her, had cemented her a place in the small circle of people he allowed himself to care about. Caring about people gave them an opportunity to hurt you, but this strong woman deserved that place.

Save her or die trying.

There was no other option.

～

January 21st
   3:51 P.M.

Stephanie had never known fear like this.

It was a blinding terror that stole her ability to breathe. To think. To function.

Rough hands dragged her away from the only safe place in the room —Trick. What she should have done as soon as she was grabbed was somehow pull herself free from the men and run for the door. But as badly as she craved safety, she found that even if she could escape—and it was really only wishful thinking to believe she could get past four huge, armed men—she wouldn't.

She couldn't leave Trick behind.

As she was shoved down into a chair, she never stopped looking at Trick. She needed something to hold onto right now, and even though she couldn't physically touch him, she needed him, needed to draw strength from his imposing presence. Even naked and chained up he was tall, big, and confident.

Everything she wasn't.

Everything she wished she was.

Here in this place, he was all she had.

The only way she even had a chance at surviving.

Instinct had her panicking when the men tried to push her into the chair. As badly as Stephanie wanted to be brave, make her brother proud, and make Trick proud of her, too, the panic was too great to fight and she began to struggle.

A fist slammed into the side of her head, right where she'd been hit when she was abducted, and pain exploded.

Stunned into compliance, she didn't offer any more struggles as she was shoved roughly into the chair. Zip ties were snapped around her wrists, binding them to the arms of a rusty metal chair. Her heart hammered so hard in her chest that Stephanie could hardly focus on anything else.

She'd promised Trick she wouldn't beg him to talk and intended to honor that.

No matter what.

But how she was going to achieve that goal she had no idea. One hit and already her body was trembling, the pain so overwhelming it threw her entire system into disarray. Panic warred with the pain which added to the trembling and the rush of her pulse in her ears.

The second blow came out of nowhere and pain exploded through her face.

Stephanie had never been hit before she'd been abducted in Mexico. Ever. She was completely unprepared for the way the pain stole her breath and barreled through her body, consuming her. It wasn't just her head and face that throbbed, somehow even though they were the only places that had been hit her entire body felt it.

Trick.

She needed Trick.

Blinking to clear her foggy vision, she sought him out. When she looked at him, she could see his entire body was rigid, his muscles tightly coiled wanting to spring, attack, do what he knew how to do, but there was nothing he could do. His expression was fierce, and his eyes aimed anger directly at their captors. When their eyes met, he softened, and she could read what he was telling her.

Hold on.

Don't give up.

Be strong.

Keep the faith.

Stephanie wasn't sure how she was going to do that, but she was determined to do her best. Survive. It seemed impossible, but all she had to do was take it one moment at a time. She didn't have to do this all at once, if she tried to think more than a couple of seconds into the future then she got too overwhelmed.

One second at a time.

If she wanted to survive this, then that was going to have to become her mantra.

"Do you know why you are here?" one of the men asked.

Since he wasn't looking at her but rather Trick, Stephanie had to assume that the question was for him and not her. Her place here wasn't anything more than a tool. Motivation, Trick had called it. She held no value other than getting Trick to talk.

If he wasn't going to talk to save her, what did that mean for her?

Presumably, Trick had the answers they wanted, so the chances they would kill him were significantly less than the chances they would kill her. If she was here for motivation and she wasn't enough to get Trick to talk—and she already knew she wasn't because he'd told her so—then she was useless. Expendable.

When Trick failed to give a response to the question, another of the men hauled back and punched her again. This time the blow was delivered to her stomach, and tied as she was to the chair with no way to protect herself, the man's fist connected squarely, shoving the air from her lungs, making her gag.

If her stomach wasn't already empty from throwing up at least half a dozen times since she awakened in this dungeon, then she would have just vomited all over herself.

Be thankful for small mercies she guessed.

"You're here for a reason, you know where the diamonds are," the man who had spoken before said and she assumed he was the one in charge of this little band of violent monsters.

Diamonds?

She had no idea this was about diamonds.

Given that Trick had mentioned a Liberian militia, she guessed that meant they were talking about blood diamonds. The militia must have been going to use them to fund whatever plans they had, and her brother's SEAL team had been sent in to stop them. Chris must have hidden the diamonds somewhere, and these men wanted them back.

Go, Chris.

Pride for her brother swelled inside her, and she smiled even as pain ravaged her face. She'd never really known any details about what her brother did since it was all classified, but hearing a little about it made her so darn proud to have had a brother like Chris who did the things he did and risked everything in the process.

"Maybe the girl knows where the diamonds are." When the man turned to her, the smile fell from her lips. She'd never seen evil like this before. Stephanie had thought her ex was the lowest of the low, dumping her when she was grieving and labeling her grief as neediness he didn't have time for. But staring into this man's dark, empty eyes she knew true evil.

Since she had no idea where her brother had hidden diamonds and had only just learned that was why she was there, she just sat there.

Taking a step closer, the man pinched her chin and tilted her face up so she had no choice but to look at him. "Do you know where the diamonds are?"

Stephanie was no Trick, she couldn't simply stare into the face of evil and refuse to speak. "N-no."

"But the man knows," the guy insisted.

She had no idea what she was supposed to say. Whether she should agree that Trick had told her he knew about why they were there but wasn't going to tell them or whether she should just feign ignorance. Deciding ignorance was her best bet, Stephanie shrugged her shoulders. "I don't know him. I've never met him before you brought us here. I don't know what he knows."

"I think the man knows," the guy said, looking over his shoulder at Trick's tense body. "I think the man will talk to stop you from being hurt."

How badly she wished that was true.

Yet at the same time, Stephanie was glad Trick was a man of honor, one who could focus on the greater good even when the smaller good was staring him right in the face. Even if he told the men what they wanted to know, it wasn't going to save either of their lives. Then they would both become expendable and they'd just be killed. Trick hadn't told her much, so she didn't know if his team would know who had taken him and come for him, but he wasn't acting like he expected either of them to get out alive, so she wasn't either.

Pulling out a knife, the man touched the tip of it to her cheek. The way he watched as her eyes widened in fear and her breath caught in her throat showed how much he was enjoying it. When she tried to lean back to pull away from the knife, he grabbed a handful of her hair and held her in place, pressing hard enough with the knife that she could feel it pierce her skin and a drop of blood bubble out.

"If the man tells me where the diamonds are you won't get cut," their captor said it like it was the simplest thing in the world.

But it wasn't.

Trick wasn't telling him anything.

When Trick's stony silence met the man's threat, he made a noise of frustration and then dragged the knife down her cheek, splitting her skin wide open.

A cry of pain wanted so badly to escape, and Stephanie wanted nothing more than to beg and plead with Trick to save her, to help her, to just tell these men what they wanted to know and find another way to stop them.

Only she couldn't.

She'd made a promise and she intended to keep it.

So, when the man moved to slice through her other cheek, she clamped her teeth into her tongue and refused to give in to the desire to scream.

CHAPTER

Six

January 21st
4:33 P.M.

"She's not so pretty now."

The mocking words said to taunt a bloody and battered Stephanie broke something inside Trick.

Your fault.

The voice inside his head mocked him the same way the Liberian militant mocked Stephanie. She had been an absolute superstar. If anyone deserved to be part of Delta Force or Bravo Team, it was her. Somehow, she had managed to keep her mouth shut while these men punched her and sliced up her face. Not only hadn't she begged him to help her and tell these men what they wanted to know, but she hadn't even screamed or cried in pain when she was being tortured.

Trick had no idea how she'd done it.

Superstar. There was no other way to describe her. She had gone above and beyond what anyone could expect of her. Stephanie had no training, no experience with this, yet she had withstood torture that could have made a highly trained operator fall apart.

But not Stephanie.

She'd held it together with a strength that not many people possessed.

Her brother would be proud of her.

Hell, he was proud of her.

In awe of her more like it.

This woman was something else, and if they had met under any other circumstances, he might very well have thrown out his remain-single-and-keep-things-with-women-casual plan and actually asked her out on a date.

Not something he could do now though.

No matter what happened, if they died in this room or by some miracle managed to survive, this would always stand between them. She would hate him. As she should. Because he was playing a role in her suffering and there was no way he could expect her forgiveness.

Knowing that this amazing, strong, fierce warrior woman would hate him soured his gut, leaving him vaguely nauseous.

Or maybe it was just seeing her covered in blood, with bruises forming on her face and torso that had him feeling nauseous. Of all the times he could develop a crush on a woman, now had to be the absolute worst. Maybe it was some kind of weird Stockholm-type thing. They were both trapped there together, their lives entwined in a way that, if they did survive, would bond them together forever. Something Stephanie was surely going to hate. Wouldn't matter that they would never see each other again, she would never be able to forget him or what he'd done to her.

Not getting the response out of him he wanted, the Liberian huffed in irritation. Keeping his mouth shut had been a whole lot harder than Trick had thought it would be. Knowing he was doing the right thing, that allowing these men to find the diamonds that would fund their plans to attack the US would get thousands, maybe millions of people killed, didn't seem to matter as he watched Stephanie so stoically accept the raw deal life had given her.

But he'd done it.

Somehow.

If Stephanie could be so brave, then he had no choice but to be as well.

It had taken every ounce of strength he possessed to keep his mouth shut but he'd managed to do it, even though it was the last thing he wanted to do, all the time wondering when Stephanie would break. Or when he would. Things were only going to get worse, and Trick feared that the more attached he got to Stephanie—and he was getting attached to her—the harder it would become.

"You'll break sometime," the man told him. "We'll come back later. Give you time to think. Cut the girl free."

At the man's order, the zip ties binding Stephanie to the rusty chair were cut, and she was picked up and tossed on the floor. She landed with a thump, and Trick couldn't help a small wince at the pain he knew her battered body had to be feeling being thrown about like that.

Somehow, he managed not to move a muscle while the four men took their chair with them and disappeared out of the cell. While he expected the lights to be shut off, once again trapping them in the darkness, they weren't, and he listened until the footsteps of the men faded away into nothingness.

The need to go to Stephanie, to hold her, beg for her forgiveness, and tend to her wounds as best as he could was powerful. Never before had he experienced anything quite like it. It had taken his team a while to earn his trust, but once they had there wasn't anything he wouldn't do for any one of them. While he always came off as easy-going and laid-back, it still took him a while to allow people in. With Beth it had been easier, given how they'd rescued her and helped her slowly recover from the horrors of her ordeals. They might not realize it, but it had taken time for him to believe that Tillie was right for Tank, and that Ariel wouldn't wind up leaving Rock and breaking his heart, although he would understand why she might walk away. If he was honest even though he'd never say it aloud, he still doubted Jessica wouldn't wind up hurting Scorpion, even though the woman had never given any indication that she would.

Trust, it was his kryptonite.

How could it not be?

When his own mother could turn a blind eye to the fact that her new husband was abusing her son it made putting his trust in anyone else next to impossible.

But with Stephanie it was different. She'd proven her trustworthiness in blood. Her promise not to plead with him to give up the intel their captors wanted had forever earned her a spot in his heart.

Which was why calling out to her was so hard. She might have earned his trust, but he had done nothing to earn hers.

He had no idea how long they both sat there in silence. Unable to speak for fear he would break down, Stephanie also lay there silently, not reaching out to him in any way. Did she hate him already?

Of course she did.

Since he couldn't avoid her forever, and she was the one who was able to move, cuffed as he was, he couldn't go to her no matter how much he wanted to. Eventually, Trick couldn't take the distance between them any longer. "Steph," he called out softly.

It took a moment, but slowly her head lifted and turned until she was facing him. The open wounds and blood streaking her pale skin had his own blood boiling, what he wouldn't give to have five minutes alone with those men when he wasn't chained up.

Keeping his voice gentle when a storm was raging inside him wasn't easy. But Stephanie hadn't done anything wrong, she didn't deserve any of this, and he didn't want her to think that even one iota of his rage was directed at her.

"Can you move, honey? Can you make it over here?" The need to touch her, soothe her pain in any way he could was too strong for him to ignore.

"I ... I think so ..." she murmured weakly.

Watching her plant her palms against the concrete floor and slowly inch her body off the ground was hell. He couldn't do anything, not even go to her, scoop her up, take her weight, and cradle her so she didn't have to worry about anything else other than surviving this hell.

Impotence was a feeling he remembered from his childhood. He'd been helpless back then as well, and he'd hated it every bit as much as he hated it now.

Unable to get up on her feet, she crawled to him on her hands and knees. Her body swayed, and from the slight wince she gave with each movement he knew she was hurting.

Not that his girl would complain.

In fact, Trick feared that no matter how bad it got, she wouldn't utter a single word of objection.

Maybe he needed her to. Maybe he needed her to beg him to save her. If she did, he might very well give in, even knowing the consequences. When he'd first realized there was another hostage with him, he'd prayed that she was going to be strong enough to do what needed to be done. He shouldn't have worried. Instead, he should have been concerned that he could do what needed to be done.

As Stephanie finally reached his side, Trick knew that he wasn't the strong one there. She was.

"Come here, darlin'," he said as he reached out and very carefully picked her up, settling her on his lap. That damn helplessness was back as Stephanie sucked in a pained breath at being moved, but otherwise didn't utter a sound. There was nothing he could do for her as he examined the cuts on her face, the torn skin around her wrists from the too-tight zip ties digging into her tender flesh, and the bruises littering her face, stomach and chest, his hatred for these men grew.

He wanted to do something, needed to, but he couldn't even clean out her wounds because they had no water.

"I'm so sorry, honey," he muttered as he leaned down and touched his forehead to hers.

A small hand reached up, curled around the back of his neck, and squeezed lightly. "It's okay, Trick. I can take it. I won't let you down."

Her sweet words cracked the ice encasing his heart. He didn't deserve her kindness, reassurance, bravery, or strength. "Try to rest, darlin'," he told her, tucking her head against his chest and curling his body around hers as much as he could to keep her warm.

Exhaustion came for her, and she went limp against him as she passed out. Trick was glad she wasn't awake to witness the tears that fell from his eyes as he was forced to accept that he was going to fail the only woman who had ever stirred up anything inside his heart.

~

January 22nd
    8:12 A.M.

"So ... umm ... I assume Trick isn't your real name ...?" Stephanie said more to break the oppressive silence smothering the room than anything else.

Not that she didn't want to know Trick's real name, because she did. She wanted to know lots of things about the man, but more than anything, she just wanted to get him talking.

She'd been right.

As horrific as it had been when those men were hitting her and cutting her, she was positive that it had been worse for Trick. He wanted to do something, she knew it, could feel it, but he was unable to stop this from happening unless he was willing to put thousands of lives at risk.

In this fight for survival, there was no room for anger, grudges, or blame. They had to focus on staying alive for as long as possible to give themselves the best chance at being rescued.

His team would be looking for him, she had to believe that. Even if nobody who had realized something had happened to her yet, it wouldn't be the same for him. Sooner or later, one of her friends or employees would realize she hadn't come back from Mexico and would alert the authorities, but she had no idea when that would be. When she got back from her vacation, she had another week off before she was due to return to the gym, and she'd been so insistent to all her friends that she needed this time alone. If it was up to her friends to help them get out of this mess, it wouldn't happen any time soon.

Trick was still her only hope.

More than that, he was the only source of comfort and security she had in this Godforsaken place.

When he didn't answer her question, she shifted uncomfortably, worried she had pushed too hard to forge a connection between them. Stephanie had to keep reminding herself that while Trick was her everything while they were there, to him, she was nothing but a burden. One he couldn't even carry because there was nothing he could do for her.

"Sorry ... I shouldn't have asked." Embarrassment for needing this man so much had her trying to pull her battered body away from him. Lying all over him and allowing him to hold her, wasn't good for her emotional health right now. He might be all she had, but she didn't want to watch him die, and if she let herself get much more attached it would hurt to lose him, and she'd already lost so much in the last year.

Tightening his hold on her to prevent her from moving off his lap, Trick sighed. A deep, sad sound rumbled through the chest she rested against. "No, it's not that, I just ... I'm afraid to get more attached to you than I already am," he admitted, surprising her. "Trauma bonds people quickly, but I can't help you. I feel so useless."

Knowing she wasn't the only one struggling with the bond forming between them, Stephanie reached a trembling hand up to cup his cheek. "You know I don't blame you, I understand why you have to keep quiet."

"You being so understanding makes it worse."

"Oh." She'd never considered that. She just assumed he'd want her to be strong and understanding, and not add to his troubles by begging and pleading with him to help her.

"Part of me wishes you would scream at me, hurl insults, tell me you hate me, but ... part of me is so relieved that you don't hate me."

If it didn't hurt her cut-up face to smile she would have offered him one. "I don't hate you," she assured him.

"Patrick, Patrick Kramer. Got the nickname Trick because I love magic tricks. Too bad real magic doesn't exist, and I can't just transport us out of here."

"I could definitely go for some magic right now," she agreed.

"Tell me about yourself, about your family, your childhood, your life."

Exhausted as she was, sleep didn't come easily. She was in too much pain to properly relax, any position she rested in wound up hurting her bruised body and waking her. Dozing was the best she had achieved in the hours they'd been left alone. Talking would worsen her already aching face, but it was better than just sitting in silence. Left alone with her thoughts too long, Stephanie was afraid they would wind up causing her to lose it.

Talking was definitely the better option.

"Dad left when I was three, Chris was nine. I don't remember much about him, I was too young, but I know he wasn't a bad guy. Well, other than abandoning his family. But he wasn't abusive or anything, more just a deadbeat. Mom would never talk about him, just pretended he never existed, but Chris told me a few things when I asked as I got older and curious about our father. Apparently, Dad kept losing jobs because he was lazy and didn't help around the house, Mom and Dad would argue about that. She'd tell him she worked all day then cooked and cleaned and took care of the kids. I guess he got sick of hearing how he needed to step up and just ... walked away."

The abandonment of her dad should maybe hurt her more than it did, but honestly, her mom had been so awesome at being both mother and father and making sure she had everything she needed that Stephanie didn't feel like she was affected by it at all. Still sucked her dad cared so little about his own children that he could just disappear from their lives and never do anything to make sure they were taken care of, but she didn't dwell on it.

"My mom was amazing," she continued. "The best mother anyone could ever ask for. She had to work three jobs to keep a roof over our heads, we struggled, I knew that even as a child. But she just loved us so much and gave us all of herself that it didn't seem to matter. I'm not saying there weren't times when I was a teenager and was upset I didn't have the same clothes as the other kids, or the latest phone, or a car when I turned sixteen, but mostly I was content. My mom ... she lived for me and my brother. Everything she did was for us and when Chris died ... she just gave up."

Since saying it didn't serve any purpose, Stephanie didn't add that it had hurt ... more than she wanted to admit ... that she hadn't been enough for her mom. She knew that her mother didn't play favorites between her son and her daughter, and yet when Chris died, she didn't want to live anymore.

Not even for the child she still had left.

"Losing them both so close together must have been so hard," Trick said, empathy in his tone.

"The worst. Those first few weeks I was a mess. Then my boyfriend, a man I had been planning on marrying and spending the rest of my life with, broke up with me because I was, and I quote, too emotional and needy. Which, of course, meant it was my fault that he went out and cheated on me."

Trick muttered a curse, and Stephanie smiled despite the painful tugs on the cuts on her cheeks. It was nice to hear someone validate her feelings and opinions on her ex. A couple of people had told her that she shouldn't be so hard on him, that he'd lost her mom, too, and he was grieving, and he had a taxing job, and she should be more understanding. Safe to say those people were no longer her friends. Grief was no excuse to cheat on the person you said you loved, and her ex hadn't even been close with her mom. Even if he hadn't broken up with her, she would have ended things because she didn't date cheaters, and she didn't date men not emotionally mature enough to support their partner.

"You're better off without him," Trick said.

"Yeah, I am," she agreed without hesitation. She wasn't lying around missing her ex and wishing things had turned out differently, she knew her own worth, and she wouldn't settle for less than a man who knew it, too. It was so much better that she found out who her ex really was before she committed her life to him and they had children together.

"You deserve a real man, one who knows how to step up when you need him, who does so without you having to ask, who knows what you need and doesn't hesitate to give it to you."

His words made her smile, but it quickly faded away as she realized what they were talking about was a moot point.

There would be no man in her future.

At least none other than their captors who wanted only to inflict pain and suffering.

And Trick. A man who would step up when she needed him, without her having to ask, a man who she knew would be intuitive to know what she needed and give it to her. A man who currently had no choice but to sit back and allow her to be hurt for the greater good. Even though she was pretty sure it was going to destroy him in the process.

CHAPTER
Seven

January 22nd
6:47 P.M.

With every second that passed, Trick grew more antsy.

More angry.

The need to do something was so strong it was almost completely consuming him, swallowing him up, devouring him, until it felt like the only thing keeping him sane was that for some reason he couldn't fathom, Stephanie seemed to need him.

She still lay right where she'd been since she crawled over to his side. The slight weight of her toned body snuggled on his lap was all that held him together. Why she didn't hate him, he had no idea, why she seemed to draw comfort from him even knowing he was the cause of her pain, he didn't get that either.

But the relief he felt when she told him she didn't hate him was far stronger than it should be given how little time they'd known one another.

Trauma bonding was a real thing. One he was currently experiencing firsthand. While it was only a couple of days at the most that they had spent together, Trick already felt closer to Stephanie than he did most of the other people in his life.

It killed him that the one thing she needed him to do for her was the one thing he couldn't.

How he was going to keep his mouth shut when their captors returned, he had no idea. Maybe it was just knowing that once he told them, not only did he become expendable, but Stephanie did as well. Her only purpose here was motivation to get him to talk, once he'd told them where the diamonds were, they would kill her.

Chances were, neither of them was getting out of there alive, but he wasn't going to do anything to speed up her death.

So he sat there, stewed in his anger, fought against his hopelessness, soothed Stephanie as best as he could each time she stirred, and prayed for a miracle.

Because that was all that was going to save them.

At the sound of approaching footsteps, his entire body tensed. Either she heard the sound as well, or it was the tension flowing through him, but Stephanie's head lifted, her eyelashes fluttering against her pale cheeks. He was worried about her, from the position of her bruises, he wasn't sure if she had cracked ribs. The wounds on her cheeks had stopped bleeding but infection wasn't just a concern it was pretty much a foregone conclusion. They hadn't been given anything to eat or drink and he knew the effects of dehydration were beginning to hit her.

Not that there was anything he could do about any of that.

"Is it them?" Stephanie asked. Although there was pure, undiluted terror in her eyes, she somehow managed to get her voice to come out calm. How any man had cheated on a woman like this, thrown her away like she was nothing, was unfathomable to him.

This woman was everything.

He was becoming obsessed with her the more she told him about her childhood, her family, and her life. It was absolutely killing him that he was going to sit there and watch her be tortured until, eventually, their captors got bored and just killed her.

"Yeah, honey, it's them," he said. Lying to her wasn't going to help, the men were going to be there any second, and while he'd love to give her a couple more seconds of peace, he knew she likely needed those seconds to prepare herself for what was to come.

"I survived what they did to me last time, I can survive this, too."

Unsure if the words were for her benefit or his, he leaned down and pressed his lips to her forehead, letting them linger there for a moment. "Yeah, you can, darlin'. I'm so sorry. I wish things were different."

"I know."

"Please, honey, if you need to cry or scream you do it. Don't hold it in for my benefit." Knowing that she was placing a higher value on his needs than her own made this so much worse. This woman didn't have a selfish bone in her body. She was everything anyone could ever want. Everything he could ever want. Everything he hadn't thought was important, didn't think existed or was interested in, that he now craved with an intensity that terrified him.

There was no time for her to respond because the door to their cell was opened and the same four men as before walked in. They had the chair with them again, and the man who was apparently their leader, at least that's what Trick was assuming since he was the only one who spoke, was playing with a huge, wicked-looking knife.

What Trick wouldn't do to get his hands on that knife.

That was all he needed to get them out of there. The men didn't appear to have guns on them, and even chained to the wall as he was, he knew he could take out all four of them before they were able to yell for help.

Like before, the men grabbed hold of Stephanie, pulling her from his arms. And like before, she kept her gaze fixed on him as they dragged her into the middle of the room. Swamped by helplessness, all Trick could do was try to infuse his own strength into her flagging body. It wasn't enough, not even close, but since it was all he could do, he held her gaze, told her with his eyes that he believed in her, and that he was so very sorry for playing a part in her suffering.

"You ready to speak now?" the leader asked as he eyed Stephanie with a hunger that had Trick's blood turning to ice as she was held between two other men.

He knew what was happening.

From her expression Stephanie didn't.

Yet.

She thought she knew just how evil these men were, but she was wrong.

Sweet, innocent, kind, sheltered even though she'd grown up poor and had a brother in the military. This woman saw—looked for—the good in people, even her deadbeat dad who had abandoned her, and her mom who he knew had hurt her when she gave up and wasted away after Chris' death.

What was going to happen next would shatter Stephanie's last belief in humanity.

At Trick's desolate silence, the leader began to unbuckle his pants. Stephanie's eyes grew almost impossibly wide, and he felt her growing panic even as she stood stock still.

Curling his fingers into fists so tightly that they ached, Trick had no choice but to watch as the man held the blade of his knife to Stephanie's neck as he pushed her legs apart and shoved inside of her in one thrust.

Her mouth opened but no sound came out.

Look at me, honey.

Focus on me.

Block out what's happening.

As badly as Trick wanted to close his eyes and let himself block out what was happening to Stephanie, he couldn't match her bravery with cowardice.

Slowly, her gaze moved back to his and stayed there. He felt her fear, her pain, her torment, and all he had to offer her was so pathetically inadequate that he almost broke down and shouted at the men to stop, that he'd give them what they wanted, but to just leave Stephanie alone.

It was only knowing he was her anchor right now, the only thing keeping her afloat, that kept his mouth shut.

Don't make it worse, don't get her killed.

Keeping quiet was the only way to keep her alive, so he pressed his lips together, and tried not to listen to the grunts of the man as he took something from Stephanie she could never get back. Nobody deserved to spend the final hours or days of their life like this, but especially not someone as good and pure as Stephanie Fuller.

When he finished raping her, coming with a howl of pleasure inside her, the man pulled out and zipped himself back up. "Girl feels good." He grinned, showing off the missing front teeth in his mouth, and even from there Trick could smell his putrid breath.

There was no way Trick could hide the fury that raged inside him, and as he directed it all at the man who had just destroyed something in Stephanie, he watched as the man faltered a little. It was one thing to know you had the upper hand because you had the numbers on your side, it was another to be reminded just how dangerous your opponent was.

All Trick needed was for them to make one little mistake and he'd pounce all over it, use it to get Stephanie out of this hellhole.

Trying to pretend he hadn't just given away an ounce of his power, the leader reached out and grabbed Stephanie's wrist, holding it tightly enough that she winced. When he moved the blade of his knife so it pressed against the bottom of her pinkie finger, once again Stephanie's eyes widened in shock.

She was smart. She knew what was going to happen next.

"Tell me where the diamonds are or the girl loses finger."

~

January 22nd
   7:07 P.M.

No.

   He wouldn't.

   Couldn't.

   This wasn't happening.

   Stephanie's gaze flew from the knife pressed against her pinkie finger to Trick and then back to the knife again.

   You couldn't cut off a finger with a knife.

   Could you?

   She had no idea, but she hoped it wasn't possible.

   But if it wasn't possible then why would the man be holding the knife against her finger and telling Trick he'd cut it off if he didn't tell what they wanted to know?

There was no other reason she could think of that he would say it if it wasn't true.

Horror over what had just happened and what was going to happen made her knees buckle and the man laughed as she fell limp in his hold.

"Last chance or the girl loses her finger," he told Trick.

The look in Trick's eyes as he stared back at her would be seared into her mind for the rest of her life.

Desolation.

Helplessness.

Rage.

Guilt.

A swirling mess of emotions she could feel from there. More than that, she could feel him wavering. He wanted to give in, she needed to assure him it was okay, that she could take whatever happened, but she couldn't make herself say the words.

How could she?

How could she tell him she was okay with being maimed?

She wasn't okay with any of this, being hit, being cut, being raped. What choice did she have though? Could she beg Trick for mercy knowing that if these people got their hands on the diamonds, they could use them to fund whatever sick, twisted plans they had? Was her finger worth more than the lives of thousands of innocent people?

The only sound that filled the small room was her own uneven breathing.

It was stupid of her to think she could do this.

She wasn't strong, wasn't brave, wasn't anything other than completely terrified.

Yanking her free from the grip of the two other men, the leader, the one who had raped her, dragged her over to the wall and shoved her up against it. There wasn't a single part of her body that didn't protest against being pressed too harshly against the unforgiving concrete. The bruises that littered her torso ached, the rough concrete tugged at the barely formed scabs on her cheeks, even the ache between her legs from being taken against her will seemed to hurt more.

Her left hand was pulled away from the rest of her body, all her fingers but her pinkie curled into her palm and crushed against the concrete like the rest of her body.

"Diamonds or finger," the man said, it was clear he was getting frustrated now with Trick's continued refusal to talk. That could only mean bad things for her.

It seemed to happen between one blink of an eye and the next.

One second, she had eight fingers and two thumbs, the next her left pinkie finger was falling toward the floor.

While she knew it didn't actually happen the way it played out in her mind, it looked like her finger fell in slow motion, almost as if it was floating. It wasn't like it was in horror movies, blood didn't squirt eight inches up into the air above the stump where her finger used to be, but blood did gush from the wound.

With no strength left in her body, when the man released her, she slumped immediately to the floor, lying in a crumpled heap.

It was all too much.

How was a girl like her, who spent her days at a gym, supposed to deal with this level of darkness and depravity?

The weight of the world felt like it was on her shoulders. How was she supposed to honor her promise not to beg Trick to save her when things just kept getting worse and worse? But how could she beg for her own salvation knowing it would cause the deaths of innocent people?

Her head spun.

If there was anything left in her stomach, she would have thrown up again.

Thankful for the first time that she hadn't been given anything to eat since she arrived there, Stephanie just lay on the floor, shivering, rocking, maybe crying, she wasn't quite sure.

A deep, vicious growl, a sound she'd never heard before rumbled through the cell. For a moment she thought she must have broken her promise and the sound was coming from her, but then she realized it was Trick.

Why was he making a sound?

He wasn't supposed to.

Suddenly too weary to worry about it, she just closed her eyes and allowed her overwhelmed and overwrought mind to carry her away.

"Stephanie. Steph. Answer me, honey. I need to know you're okay. Stephanie."

Like through a haze, the words pierced through the fuzzy state of consciousness she seemed trapped in.

Not quite awake, but not quite asleep either.

Hovering.

In a place filled with nothing but pain. A place she wanted to escape so badly. A place there was no escape from.

"Please, darlin', let me know you're okay."

It was only the fear in Trick's voice that prodded her out of the bubble of pain and terror she was trapped in. Trick was worried, she had to answer him. The need to assuage his fear was unexplainable, all she knew was that he was suffering, and something deep inside her didn't like it.

"I'm ... 'kay," she mumbled.

"Honey, don't scare me like that again." Although there was a small amount of reprimand in his tone it was mostly relief. Relief so great she could feel it. He'd been genuinely terrified for her.

The sound of the chain keeping him tethered to the wall being violently shaken prompted her to lift her head and she saw Trick fighting with it.

What did he think he was going to be able to do?

Suddenly break it?

A roar of frustration so loud, so powerful, it made her flinch, echoed through their cell.

This wasn't the Trick she was used to seeing.

No longer was he in control, he looked like a wild man, his eyes seemed too big for his face, and he was breathing hard, doing crazy things like acting as though it was possible for him to break through metal with his bare hands.

She needed him to stop.

Needed him to be calm.

Needed him.

"Trick." The word sounded weak and hurt to speak, but she

couldn't let him go on like that, he was going to hurt himself ... or give himself a heart attack.

At the sound of her voice, he froze.

Like he could read her mind, she could see him physically pull himself together, his big chest expanded with a controlled breath, and he raked his fingers through his hair before his gaze softened as it landed on her. "Come here, honey."

Stephanie would have sworn that moving was beyond her. Burning pain consumed her hand, her head throbbed with a headache, the cuts on her cheeks stung from her salty tears, and her battered torso made even breathing difficult. But she felt a pull toward Trick like an invisible string joined them together and she was powerless to do anything but go to him.

Cradling her injured hand against her chest, she shifted so she was on her right hip and somehow managed to drag herself across the floor. Each drag took off a layer of skin, but she didn't care. She just wanted to get to Trick.

Nothing else mattered.

Once she was close enough, he reached out and snatched her up, cradling her against him and rocking her from side to side like she was a small infant.

Waves of helplessness washed over her. His, hers, she wasn't sure anymore.

"Honey, I'm so sorry," Trick whispered as he sat and settled her on his lap. His gaze landed on her bloody, maimed hand, and anger sparked in his dark eyes. Another growl rumbled through his body. "I'll kill every last one of them for doing this to you. Damn, darlin', damn ... I don't even have anything to stop the bleeding. I'm so sorry ... so sorry."

She wanted to comfort him, but truth was, her well had run dry and she didn't have anything to give him right now.

"What can I do, honey? Anything. Give me something. Whatever you need I'll give it to you."

They both knew he couldn't give her what she really needed. Food, water, medical supplies, her finger back, her rape erased, or a way out of this hellhole. Since she couldn't have any of those things, Stephanie took the only thing she could have.

Trick.

For the time being the men were gone. She didn't have to brace herself for pain and find a way to hold it all inside.

"Hold me," she whispered as she pressed her shivering body closer to the only source of warmth in the room.

Trick's arms closed around her, and he somehow seemed to curl his body into a protective cocoon, keeping her safe and protected. Reaching a brick wall, her mind and body crashed, but before she slipped away, Stephanie prayed one more time for a miracle.

CHAPTER
Eight

January 23rd
2:05 A.M.

He was done with this.

Flat out done.

Trick was going to find a way out of this place.

Staying here wasn't an option. Stephanie couldn't take much more of this and neither could he.

Watching her be raped and then have her finger amputated had killed something inside him. There was no way to pretend he wasn't partially responsible and even if he survived this, he very much doubted he'd ever be able to look himself in the eye again.

He should have done more.

Should have found a way out sooner.

This was on him.

Glancing down at the unconscious woman in his arms, he knew it was now or never. If he didn't find a way out, there would be no point, they were both going to wither away and die. If he wanted to at least give them a chance, he had to make a move.

Exactly what that move was he had no idea yet, but he would figure something out.

He had to.

Nothing else was acceptable.

Stephanie's cold skin pressed against his, even though he was sharing his warmth with her, curling his body around hers as much as possible, he feared it wasn't enough. Her system had been thrown into turmoil, beaten, cut, starved, denied water, raped, and then maimed, it had all been too much for her and she had been floating in and out of consciousness ever since she dragged herself across the floor and into his arms.

Those minutes she had laid there after the men left them alone in their dungeon cell had been the longest of his life. No matter how many times he called her name, begged and pleaded with her to answer him, to let him know she was okay, she had remained silent. Deathly silent.

But she wasn't dead.

Not yet anyway.

And if he wanted to keep her alive, he had to figure something out. He wasn't going to fail her again. No matter what it took he was going to get her out of there.

Stirring in his arms, red-rimmed eyes opened slowly and looked up at him. For a moment he saw pain, hopelessness, and emptiness. It terrified him. Scared him even more when she blinked and cleared all her emotions from her gaze, instead, reflecting out at him what she knew he needed. Strength and bravery. While he needed to know she had what it took to survive, he felt a piece of Stephanie slip away each time she gave him what he needed instead of taking care of what she needed.

"Hey, honey, how you doing?" he asked, forcing his voice to come out soothing and calm despite the fury that raged unabated inside him. Every time she woke, he asked her how she was doing and each time she told him she was hanging in there.

"I'm okay," she assured him in that weak voice that told him she was anything but.

Unable to take her valiant grace a single second more, he jostled her —would have shaken her if he didn't know how much pain she was in despite her trying to hide it from him—and shifted her so she was sitting more than lying across him. "Don't. No more lies."

"What do you want me to say, Trick?" she asked so wearily his eyes stung. "That I'm hungry? Can you do anything about that? So thirsty I can hardly think of anything else, even the pain? Can you do anything about that either? That I'm in pain, that I'm traumatized, that I'm struggling, that I'm trying my very best to be brave even though this is the hardest thing I've ever had to do, you know all of that. Saying it doesn't help."

"Holding it in doesn't either," he said softly. Even knowing it was a bad idea, he was attached enough to this woman as it was and it was getting harder and harder to keep his mouth shut, Trick reached out and smoothed a stray curl off her cheek, tucking it behind her ear. The only place left on her face that wasn't sliced open and smeared with blood was her forehead, so he brushed his knuckles across the smooth skin there, and then slid his hand behind her head, gently massaging the tight muscles in her neck.

"I ... I want to go home," she whispered so forlornly that he had no choice but to tighten his hold on her and bring her closer. Tears shimmered in her eyes, but his strong girl didn't let them fall. Wouldn't. She was hellbent on holding those emotions in and not allowing them to escape because she knew he was struggling to do the right thing.

"I'm going to get you home, honey," he said fiercely.

"Trick ... you know you can't promise me that." There was tenderness in her gaze instead of the loathing he should see when she looked at him. Damn, he hated himself for putting her through this and would do anything to take it all away and make it better. Knowing there was no way to undo the damage even if he did somehow manage to get her out made it almost impossible to breathe.

Shoving away his self-loathing, guilt, and fear, Trick focused himself like he had been trained to. "I can promise you that and I have."

"But ..."

"No, darlin', no buts."

"However—"

"Fancy but," he told her and shot her a grin.

A small smile curled her lips up and some of the pain, fear, and hopelessness in her eyes faded. "Cute. Nevertheless—and don't you go and tell me that's an even fancier but—you know we can't get out of here. You're chained up, the door is locked, there are more of them than there are of us, and we're both weak and dehydrated. We're not getting out of here."

"I won't let you give up hope," he said fiercely.

"Trying to be realistic."

"Then don't. For a moment just believe that all things are possible. Please, honey."

For a long moment, Stephanie studied him as though trying to figure him out. Then, finally, she gave a small nod. "I suppose it isn't outside the realm of possibility that you could find a way out for us. I mean, after all, guys like you are the closest thing to superheroes that exist."

"Sure are," he readily agreed. While Trick certainly didn't feel much like a superhero, he felt an infusion of strength from Stephanie's words. She was counting on him, and somehow, that seemed to make him feel like he really could be a superhero, like nothing was off the table because his girl needed him to be able to do the impossible.

Both their heads snapped toward the door to their cell when they heard footsteps.

Any progress he'd made lifting Stephanie's mood immediately evaporated. "They're back already?" she asked in a panic.

"Try to relax, darlin', you got this." Trick wished there was more he could say, more he could do, but honestly, he'd expected to have more time before the men came back. Dehydrated as she was, and then with the blood loss from her hand, certainly not a life-threatening amount on its own, but combined with everything else, he was terrified she wouldn't survive another round of torture.

When the door to their cell was opened, he was surprised to see only one man there, different from the four who had come both times before. This man had a couple of bottles of water in his hands and what looked like a couple of old, stale pieces of bread. Guess their captors decided if they wanted to continue trying to get answers, they had better give their hostages something to eat and drink.

What Trick cared more about, though, was that there was a padlock on the other side of the metal bars, and once the man had unlocked it, he shoved the key into his pocket. Since Trick was chained up and Stephanie was weak and injured, the man obviously wrote them both off as a threat because he left the door open, the padlock hanging on the lock.

It took all his control not to scream at Stephanie to run, but having her go running blindly out into the unknown on her own and in her condition was sending her on a suicide mission. They needed to go together, and he knew exactly how they were going to do that.

That bit of magic they'd been hoping for was right within his grasp.

Sliding Stephanie off his lap, Trick propped her up against the wall and then stood, drawing himself up to his full six-foot-four height.

Younger and smaller than the men who tortured Stephanie, this man shuddered at the sight of Trick, and scurried across the floor to hand them the bottles of water and the scraps of food.

Sleight of hand.

How many times had he done this trick? Since learning it at the age of seven he would have to guess at least a thousand. In fact, he did it so often that his team was sick of him taking things without them realizing it and then pulling those things out from behind their ears. The only one who thought the trick was fun was eight-year-old Andy.

This time the trick was going to save his life and Stephanie's. There would be no pulling the key out from behind the guard's ear, but as he took the food and water from the man, he swiped the key with the practiced hand of someone who had worked hard to perfect the simple magic trick.

∾

January 23rd
   2:42 A.M.

The door closed behind the man who had brought them food, and Stephanie felt like their only chance of escaping had disappeared with him.

Why hadn't Trick done something?

Just because he was chained up, it didn't mean he was completely helpless, and this man had been younger and smaller than the others. Surely, there was something Trick could have done to take him down and at least given them a shot at escaping.

Weariness weighed her down, and she sunk back against the wall, allowing every muscle in her body to go completely limp. It was taking too much effort to keep ... going. Everything was hard, keeping her mouth shut, dealing with the pain, pretending she hadn't been violated, blocking out the consuming need for water.

When she felt Trick kneel beside her, she didn't bother to open her eyes. He needed her to be strong, she knew that, but in this second, she didn't have any strength to spare that wasn't being used to just survive.

"Open your eyes, darlin', we don't have long before they realize."

She had no idea what he was talking about, but something in his voice had her reaching deep down inside herself for strength she didn't think she possessed and somehow she managed to pry open heavy eyes.

"Drink, not too much or you'll make yourself sick." Trick held one of the two water bottles to her lips and a part of her wanted to refuse. Because as thirsty as she was, she was way too nauseous to keep anything down.

"You take it, I'll just throw it right back up," she murmured, allowing her eyes to fall closed again. All of a sudden death seemed awfully close. Not close enough to take her, but she could feel it circling, just waiting for an opportunity to pounce.

The shake Trick gave her was enough to make her moan in pain.

What was he doing?

Why couldn't he just leave her be?

Finally, she was numb enough that she could rest without being in so much pain she kept constantly waking, attempting to shift into a position that didn't hurt even knowing there wasn't one. Now she was weak enough that her brain just checked out, a blessing in disguise, it had gotten to the point where Stephanie treasured those moments of blissful nothingness.

"Oh no, you don't," Trick said, giving her another shake. "You are not checking out on me now, not when I finally have a chance at getting you out of here."

"Huh?" Her eyes popped open and when Trick tipped the water bottle to her lips, she opened them automatically and drank the couple of mouthfuls he allowed her. "What do you mean a chance at getting out of here?"

A huge grin unlike anything she'd seen on his face so far turned him from handsome to downright sexy, panty-melting, attractive. He reached behind her ear, and then the next thing she knew, he held something up that glinted in the dull light of their cell. Something that absolutely hadn't come from behind her ear.

"Is that ...?"

"Guess all my hours of practicing magic tricks actually paid off. Took it from the guard's pocket. Sooner or later, he'll realize it's missing, so we need to hurry. Eat one of these, then keep the rest for later." He handed her a loaf of stale-looking bread cut into slices. As much as she didn't feel like eating it, she took one piece and nibbled at the corner.

As she did so, Trick very gently took the wrist of her maimed hand and lifted it away from where she had it tucked protectively against her body. So far Stephanie had avoided looking at it as much as possible. Blood she was okay with, gore too. She liked horror movies and she knew first aid, had even been first on scene at a terrible car accident once. According to the first responders, her quick thinking actions had saved the life of one of the injured.

But this wasn't a horror movie, it was real life.

Her life.

Her hand.

And the sight of the bloody stub where her finger used to be was too much to handle.

"This will probably hurt," Trick warned as he held the other bottle of water above her hand.

"Not worse than when it happened," she murmured, and he winced at her words.

"It's not much, but at least it'll clean the wound out a little," he said softly.

The water hitting her stump sent a fresh wave of pain cascading through her body, and she couldn't stop a couple of tears from squeezing out as she scrunched her eyes closed. She was so tired of living in pain, she wanted a break from it.

"There, honey, all done." Trick set her hand back against her chest. "Come on, darlin', eat that up, you need the strength. This isn't going to be easy, and I'm going to need you to stay strong for me. Can you do that?"

If it meant getting home, she could do anything.

A new wave, this time of energy, hit her and she opened her eyes and straightened her spine. What was the point of surviving beatings, rapes, and torture if she was going to give up now when this could be their only chance at getting out of there?

"I won't let you down," she promised.

"There's my girl." Trick's smile was soft and warm this time. He reached out, pressed his calloused fingertips to her forehead, and very gently caressed her skin. It was the only place on her face that wasn't marred with gashes, and he'd taken to stroking it. She liked it. Probably more than she should. "You ready?"

When she nodded, he took her elbow and helped her stand. Only then did she realize he had already unlocked the metal cuff around his ankle.

With the two bottles of water and the rest of the bread balanced in her good arm, she followed Trick to the door of their cell. There wasn't a lot of space between the metal bars, and she had no idea how he was going to reach between them to use the key to get them out.

Turned out she shouldn't have doubted him.

It took less than a minute for his long, nimble fingers to slip between the bars and make quick work of unlocking the padlock. After ushering her through the door, he locked it behind them, leaving them in a long, dark passageway.

Moving his lips so they were right above her ear, he whispered, "You stay behind me. Do what I tell you when I tell you to do it, no discussion, no arguments."

If he was expecting her to pretend she knew more about how to get them out of their situation than he did when he was the one with the training and experience, he was crazy. "I won't mess this up," she assured him. "I trust you. I'll do whatever you tell me to do."

Something passed through his dark eyes, but it was gone before her sluggish mind could figure out what it was. "You're amazing, Steph. I hope you know that."

It was nice to hear that she hadn't let him down, that he thought she had done a good job of being his partner in this mess they were both trapped in. When he pressed his lips to her forehead and held them there for a moment, she found herself lifting onto her tiptoes, seeking more of his touch, more of his warmth, his strength.

The moment passed far too quickly, and then Trick was tucking her in behind him and leading her down the passageway. There were other cells like theirs down there, although all of them appeared to be empty. At the end of the long corridor was a door.

For a second, she thought it was going to be locked. That this was all for nothing. That they weren't ever getting out, but when Trick grasped the doorknob and turned the door swung open.

They were met with a staircase, and her anxiety mounted as she forced her heavy legs to carry her up each step. Stephanie kept as close to Trick as it was possible to be without actually climbing onto his back. He was her lifeline, her only hope, her only protection, and she was terrified something was going to happen to him.

If it did, how would she survive on her own?

At the top of the stairs was another corridor, this one led to a door underneath which she could see a sliver of light.

Someone was on the other side.

Likely, multiple someones.

If Trick was worried, he certainly didn't show it. His steps were calm and measured as he headed for the door, and when he ripped it open and sprang into action it was unlike anything she had ever seen before.

Three men were in the room, but Trick didn't hesitate to take them each on. He seemed to have a plan, and all she could do was stare at him in shock as he killed first one man, and then another, and then the last. He was like some sort of avenging angel, and she couldn't help but feel that, somehow, he'd been sent here for a reason, like even in death her brother was looking out for her and had made sure the best of the best was the man the militia had targeted.

Trick was her very own superhero.

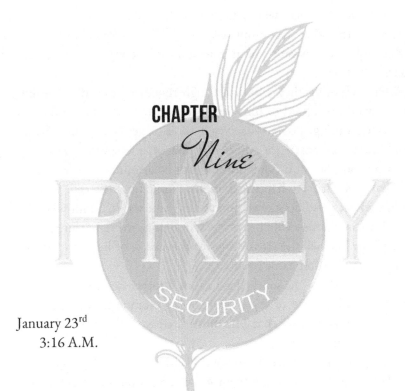

CHAPTER

Nine

January 23rd
   3:16 A.M.

Trick approached her slowly.

All too aware of the horror etched into Stephanie's features.

On top of everything else she'd had to go through, she'd just watched him kill three men like it was nothing, a walk in the park. No wonder she was staring at the bodies with wide eyes and fine tremors wracking her body.

He hoped it hadn't changed how she saw him. The last thing he wanted was for her to think he was no better than the men who had hurt her, so easily able to inflict pain and take lives like it was nothing.

Only for him it wasn't nothing.

It wasn't that he enjoyed killing, it was that these men were the enemy. They were involved in torturing a woman who mixed him up inside, and there wasn't anything he wouldn't do to protect her.

Stephanie was his priority.

Whatever it took to get her home, he'd do.

And if there was a part of him that would have enjoyed inflicting the same pain on the men who had tortured Stephanie that they had brought her, then that was completely normal if you asked him.

But right now wasn't about punishments, it was about getting Stephanie to safety.

After everything they'd been through together Trick didn't think that she would be afraid of him now. She had to understand that this was about escaping, doing whatever it took to get out of her. So he shoved aside his conscience whispering that in the short time they'd known one another he'd done nothing but be a source of pain to her. Trick hated what had happened in that underground cell, but he couldn't go back and do it over, and as hard as it was to admit when he looked into Stephanie's wild brown eyes, he'd done the right thing.

Just hurt like hell the right thing for thousands of innocent people had been allowing Stephanie to suffer.

"It's okay, honey," he soothed as he took another step closer, moving so he blocked her view of the bodies she was staring unblinkingly at. "I'm sorry you had to see that," he murmured when he stopped about three feet away from her.

A long, slow blink cleared her gaze. "Huh?"

"Had no choice but to kill them so we can get out of here, but you know I'd never hurt you." Maybe a part of him needed to hear her say it out loud. Maybe if she did, he'd be able to sleep at night if he got her out of this mess alive.

"Of course I know that." Shifting so she could see the dead bodies that littered the room, her face broke out into a grin. "That was amazing."

"Huh?"

"I never really knew what men like my brother were capable of. I mean, I knew Chris was trained to use weapons and to kill with his bare hands, but ... I guess knowing it in my head and seeing it in real life are two different things."

"You're ... okay with seeing me kill three men?"

"Three monsters who are responsible for what happened to us even if they weren't the ones in the room." Cocking her head to the side she shot him a confused frown. "Why would I be anything other than grateful to you right now? You killed those men for me. For us. To give us a chance."

"I don't want you to think I'm like them."

Her gaze softened. "Trick ... you gave me strength in that dungeon, I tried to hate you at first, but I couldn't. All it took was one look into your eyes and I could see how badly you wanted to save me. It's not your fault you couldn't. You're saving me now though. I don't think you're anything like these men, you're my superhero."

Stephanie's words were sweet and heartfelt and everything he wanted—everything he needed—to hear. "I'll do whatever it takes to get you home," he vowed. Not a promise he should make given he didn't even know where they were, but anything less wasn't acceptable. "Before we get out of here, I need to try to clean you up a bit."

As he guided her over to the table where two of the three men had been sitting when they came into the room, he couldn't help a flash of worry. Just because he got her out of the cell, it didn't mean they were out of the woods. Trick was genuinely concerned about infection. The wounds on her cheeks were red and angry looking and the stump on her hand was practically inviting infection.

The room wasn't much, it was a small wooden structure with a tiny kitchen and what he assumed was a small bathroom. Heading there first, he found a couple of dirty towels and a bar of soap that had seen better days. Still, it was all he had to work with, so he filled a bowl with water and brought it to the table.

Stephanie didn't speak as he wet the towel, smeared some soap on it, and gently grasped the back of her neck, but she did suck in a breath when he made contact. Since she quickly averted her gaze, he had no idea if it was a pained breath or if his touching her brought back memories of her rape, or if ... maybe she liked his touch.

He liked touching her, and holding her, and couldn't deny that if their situation weren't so messed up, he would have already asked if he could kiss her. Something about this woman called to him like a flame to a moth.

Although she winced and stiffened as he cleaned the wounds on her face as best he could, she didn't utter a single sound of complaint. Stephanie had nerves of steel, he was honestly in awe of her. Most special forces operators couldn't hold in their pain, fear, and anger when they were hurt the way she had been.

It also made him angry though. He didn't deserve the kindness she kept showering upon him.

By the time he had her face clean, he noted the cuts weren't as bad as they had appeared when they were all smeared with blood. They would leave scars though. If she'd had immediate access to a hospital and plastic surgeon, the damage would have been minimized, but by the time he got her to any sort of help it would be too late to do anything to hide the wounds.

"I'm going to bandage your hand," he told her as he prepared another towel by ripping the material into strips. "Do the best we can to prevent infection getting in."

"I can't look at it," Stephanie said, voice slightly trembling as she turned her head to the side so she faced the far wall.

"Not a failing, darlin'," he reminded her. As he did his best to clean her hand without causing her too much pain, his jaw began to ache from gritting his teeth together. He was beginning to hate the way she held in her emotions like she didn't want to bother anyone else with them.

He knew why she did it.

That jerk of an ex of hers cheated on her and broke up with her when she was grieving the loss of the only family she had because she was behaving like any normal person would when they'd had two loved ones die so close together had really messed with her head. Now she seemed to see any display of emotion on her part as a turn-off to others. She was taking her promise not to plead with him to give the militia the intel they needed to the absolute extreme.

Now wasn't the time to address that issue though.

Not that there would ever be a time for them to discuss it. It wasn't his job to help her with her issues, she wasn't his, not really. Stephanie was just a woman he had to get to safety and then he'd walk away and leave her in the care of her friends.

An unsettled feeling at the thought of just handing her off and walking away settled in his gut, but he brushed it off. He didn't even want a relationship, so why should walking away from this woman be any different from leaving behind the women he slept with?

Because she's different.

Because you're different when you're with her.

Because this whole mess has made you look at the world differently.

Ignoring the voice in his head, he fastened the bandage and then looked around the room. This place seemed to be purely for torturing people. There were no beds or anything in there, and this room was just for the guards to hang out in until shift change.

Which could be happening at any moment.

They had to hurry up and get out of there. While tending to Stephanie's wounds was unavoidable, they'd already spent more time there than they should. Stripping off the clothes of the largest and smallest of the men, he quickly threw on the bigger man's clothes. They were a little tight, but they'd do, and then crossed to the table to give Stephanie the other set of clothes.

"Sorry, best I can do, better than walking around naked," he said.

Although she grimaced, she nodded. "Definitely better than naked."

He had to help her dress, her hand was too painful for her to do much with, and there were still bruises, now dark black and blue, all across her torso. After checking for keys to a vehicle and coming up empty, he gathered all the food he could find, commandeered all the bottles of water, and collected anything else he thought might be useful. He put it all into a pack along with the guards' weapons. Then they were ready to go.

With the pack on his back and one of the guns in his hand, with his other he took Stephanie's good one and helped her to her feet. It worried him that she wobbled precariously before catching her balance, but as much as he wanted to give her time to rest, to eat and drink, and get some sleep, they had to put as much distance between them and this place as they could.

They both froze when he opened the door.

"What now?" Stephanie asked, a hint of trepidation in her tone as they looked at the thick expanse of jungle surrounding them.

"Now we walk." It wouldn't be easy, but he wasn't giving up.

Stephanie's life depended on him, and he wasn't going to let her down again.

~

January 23rd
5:39 P.M.

Now we walk.

It all sounded so simple.

But what had seemed so simple when Trick said it well over twelve hours ago now seemed like the impossible.

Naïve of her, but Stephanie had thought when Trick busted them out of that cell, then killed the guards, and they walked out of their prison free that their ordeal was as good as over.

How she thought that she had no idea.

Of course, it wouldn't be that simple. They were still trapped in the middle of nowhere. Worse than that, this was the militia's territory, they knew it like the back of their hands while she and Trick were walking around blind. He was certain they were in Liberia, but even if that was true—and honestly, she didn't doubt him about anything—that didn't really help them.

Where were they and how could they get to a safe place so Trick could call for help?

That's what they needed to know, and yet hours later—hours of trudging through jungle so thick it was like trying to force your way through wall-to-wall plants, only there were no ends to the walls, they just went on and on forever—they were no closer to getting any answers.

Trick said this whole area was likely under the militia's rule, so it wasn't even as simple as just getting to a village or town and asking for help. They were going to have to hide out, slip in somewhere, find a phone, steal one if they had to, whatever it took to get a message out so they could get home.

She said "they" but what she really meant was Trick.

She was nothing more than dead weight.

Dead weight that wasn't sure it could keep walking much longer. Trick moved slowly on her account, he made sure they stopped regularly. He made her eat and drink some of their water even if she protested, but she was getting weaker and weaker. They both knew it although she was sure Trick would deny she was holding him back if she brought it up.

There wasn't a single part of her that didn't hurt.

From the soles of her feet to the top of her head, she just ... hurt.

The boots she was wearing were several sizes too big for her, and her feet slipped and slid about in there with every step she took leaving her with blisters. After days of nothing to do but sit in their cell, her muscles were protesting big time having to traipse for hours through rough terrain. Her entire torso hurt from all the bruises marring it, and her maimed hand was pure agony, no other way to describe it. Add in a headache, and all she wanted to do was curl up and sleep, even sleeping in the jungle wasn't enough of a deterrent, although she'd love a nice, warm, cozy bed.

"Okay, time for a break."

Although her entire body screamed at her to stop, to let Trick find a safe place for her to sit that wasn't crawling with dangerous bugs or snakes or something else equally as icky, Stephanie was afraid that if she stopped now she wouldn't be able to get going again. Already pushed beyond what it could handle, it was only a matter of time before her body gave out on her.

"I can keep going," she said. Although since it came out as a pant as she struggled to catch her breath, it didn't really sound all that convincing.

"You need rest," Trick said in the tone she associated as his don't bother arguing I've already made up my mind voice.

"Trick ... I ... I don't think I can get going again if I stop," she admitted. For some reason it hurt to make the admission. It shouldn't, while he knew she ran a gym, Trick also knew that working out in the air-conditioned safety of a gym wasn't the same as walking through thick jungle in the humidity. He knew she was weak and injured, healing from a concussion, then cuts and bruises, dehydrated, starved, and exhausted, he didn't expect her to be superwoman. Yet ...

Still, she felt like she was letting him down.

"Maybe if—" she started only to be cut off by Trick.

"Hop on my back for a while."

"Huh?"

"I'll carry you for a while. I want to put a little more distance between us and them before we find somewhere to sleep for the night."

"You can't carry me and walk through this." Stephanie waved a hand at the miles of jungle surrounding them. "And keep an eye out for the militia and any animals or bugs that want to hurt us."

"Not sure the animals and bugs want to hurt us," Trick teased.

Somehow his easy-going manner managed to pull a smile out of her. "Still, there's no way you can carry me through this."

"You insulting me, darlin'?"

"Umm ... no?" Why would she? She was pretty sure there wasn't anything this man couldn't do.

"Course I can carry you and keep us safe at the same time. I'm a superhero, remember?"

How he kept doing it she had no idea, but his laidback attitude in the midst of a terrifying ordeal and his gentle teasing managed to make her smile again. "My superhero," she agreed. It hurt in a weird kind of way to know that Trick wasn't really hers. They might be going through this ordeal together, he might have tended her wounds as best he could, held her in his arms and offered her comfort when they were alone in their cell, and they might be traipsing side by side through the rainforest, but none of that made him hers.

For some reason that made her heart ache.

Stupid.

She had way bigger things to worry about than that a man she'd just met was going to walk right on out of her life as soon as they got home.

"Come on, honey. Hop on. I got you."

Even though she knew he was just trying to keep her calm, that he didn't mean it as anything more than his desire to make up for not being able to protect her while they were trapped in hell, her heart did a weird little flutter when he said I got you.

Part of her wished he really did. That he wouldn't leave as soon as she was safe. How was she supposed to go back to regular life after this?

None of her friends could understand what she'd lived through, how it had changed her.

Grasping her forearms, he moved in front of her, stooped, and hoisted her up. Doing her part, Stephanie wrapped her legs around his waist, and her arms around his neck. Avoiding the bandage on her hand, she gripped her forearm, her fingers brushing against Trick's, sending a tingle up her arms.

She ignored it ... kind of. But also wondered if he'd felt it, too.

Despite her fears that he wouldn't be able to carry her through the thick jungle on his back, Trick was actually able to move faster than when she'd been walking on her own. Guess she'd underestimated her superhero.

Time kind of blurred as she perched on Trick's back, lulled into a semi-sleep state by the methodical bounce of each step he took.

"Steph, wake up, honey." Trick's voice tugged her out of sleep she hadn't even realized she had fallen into.

"What is it?" she asked, lifting her head from where it had been tucked against his neck, her cheek pillowed on her arm. Had he found help?

"A car," he said, excitement in his voice.

That excitement was catching, and she straightened, planting her feet on the ground when he slowly lowered her down.

"Stay here," he said, guiding her to duck behind a tree.

"Why?"

"Abandoned car, got to check it out, make sure there's nobody nearby." Pulling out one of the weapons, he pressed it into her good hand. "Use it if you need to. No hesitation. Promise me."

The thought of shooting someone filled her with dread, but she gave a shaky nod. She hadn't survived everything she had to not follow through on whatever needed to be done. If it came down to it, she would protect herself and Trick by killing.

"Be right back."

After giving her a quick kiss on the forehead, Trick disappeared. Like he was performing a magic trick he faded into the jungle, and even though she looked for him, Stephanie couldn't find a trace of him.

Alone out there, she was suddenly aware of just how huge the jungle was. How remote. How dangerous. Everywhere you turned there was something that could hurt you. More than that, things that could kill you if you weren't careful.

Add to that the fact this was likely still the militia's territory, and that they probably knew she and Trick were gone. That meant they were out there, too, hunting them, and she didn't want to think about what would happen if they were caught.

Seconds ticked by feeling more like hours.

Even though she could just make out the car, mostly hidden by the thick vegetation, she couldn't catch even a glimpse of Trick.

It was getting dark with hardly any sunlight left making it through the trees to where she was crouched, leaning against the trunk of the closest tree. All the nocturnal predators would soon be coming out, and she could only hope that the militia were going to take a break for the night.

Anxiety mounted inside her, she wanted Trick to come back, needed him, he was the only safe place she had.

Where are you?

Please come back.

Just when she was about to lose it and do something stupid, like stand up and start screaming at the top of her lungs, a shadow moved toward her.

A startled gasp was thankfully the only sound she made as she swung the gun toward the moving figure.

"Don't shoot, Steph. It's only me."

At the sound of Trick's voice, she immediately relaxed, sinking back against the tree trunk. "You're okay?"

"Fine, honey," he assured her. "Bad news or good first?"

"Bad."

"No key, and I'm not sure I'm going to be able to get it started. Even if I can, I don't know how I'm going to drive it out of here, I don't even know how it got here. Good news is it's unlocked, we can spend the night in there and you can get the sleep you need."

She supposed that was better than nothing, definitely more good than bad. At least for now, tomorrow morning she might see it differently, and she was so tired.

A huge yawn tugged at the cuts on her face, but she hardly felt the sting.

Sleep.

She needed sleep.

"Come on, darlin', let's get you tucked in so you know you're safe for the next few hours."

As Trick scooped her up and carried her toward the car, Stephanie knew it wouldn't be the car making her feel safe tonight, it was the man holding her in his arms. Trick was the only thing that made her feel safe, and as rescue slowly became more of a possibility, the thought of how she was going to survive the aftermath of her ordeal without him by her side utterly terrified her.

CHAPTER *Ten*

January 24th
6:02 A.M.

He didn't want to wake her when she looked so peaceful and he knew she was finally out of pain, but Trick didn't have a choice.

The longer they stayed there, the more they were tempting fate.

Given how slowly Stephanie had been moving, Trick knew there had to be someone watching over them because it was the only reason they hadn't been found already. As soon as a shift change in the guards occurred or their torturers returned for another round of questioning, they'd know that the two of them had escaped. Once they did, they would go all out searching for them. Those men knew this jungle a whole lot better than he did, and he knew they were leaving more of a trail than they would if he was on his own.

But hours had passed, and he hadn't heard any signs of them being followed.

Somehow, they'd even avoided coming into contact with any dangerous animals he knew called this rainforest home.

Not wanting to tempt fate any further, Trick knew he had to find a way to get this car working so they could drive out of there. Stephanie couldn't walk much further before her body gave out completely, and while she was small, and carrying her meant he could walk faster, it also meant he was less able to protect them, either from humans or animals.

"Wake up, darlin'," he said as he stroked the pad of his thumb across her forehead. Once he'd gotten her settled on the vehicle's backseat last night, she'd crashed. While there wasn't really enough room for both of them to lie on the seat, there was no way he wasn't going to sleep holding her in his arms. So, he'd laid on his back and draped Stephanie across him. With his weapon on the floor by his side, he'd felt confident enough that he could protect her if the need arose.

"Mmm, not yet. Five more minutes," Stephanie mumbled sleepily as she burrowed closer against him.

The ache in his heart intensified. She was so peaceful at that moment. The reality of their situation, of all she'd been through, of all she still had to go through had yet to seep into her consciousness. Trick wished she could be like this always, carefree and innocent. But she couldn't. Her body and soul were already scarred for life and there was nothing he could do to take that away from her.

She was going to hate him.

That she didn't at the moment was cold comfort because Stephanie knew she needed him for survival. It wasn't that he thought she was pretending to offer reassurance and comfort, he knew she believed it. But when they were home, and the full reality of what had happened sunk in without the adrenalin of trying to survive blocking it out, Trick was sure she would feel differently.

How could she not hate him?

Simple things like curling up in a man's arms would never be as simple again asin this moment.

"Sorry, honey. No more minutes," he said, jostling her enough to nudge her out of sleep.

Lifting her head, she gave a sleepy blink and stared at him with the fogginess of not quite being awake and aware yet. Damn, she was adorable all sleep rumbled like this, with her hair tousled about and a cute dopey look on her face. The wounds on her cheeks didn't take away from her beauty, but he knew she wouldn't see it that way for a long time, maybe ever.

Trick could see the exact second reality hit, and she remembered where they were and everything that had happened.

"Morning already," she said.

"Morning already," he agreed. "I'm going to try to see if I can get this car going. Why don't you eat something?" She'd had little appetite, and he knew that if he didn't make her, she wouldn't eat at all. But she of the two of them needed her strength. Other than the head wound from when they'd knocked him out and abducted him, he hadn't been physically assaulted. It was Stephanie's body that needed healing, and to do that it needed fuel.

"I need to go pee first," she told him.

Shifting with her in his arms, he reached behind him and opened the door then pulled them both out of the vehicle, setting Stephanie on her feet and keeping an arm around her waist until he was sure she wouldn't topple over. "Go where I can see you," he told her. Given how they'd shared a cell with no privacy, seen each other's naked bodies, seen each other do everything, there was no modesty between them anymore.

"Okay," she agreed without protest, and since it seemed like she wasn't going to fall, he let her go, keeping an eye on her as she walked a little way aways.

Keeping half his attention on Stephanie and their surroundings, Trick popped up the hood of the SUV and examined the engine. He'd already checked to make sure the vehicle had gas, there was no point in wasting time on it if it didn't since there was absolutely nothing he could do about it.

The vehicle gave him hope. It hadn't gotten itself out there, someone had driven it. There was no way to know if it had been a member of the militia or someone else, but he had to believe there was a village or better yet a town nearby.

Just as he was about to start fiddling with the engine to see what he could do, something made him look up.

When he did his heart stuttered in his chest.

No.

Standing in the trees, watching its prey, was a leopard. Dangerous, fast, vicious, strong, agile, and known to attack humans, not an animal you wanted to mess with, and it currently had Stephanie in its sights.

"Steph, honey, don't panic," he called out, attempting to keep his voice calm even though his heart was trying to beat its way right out of his chest.

She froze with her pants half pulled up. "What?" Although there was panic in her tone she didn't move, spin around, or come running toward him, which would be the worst thing she could do in this situation.

"There's a leopard with you in its sights," he said, still maintaining a level of calm he certainly didn't feel.

"A leopard?" she asked, voice gone shrill.

"Don't run, Steph," he said quickly. "You want to wave your arms and yell as loud as you can." It was his first encounter with a leopard although he'd come face to face with other dangerous animals in his career in Delta and then at Prey, but he knew what to do with any animal you might come across to give yourself the best odds of surviving.

"Y-yell?" she squeaked.

"Loud. And wave your arms as best you can, you want to try to convince it that you're bigger, stronger, and more dangerous."

"But I'm not."

"All about appearances, darlin'. You showed those men in that cell that you were a force to be reckoned with, and you can show this leopard, too. Go, honey. Now." To make his point, Trick took all gentleness and coddling out of his voice, making the word a command she had no choice but to obey.

Letting her pants drop, Stephanie tucked her maimed hand to her chest, dragged in a breath, and then let out an ear-splitting scream. He wasn't the only one who startled, the leopard pulled back as well, and when Stephanie began to jump up and down, waving her good arm all over the place and continuing on with the piercing screams, it studied her for a moment, then obviously decided she was more hassle than she was worth and turned and slinked away.

While he let out a breath as he watched the gorgeous animal turn and disappear into the trees, Stephanie obviously didn't notice it had gone. "Okay, darlin', it's gone," he soothed in a loud voice to be heard over her screaming as he headed over to her. "You did it. Scared it off, just like I knew you would."

"I-it's gone?" she asked, stopping with the yelling but continuing to jump about as though she wasn't quite sure he was right and that the big cat could still be lurking somewhere ready to pounce.

"It's gone," he repeated, placing his hands on her shoulders to still her.

"I did it? I scared it off? Or did you do something?" Her brow made the most adorable furrow, and he laughed and leaned in to kiss it away.

"All you, little superhero in training."

The smile she gave him was bright and sunshiny. "Superhero in training, I like that. I love cats, especially big cats, I wanted a pet cat as a kid, but we couldn't afford it. Now I don't think I ever want to meet one of those guys that up close and personal again."

"Then we better go see if I can get that car started." While he didn't say it out loud, didn't want to bring Stephanie down from her momentary high, he was worried all her yelling and screaming—while completely necessary—might have alerted anyone close enough that they were there.

～

January 24th
6:28 A.M.

It was too early in the morning for this.

Stephanie was trembling as she managed to yank her pants up, not an easy thing to do with the use of only one hand. On top of everything else she'd been through, she'd almost been a snack for a leopard.

A leopard.

After a lifetime of loving cats, of desperately wanting a pet cat as a child even knowing they couldn't afford the added expense, of wishing she had the time for one when she moved into her own place as an adult, of dreaming of a safari in Africa where she could meet lions, she was now completely rethinking the whole thing. Cats weren't so great after all, at least not the big ones, they were downright terrifying.

As she walked back over to Trick and the car, she had to lock her knees to stop them from knocking together. It wasn't just the fright that she'd had, but the jumping about had started a roaring agony in her hand, and her chest and abdomen were also going out in protest of all the movement. Since they had no painkillers, there was no point in complaining about the pain, she had no choice but to endure it.

It was just ...

She was so tired of enduring.

Tired full stop.

Despite the food and water Trick kept pushing on her, and the good night's sleep she knew she'd had draped across his hard, muscled body—which in theory should have been no more comfortable than the concrete floor of their cell, but its warmth and security made it better than her bed at home—she was feeling worse this morning. A fogginess in her head told her something wasn't right, and she was hot and sweaty. Stephanie feared it was infection setting into her wounds but was too cowardly to unwind the bandages of her hand and take a look.

Even though she was doing her best, it was getting harder and harder to hold onto control. She was so scared, and the pain was difficult to ignore, and she just wanted to know she was safe, this living in constant fear was wearing her down.

But she didn't want to complain.

Trick was dealing with enough, the last thing he needed was an overly emotional woman having a breakdown.

Hold it together.

You can do this.

The mental pep talk obviously wasn't working because when Trick looked up from whatever he was doing to the engine his brows snapped together. "Everything okay, Steph?"

Pasting on a smile she certainly didn't feel, she forced herself to hold his gaze. "Yep. Just a little jittery over the leopard."

For a moment a frown crossed his features, and she froze.

Did he know?

Did he realize how badly she was struggling?

Was he annoyed with her for not being calmer? For letting her emotions get the best of her?

She didn't want to let him down, she had to do better at keeping her emotions locked tightly down inside.

Wiping the frown from his face, he replaced it with a grin. "I know what'll make you feel better." Closing the hood of the car, he walked around to the driver's door, leaned inside, and fiddled around for a moment, then the next thing she knew the engine had sprung to life.

Genuine delight wiped away some of her weariness. "You did it," she exclaimed. For a moment, she almost went to clap her hands together before realizing that one of her hands was bandaged and would never be the same again.

Dismay threatened to steal her moment of joy, but Stephanie shoved it away with a ruthlessness she hadn't even known she possessed. She had to, for Trick, there was no other choice. He needed her to be strong so she was going to be as strong as she knew how. Stronger. Because anything else was a failure.

"Come on, let's get out of this jungle. Get you home."

"Home." She sighed. It had taken on an almost ethereal, magical sort of quality. Like it was some lost city that had been gone for thousands of years instead of the place she'd always known.

Like the gentleman he was, Trick rounded the car, took her elbow, and helped her into the passenger seat. He buckled her seatbelt for her and then paused before closing her door. As he looked down at her, she couldn't discern the expression on his face, all she knew was that it was soft and radiated warmth. A nice warmth, not like the too-hot feeling her body had been emitting ever since she woke up.

When he leaned down and touched a kiss to her forehead, she closed her eyes and gave another sigh, this time one of contentment. They might not be safe yet, not even close, but Trick was here, and somehow, that made everything okay.

"What's the first thing you're going to eat when you get home?" Trick asked as he slid into the driver's seat and buckled his seatbelt.

Her stomach turned at the thought of eating, but she couldn't tell him nothing, that she was way too nauseous to get any joy from thinking about food. "Umm ... comfort food I guess," she answered vaguely. "Mac and cheese, or mashed potatoes, or something like that. What about you?"

Trick laughed. "Not sure you want to ask that question, darlin'. Ask anyone who knows me and the two things they'll tell you about me is that I love magic tricks and I love to eat."

The sound of his voice was soothing, and she'd rather listen to it than the fears and anxieties running rampant inside her head, even if they were talking about food. Shifting so she could see him better, she ran her gaze over the solid wall of muscle she knew was hidden beneath his clothes. "I can see why. You're a big guy."

Maneuvering through two huge trees, he turned his head to shoot her a smile that managed to be charming, sexy, and sweet all at the same time. A smile that was impossible to resist.

"A big guy who loves his food. First thing I'm going to eat is a burger and a huge plate of fries. Then I'm thinking pizza, all the toppings, everything they can throw on there I want. Maybe something sweet after that. Brownies or cookies and a big bowl of ice cream. Lots of soda, too, and nice steaming hot coffee, the kind that burns the whole way down. After that—"

"After that surely you'll have a belly ache and have to take a break," she said, mouth and eyes round as she tried to comprehend eating so much food in one go.

Trick just laughed at her. "You'll learn."

As though realizing that once they got out of there they weren't going to see each other again, the smile dropped from his face. Her smile dropped, too.

She wanted this to be over more than she wanted her next breath of air, but she didn't want to lose Trick.

It would hurt.

It didn't matter that they hadn't known each other long, it only mattered that they had lived through hell with only one another to rely on. That bond that had formed between them defied logic, defied understanding, it simply ... was.

Both drifting into silence, Stephanie stared out the window as Trick somehow once again managed to do the impossible and navigate the vehicle between trees, over stumps and undergrowth, and then finally, after what felt like forever, out onto a road.

"You did it," she said, a little in awe of this man. Okay a whole lot more than a little. She was completely and utterly impressed by him and everything he was and everything he knew how to do.

"Had to, honey. No other option. I'm getting you home." He said it with such conviction like it was already a foregone conclusion that she believed him.

For one blissful moment anyway.

Stephanie was so tired, and the gentle rocking of the car must have lulled her off into sleep because the next thing she knew was Trick's urgent voice calling her name as he shook her shoulder.

"Hmm? What's wrong?" she asked, trying to blink the sleep out of her eyes and her mind as quickly as possible. Trick's anxiety felt like a living, breathing being sitting in the car alongside them.

"Roadblock," he announced, nodding up ahead of them, and when she looked out the windshield, she could see that there were at least half a dozen men dressed in military uniforms holding machine guns blocking the road. Somewhere along the way they'd left behind the thick jungle, and now the road they were on was more populated, not busy per se, and there were still trees lining the road, but there were other cars in the line waiting to be checked by the soldiers.

There was no way to know if the roadblock was about them. She didn't know much about this militia, but it made sense that they might have connections they could call on to find their missing prisoners.

Whether it was about them or not, it didn't matter.

She and Trick didn't belong there.

They were the very epitome of the 'One of These Things Is Not Like the Others' song from Sesame Street.

When they reached their turn, it would all be over. They'd be killed on the spot or returned to the militia for more suffering before death. Neither option was good.

Their desperate fight for survival was about to come crashing to a halt.

CHAPTER
Eleven

January 24th
1:44 P.M.

"They're going to kill us, aren't they?" Stephanie asked. Her eyes were almost impossibly round in her pale face, and her bottom lip trembled as she struggled to keep a rein on her emotions.

As badly as he wanted to promise he wouldn't let anything happen to her, Trick couldn't. Well, he could but it would be a lie, and they would both know it.

Still, he had to erase her fear.

It ate at him, destroyed something inside him.

Whatever it took, lie or not, he had to soothe that terror.

Reaching out, he cupped the back of her neck, tugging her closer until their faces were only inches apart. "Hey, listen to me. I will do everything I can to keep you safe. You hear me? Whatever it takes."

"H-How will you convince them to l-let us through the roadblock?" she asked. "As soon as they see us, they'll know who we are."

"If they see you, they'll know, but I'm wearing a uniform, I can blend in. You need to get down on the floor and cover yourself with the backpack." Trick was eternally grateful that he'd grabbed it before leaving the building. He'd taken it just to carry the spare weapons, food, and water, but now that he had it, he could use it.

"They'll see me," Stephanie protested.

"Not if you open the pack first, pull some things out and spread them half over you and half over the passenger seat. It will just look like I'm messy and was rummaging through the pack." He was also grateful he'd taken the third guard's clothes. He'd taken them because if it got cold, they were an extra layer of warmth, but now they could provide the hiding place Stephanie needed.

"Maybe I should get into the back seat, hide there."

Trick shook his head. "Back seat is where they'll look. You're small, if you get down there, curl in on yourself as tight as you can, let me cover you with some things, I don't think they'll spot you." At least that's what he was praying for.

Because if she was spotted, it would be all over for both of them.

They might not be killed outright, likely wouldn't. They would be returned to the militia, punished for escaping, then executed. Since they hadn't gotten the answers they wanted, the militia could go after another family member from the SEAL team to replace Stephanie, and after another member of his team. They had to know about Bravo Team since they'd come after him, and they also had to know where he and his team lived. While he didn't remember the details of his abduction, he knew he hadn't been grabbed when they went to the farm because he was the only one of his team who had been taken. They must have returned and then split up, and he'd been grabbed somewhere close to the compound.

The last thing Trick wanted was another member of his team trapped in this hell. Axe had Beth, Tank had Tillie, Rock had Ariel, Scorpion had Jessica, and Panther had Andy. He was the only one who had no one he would be leaving behind, and he was grateful he had been the one the militia targeted.

"Trust me, honey. Please." The last came out whispered and border-line desperate, but he needed to know she could still trust him after everything he'd done to her. While he hadn't laid a hand on her, he had stood by and done nothing to stop what was happening to her. She said she didn't blame him, but he didn't see how that could be true. In this moment, even with time ticking out and their turn at the roadblock edging closer, what he needed the most was for Stephanie to be able to put her trust in him. It meant more than she could ever realize.

"I do," she murmured. Then he felt her physically pulling herself together. "I will."

With that, she fumbled with her seatbelt and slid down to the floor, tucking herself beneath the dashboard as best as she could. This was a risky move, Trick wasn't denying that. If the men looked closely, they'd spot Stephanie, and while he might be able to blend in a little better as soon as they spotted her and saw her wounds, they'd know who she was. But he believed he could keep most of the men's attention on himself and that this was their best shot at getting through the roadblock unscathed.

Reaching behind him for the backpack, which was not quite as large as the one he would have used if this was a regular mission but still pretty big, he stuffed it down into the space in front of the passenger seat along with Stephanie. It covered most of her body, and by the time he opened it, threw some bottles of water onto the seat along with some of the food, and then strategically placed the spare items of clothing so they were draped haphazardly about like he'd just slung then there when in reality, they blocked even more of the view of Stephanie.

Fiddling with the radio, he managed to find something to play, then adopted a bored expression as he inched closer to the checkpoint.

Ten minutes later, he was pulling up alongside half a dozen armed men. While these men were in the military, they obviously had a connection to the militia because there wasn't a doubt in his mind that this particular roadblock was about him and Stephanie. The timing and the location were too coincidental. There were only so many roads leading in and out of the part of the jungle they'd been in, and he was sure every one of them was currently doing random vehicle checks.

One of the armed men approached and motioned for Trick to roll down the window. He did so with the calm, confident attitude of someone with nothing to hide. Didn't matter that he had everything to hide and everything riding on this, it was all about perception. If he let on that he was close to the most anxious he'd ever been, he would tip the man off that he wasn't who he was pretending to be.

Accents weren't his forte, but he did his best to inject a West African accent into his words when he spoke. "They been found yet?"

Obviously, his outright asking caught the soldier off-guard, and he froze for a second, taking a look at the uniform Trick was wearing and the stuff strewn about the front seat.

Seconds ticked by feeling like hours.

Tension radiated off Stephanie even if he was the only one who could feel it, and honestly, tension was mounting on him as well.

If they were found, there wasn't much of a chance he could take out six armed men when all he had was a couple of handguns and they had automatic rifles. Still, if it came down to it, he'd certainly try. He could even use the car as a weapon if he had to.

Whatever it took to get Stephanie to safety.

Finally, the soldier relaxed. "No sign of them yet, but they're in there somewhere." He waved a hand at the rainforest surrounding them. "Where they going to go?" When the man laughed, Trick laughed along with him, all the while thinking, you underestimate your opponent you hand them a chance to beat you.

And he was going to beat them.

When the stakes were this high failure just wasn't an option.

"I'm moving to a different search grid," he explained.

"Better hurry up, your boss is furious."

Trick nodded his agreement, he bet the militia were hopping mad. Not only had they lost the diamonds that would fund their campaign, but they'd lost their best and possibly only chance at finding them. Then there was the humiliation that came with having two prisoners escape and kill three of your men before disappearing into the jungle.

Took everything he had not to grin.

"Yes, sir," he nodded.

With a nod back, the soldier took a step away from the car, but not before Trick watched him check the backseat and he inwardly sighed in relief that he'd not stashed Stephanie there.

Rolling the window back up, he drove off down the road, not

daring to stop until he was completely out of sight of the roadblock, only then did he pull over to the side of the road.

"You did it again," Stephanie said in awe as he pulled the backpack away and reached out to help her climb back onto her seat. The way she looked at him ... it made him wish for something that he was sure could never be.

"We lucked out," he agreed.

"Wasn't luck, Trick, it was you. Somehow, it doesn't seem to matter what obstacle we face you know just how to overcome it. Maybe you really are a superhero."

"Just a regular old human." She was putting him on a pedestal he certainly didn't deserve after what he'd allowed to happen to her.

"All men and women who put their lives on the line to serve their country are superheroes," she said softly.

Couldn't argue with that.

While it was hard to put himself in that same category, he respected the hell out of the military men and women even if he had moved to the private sector.

"What next?" Stephanie asked.

"Next we find a town. Somewhere to lie low so I can call my team and wait for them to come and extract us." While making it through the roadblock unscathed was a relief, it was only one of many obstacles they were going to have to face to get back home. Hopefully, he had enough superhero powers left to get Stephanie back where she belonged.

January 24th
    5:05 P.M.

They'd been driving for hours.

Literally.

Every muscle in her body was cramped and uncomfortable. Her stupid hand still throbbed with an unrelenting beat that didn't give her a moment's peace even when she passed out into a fitful sleep. Stephanie was too hot, her skin felt too tight, her cheeks ached every time she spoke, and a headache roared between her temples like the leopard from earlier had set up residence inside her skull.

Did leopards roar?

She assumed they did.

Didn't all big cats?

Pretty sure she should know the answer to that question, but for some reason, her brain didn't want to cooperate and connect. It hurt too much to think, to concentrate, to do anything at all, even breathing sucked.

She let her mind drift away because there was nothing else to do—nothing else she could do. It didn't quite make it all the way to sleep as proper decent sleep continued to elude her, but at least it took her a little bit away from the car, the road, and the endless hours of driving.

They'd left behind the dense jungle, and as the trees began to thin out, the busier the roads became. She was sure they would have to make it to a town eventually, but after hours of driving she began believing that Liberia was devoid of towns. Of course, she knew that wasn't really true, but she ached to get somewhere. One step closer to getting home. The more hours they spent driving, the more it felt like they were just going in circles rather than making progress in returning to the US.

A sound rumbled somewhere nearby, but she didn't have the energy or the desire to open her eyes and see what it was.

Something brushed against her shoulder and then her forehead, and she weakly lifted her good hand to swat it away.

Couldn't she have a few minutes of peace?

Pain and fear had become her constant companions since she'd woken up in that cell, and all she wanted was a reprieve from both. A moment to just be without the crushing pressure of trying to hold it all together and the fear of failing.

"Come on, Steph. Wake up for me, honey."

The voice penetrated her hazy consciousness, maybe because it sounded so concerned. It was Trick, she knew that even as she was struggling to get her brain to cooperate, and she didn't want him to worry, so she forced her eyes open and lifted her head.

"Sorry, must have drifted off," she mumbled as a way of an explanation.

A small frown creased his forehead. He opened his mouth like he wanted to say something but snapped it shut again without uttering a word. "It's fine," he said when he finally did speak, although she was pretty sure that hadn't been what he was going to say.

He'd been going to tell her to pull it together, that he needed her to be strong, that there was no time for her to be emotional and fall apart now.

All of which she knew.

So somehow, she managed to find the strength to straighten her spine and pasted on a small smile. When she caught a glimpse of the scene outside the window that smile quickly became genuine. "We're here. A town. You found a town."

"Yep, that's why I was waking you." Trick smiled back at her, and she basked in the warmth that smile sent straight to her soul. She needed the revitalization more than she could say.

"What now?" she asked excitedly. "Do we go find a phone to call your team? Or somewhere to hide out first?"

"We don't do anything. You'll stick out too much. Chances are the militia has people here, as soon as they see you, they'll know who you are. I need you to stay in the car, keep your head down, while I get us clothes and food, and then we'll find a place to hide out. Once I have you settled somewhere, I'll find a phone and call my team."

A part of her wanted to argue, to say she was fine to go with him, and she'd hide her hand and let her hair cover her face, but Stephanie knew that would be crazy. Her wounds were too visible—would always be visible even once they healed and scarred—and she wasn't going to put both their lives in jeopardy just because she was excited that they were finally making real progress toward getting out of there.

"Okay," she agreed.

"I'll be as quick as I can." Trick leaned in to kiss her forehead like it was the most natural thing in the world.

It would have been nice to bask in the glow of his sweet gesture, but as he pulled back, she saw the worry in his eyes. He'd felt how hot she was and knew she wasn't doing as well as she was pretending. Not that she was doing a fabulous job of pretending, but she hadn't told him just how badly her hand throbbed, or how hot she was, how sweaty she felt, or that every so often she'd get a chill so cold it felt like someone had thrown a bucket of ice water over her head.

Sooner or later, she would have to tell him, but not until they were somewhere safe and he'd called his team. The last thing she wanted to be was a distraction. It was bad enough that she was a burden without her distracting Trick from what was most important. Getting home.

"I'll be fine," she assured Trick as he climbed out of the car. Although, as she watched him walk away her chest ached, and not because of her bruises.

It hurt to watch him walk away.

If it hurt this badly when she knew he was only going to be gone a short time while he got them the things they needed, how was she going to cope when he walked away for good?

It was stupid to hope that he might stay because she knew he wouldn't.

What would a man like Trick want with her?

Maybe before all of this, he might have been interested. She kept in great shape thanks to her job, and while she didn't think she was pretty, per se, she also didn't think she was unattractive. She wasn't super outgoing, but she was confident in herself and the person that she was. She liked to hang out with her friends, and while she preferred sex in a relationship to sex with random guys, she'd had the occasional one-night stand.

But now ... now she had scars on the outside and the inside. Scars would forever mar her face, a sign to anyone who saw her that she'd been through an ordeal of some kind. One of her fingers was missing, it would be noticeable to everyone. They'd see and wonder what had happened to her. On the inside she had more scars, ones no one would see, but that would impact her every interaction. Fear would have her doubting anyone she saw, wondering if they were going to hurt her. Being raped would change how she viewed men and relationships for the rest of her life.

Who would possibly want a woman people would stare at, who was no longer beautiful, who would always be afraid, and who might never be able to be intimate with a man?

Certainly not someone like Trick.

He was too strong, too confident, too handsome to be with the woman she was now.

Curling in on herself, Stephanie tucked her face against her good arm and allowed her tears to flow now that she was alone. Doing her best to keep them silent so no passersby would hear her weeping, she allowed all the emotions she'd been clutching close to her chest to flood out of her.

She wanted this to be over, but with each step closer to getting home, Stephanie was realizing more and more that this was never going to truly be over. There would be surgeries and medical treatment she'd need once they got home, she'd need counseling, too. There'd be nightmares and probably flashbacks, too. Over time, her fear might fade, her scars, too, but it would always be there.

This ordeal was a part of her now.

There was no changing that.

No wishing it away, no ignoring it, and knowing she had to find a way to go on having lost such a huge piece of who she was before was as overwhelming as it had been when she first woke up in that underground cell.

How did she do this?

How did she keep going forward when it felt like her soul—everything that made her Stephanie Fuller—had been so viciously and so irrevocably ripped away from her?

CHAPTER
Twelve

January 24th
5:51 P.M.

She'd been crying.

Trick knew it as soon as he got back into the car. Her red-rimmed eyes were a dead giveaway, as were the tear tracks on her flushed cheeks.

He absolutely hated that as soon as she heard him return, she shoved her emotions back down, burying them deep where there was no chance of anyone else seeing them.

But he saw.

He saw and he felt them. Knowing that her ex had scarred her badly enough that she was afraid of anyone using her emotions against her made him want to track down the ex and spend a few minutes alone with him, teaching him what it felt like to be hurt so badly it couldn't not affect you. If he didn't waste his time on people who didn't deserve it, he'd do that first thing when he got home, but more than he wanted to punish the ex for hurting her, he wanted Stephanie to learn that she didn't have to hide that she had emotions.

Of course, she did.

Of course, this whole ordeal was messing with her head. How could it not?

There was absolutely no reason for her to hide that she'd been crying from him, and he hated that it wasn't her natural instinct but a behavior learned the hard way when someone had thrown her emotions—perfectly reasonable ones—in her face.

As much as it pained him to see her shut down like that, and as badly as he wanted to help her relearn to be the woman she'd been before her ex hurt her, it wasn't his job. Sure, there was part of him that was more than happy to sign up for it, but he was still convinced that as soon as she was safe, Stephanie would realize how badly he had hurt her and want nothing to do with him.

Besides, they had bigger concerns than Stephanie wanting to hide her emotions.

Like the fact that she was burning up, her eyes holding that feverish glaze, sweat dotting her brow, and a flush to her cheeks that wasn't just because of the torn skin there but because she was running a temperature.

Infections.

There was no point in pretending they'd managed to avoid infection settling into her wounds. There had never been any doubt it was going to happen. Between the unsanitary knife that had cut up her face and then removed her finger, to the even less sanitary conditions they lived in their cell, and the fact her wounds hadn't been properly cleaned, it had always been a foregone conclusion. The fact that she wasn't properly hydrated, that she was barely eating, and was in constant pain wasn't helping. Her body had been so battered down that it simply didn't have what it needed to fight off an infection.

"Trick?"

"Yeah, honey?"

"What's wrong?"

"Nothing. Why?"

"You're just sitting there staring at me." Her eyes dipped and he saw shame in them when she slowly lifted them to meet his. "I was quiet, I didn't let anyone know I was crying."

Damn.

She thought he was judging her.

That couldn't be further from the truth, but he had no idea how to convince her of that.

"It's okay to cry, Steph. I'm not going to hold it against you. And nothing is wrong. I got clothes, blankets, some food and water, and organized a place for us to stay. It's a small hotel but they have vacancies. Probably not as nice as your hotel in Mexico was but a definite upgrade from our last accommodations," he teased, hoping to get a smile out of her.

Rewarded with a small one he relaxed a little. It would take time, but Stephanie would recover from the wounds inflicted by her dirtbag ex just like she would recover from the wounds inflicted by the militia. Time certainly didn't heal all wounds, but it did help you learn to live with them. The wounds she'd received there, both physical and psychological, would change her, but she was strong, determined, and a survivor. She would make it through this and out the other side.

Trick had to believe that.

It was the only way he'd be able to walk away once he knew she was safe.

"Anything is an upgrade from the last accommodations," she agreed as she rested her head against the window as though it were too heavy for her to hold up a second longer.

Worry burned in his gut as he followed the directions the man in the store had given him, and fifteen minutes later, they were pulling up outside a run-down but not as bad as he'd thought it would be, hotel. Three stories high, and despite the building having seen better days, it looked clean, and it would offer them the space they needed for Stephanie to rest, and for him to call his team. The store where he'd bought their clothes didn't sell cell phones, and he couldn't ask to use the hotel's phone because he didn't want to bring trouble on them if the militia had enough resources to track phone calls to the US.

Once he got Stephanie settled, he'd go back out to find a phone. He hadn't wanted to leave her alone in the car too long, not just because the militia could have spies there but also because he knew she wasn't well. If she thought she'd hidden that fact from him, she was sorely mistaken.

"Okay, honey, time to get you inside," he said, reaching out to softly smooth a lock of hair off her cheek.

When she went to reach for the doorhandle—apparently forgetting her seatbelt was still on—Trick stopped her. While he could blend in reasonably well with his dark hair, dark eyes, and tanned skin, Stephanie may as well be a billboard proclaiming that she didn't fit in.

All it took was one person to see her, realize that she looked out of place, and mention her to someone else, and their cover would be blown. With Stephanie sick, it meant they needed to be able to hunker down and hide out until his team could get there.

"Hold up, darlin'. Don't want anyone seeing you. I'm going to tuck the blanket around you and carry you in."

Her brow scrunched in confusion, then she winced like the movement had caused her pain. "Won't people look at us if you're carrying me?"

"Probably. But all they'll see is a man carrying his woman in, they might think it's odd, wonder if you're sick or hurt, but the important thing is they won't be able to see you."

Settling back into her seat, Stephanie offered no protest when he unbuckled her seatbelt for her. Grabbing the rest of the stuff he'd bought and the backpack with the weapons, Trick got out of the car and rounded it, opening Stephanie's door and reaching for her. After making sure she was covered with the blanket, he lifted her into his arms and stood, bumping the door closed with his hip.

"Keep your face turned into my neck," he whispered to her as he started walking toward reception.

There were a few people about, and some of them shot curious looks their way, but so long as no one recognized him and Stephanie, he didn't care if people wondered why he was carrying her.

"Looking for a room for a few days," he told the young woman at reception.

"Is everything okay?" she asked, worried eyes on Stephanie.

"My wife is sick. We need a place to stay so she can rest and recover before we can continue our vacation," he replied, holding out some of the wad of cash he'd swiped from the guards before he and Stephanie had hiked into the jungle.

Thankfully, the woman took the money without further question and handed him a key along with directions to their room.

A couple of minutes later, he was locking the door behind them and setting Stephanie down on the bed. The room wasn't large, and the décor was definitely dated, but it was clean, quiet, and exactly what they needed.

Stephanie was shivering, and from the tight way she pressed her lips together he knew she was in pain and trying to hide it from him. He was going to have to do something about her pain. She hadn't given a single complaint at all since she'd received the first strike which only made him respect her that much more, even as he hated that she didn't feel free to be honest with him.

Perching on the edge of the bed, Trick pressed his palm to her forehead. "You're burning up, darlin'," he mumbled.

"S-Sorry," she replied through chattering teeth.

Closing his eyes he dragged in a ragged breath. "Oh, honey, you don't have to apologize for that. Stop holding everything inside, Steph. Do you know what happens when you keep all your emotions, all your fear and anger bottled up inside? Sooner or later, you end up exploding. Trust me, I've been there, done that, and it almost cost me my freedom and my future."

~

January 24th
6:38 P.M.

Everything inside her went still.

Never before had Trick opened up about himself. While they'd been in their cell, they'd talked a lot. Stephanie had told him about her childhood, her family, her business, and the things she liked and didn't like. But Trick had been mostly closed off about his past. He told her random things about himself, like favorite foods, and favorite music, what sports teams he liked, and trivia like that.

Nothing meaningful though.

Until now.

Feeling like he'd given her a gift, Stephanie pushed away the fogginess and reached out to curl her fingers around the hand still resting against her forehead.

"Why were you angry and scared?" she asked.

For a long moment, he just stared at her, saying nothing, and she was sure he wasn't going to answer, but then he turned his hand over, cradling hers as his thumb swept across her palm, more to soothe him than her, she suspected.

"My dad left when I was young, too. Still a toddler, I don't remember him at all. My mom didn't take to being a single mom like yours did. She didn't want to have to work hard on her own to put a roof over our heads. She married the first man she came across. He was well off, a businessman, he drove a nice car and had a nice house. He wasn't rich by any means, but he lived a comfortable life and made enough to take care of her, so she didn't have to work."

There was bitterness in Trick's tone, which told her he held a lot of resentment toward his mother.

"My stepdad enjoyed only one aspect of having a son. Beating on him. The man wasn't a drunk or an addict, he didn't even do it out of anger. He just liked to beat on someone smaller than him. Working out his own issues I guess."

"Oh, Patrick," she said softly, squeezing his hand, everything else forgotten, even her pain. How awful it must have been to be a child and have someone who was supposed to be responsible for caring for you, guiding you, helping you find your way be the one to inflict such suffering on you.

He gave her a funny look she couldn't decipher, and she had no idea why. She would have asked, but he kept talking, so she just listened.

"I told my mom the first time it happened. I was around four, and I was sure she would pack us up and take us away. I was naïve. She told me not to do whatever I'd done to provoke him again and then sent me to bed without any dinner as a punishment for complaining when her new husband was giving us both so much. The older I got the worse it got. Beatings became more regular, got worse, even a couple of broken bones, but mostly he hit me where no one would see. My mom witnessed several of them and it took till I was about ten for me to realize she was never going to step in and stop it. She cared more about the comfortable life she lived to jeopardize it by telling her husband to stop abusing her son. By the time I graduated elementary school, I was filled with anger."

"Of course you were," she readily agreed. How could he not be? His mom was allowing someone to hurt him and making it seem like he deserved it.

"I was embarrassed about what was happening at home, and I'd lost faith in adults to do anything to help. So, I was angry. At my mom, my stepdad, adults in general, and other kids because they didn't have to go home and get beaten just because they existed. I got in a lot of fights and very nearly wound up getting arrested and going to juvie. Turned out to be the best thing to ever happen to me. I finally had someone who cared enough about me to want to help me, set me on a path where I didn't self-destruct." Trick's gaze turned anxious. "You know what he told me? He said never bottle up what you're feeling, find a way to get it out in a safe way, because if you don't it's going to turn to poison and destroy you from the inside out. I see what you're doing, honey. That ex of yours has you thinking you can't show your emotions because they'll be used against you, but he was wrong. He was using that as an excuse for an out. Everyone feels, darlin'. Everyone."

Tears blurred her vision. How did he understand her so well when they'd only known each other such a short time?

"I see you, Stephanie Fuller. I see you trying to hold it all in. I see you worried about how I'm going to react if you tell me you're scared, or hurting, or losing hope. I see you and I'm here. You don't have to hide."

The trembling in her body increased and it wasn't all because of the fever she knew was raging inside her.

She felt him seeing her, felt him reaching down inside her soul and examining every bit of pain in an effort to find out how to soothe it.

Tears leaked out the corners of her eyes, and for the first time since her ex had shattered her heart, she didn't try to hold them back.

"I-I'm terrified," she whispered.

"Me too."

"The pain ... it's so bad I almost can't breathe."

"I'll never forgive myself for letting you get hurt."

"I don't want that."

"Doesn't change anything. I'd take that pain from you in a heartbeat if I could."

"I know you would. I ... I want to believe we'll get home ... but ... I'm not sure I do believe it."

"I will do everything in my power to get you back home where you belong."

A rush of heat so hot it felt like a fire was literally burning through her veins stole her ability to think of anything but the raging pain and the fever, and she moaned and scrunched her eyes closed. Her body moved restlessly as though it could outrun the heat even though it was inside her.

"You're burning up. We need to do something to get your temperature down."

Trick's voice sounded far away, but she wasn't so far gone that she couldn't hear the raw fear in it.

"Have to get your clothes off, darlin'," he said, and she felt his hands on her, stripping off the boots, socks, pants, and shirt that he'd stolen from one of the dead guards.

Given their history, she had no qualms about him seeing her naked body. At least half the time they'd spent together they'd been naked.

With the clothes gone, there was little relief from the relentless waves of heat that buffeted her weak body.

Arms slipped under her legs and behind her back and she was lifted.

It felt more like she was floating as Trick carried her through the bedroom and into the bathroom.

There was sweet relief when he set her down in the bath, and the cool porcelain against her burning skin was nothing short of pure bliss.

But when Trick turned on the tap and cold water began to flow over her body a sudden chill had her crying out and trying to move away from the cold.

"Sorry, honey," Trick said, sounding distressed as his large hands clamped onto her shoulders, holding her in place.

"Cold, too cold," she cried as the freezing water continued to flow over her body.

"I know, darlin', I know, but we have to get your temperature down."

She just couldn't catch a break. Infection on top of everything else, and now switching from burning hot to freezing cold like the flip of a switch.

When Trick released her, she cried out on pure instinct. "Don't leave me!"

"Shh, honey. I'm not going anywhere," he soothed.

Through bleary eyes, she watched as he stripped off his own clothes, letting them fall on the floor beside hers, then stepped over the edge of the bath and sat down behind her. He stretched his legs out on either side of her and settled her back so she rested against his chest. He scooped up water with his hands and then let it fall over her head.

Although the cold no longer felt nice against her overheated skin, Stephanie did her best not to flinch each time the water touched her.

Just when she thought she couldn't take another second of the cold, it vanished like a puff of smoke, and the heat was back. Unrelenting as it spread inside her, claiming every inch of her body.

She whimpered and squirmed, wanting so desperately to escape the fever's clutches but knowing it was impossible.

"It's okay, honey, it's okay. I'm right here, just relax, try to sleep. I got you."

I got you.

Were there more reassuring words in the English language?

Reaching its limit, her mind was already searching for the peace only unconsciousness could bring. Before she went under, she clutched at Trick with her good hand. "Don't leave me, Patrick."

CHAPTER
Thirteen

January 25th
3:22 A.M.

Nothing was working.

She was getting worse not better.

Trick was getting dangerously close to panicking. Watching Stephanie slip further and further away from him was utterly terrifying. He'd promised her that he would do whatever it took to get her home, and while he'd known there was a chance he wouldn't be able to follow through, he hadn't expected to be forced to sit helplessly by as she slipped away a second at a time.

This woman who left him in awe of her bravery and strength was drifting further away from him, and he didn't know how to cross the chasm between them.

First aid training was all well and good, but it didn't equip him for this. Tending wounds in the field he could and had done, but then he usually passed the injured person off to a medical team who took it from there.

But there was no one else to pass Stephanie off on.

No one there but him.

And he was woefully inadequate.

What Steph needed was IV fluids and antibiotics, something to bring her fever down, and a surgical team to clean and close the wound on her hand where her finger used to be. She needed a safe, sterile environment to rest and recuperate.

The cold water in the bath had helped a little, at least at first. Now he had her in the bed, every time he tucked the covers up around her, she began to moan and thrash, desperate to get them off. But as soon as she had them off, within minutes, she would be shaking violently as chills wracked her body.

She looked so small and fragile lying in the middle of the bed, even though he knew she was far from weak.

There was no point in pretending he wasn't becoming completely and utterly obsessed with this woman. He couldn't get enough of her. Even as he sat perched on the edge of the bed, he had to be constantly touching her. Alternating between holding a cold cloth to her forehead, blotting at her sweat-dotted brow, and touching his fingertips to her wrist to check her pulse.

Elevated as it was, it was somehow still reassuring in the very fact that it was still there. Returning home without this woman didn't seem to be an option. Losing her to infection somehow seemed worse than losing her back in that hellhole would have been because the more time they spent together the more attached he got.

Trick was so attached now he'd told her about his childhood. Wasn't like it was a secret exactly, his team knew his stepfather used to beat him up for fun and that he'd almost ruined his own life by choosing a path that would have led him directly to prison, but it wasn't something they talked about. None of the women who had entered his life knew about his past, it wasn't something a one-night stand needed to know. Sure, some women he slept with lasted a little beyond a single night, but never more than a handful of times.

They might not have had sex, but he'd gotten closer to Stephanie than any of them and allowed her to get closer to him, too. They'd formed a bond he knew could never be broken, and there was a part of him that, if they got out of this, wanted to ask her for more, but how could he expect her to give him anything when there was so much standing between them?

When she moaned, he felt her pain like it was his own, and dipped the cloth into the bowl of cold water sitting on the nightstand. After blotting it against her neck where her lymph nodes were swollen, he draped it across her forehead.

He had to do something.

Sitting there watching her suffer was no longer a viable option.

Taking her to a doctor was risky. He still had some cash left, but as soon as anyone saw her wounds, word would spread about the white woman with a missing finger. Explaining away the injury would be hard enough without them thinking he'd done it if they weren't associated with the militia. If they were associated with them, they would immediately call in his location, and he and Stephanie would be captured again. Having the cops called to arrest him or the militia getting word of the vicinity in which he was hiding out would both pretty much end up the same way. He would not trust the cops knowing how deep the militia's reach went.

Deep enough to find out which team had come in after the SEAL team and where he and Bravo team lived.

Those ties didn't just run deep here in Liberia but back home as well.

That was a problem for another day though.

Right now, his priority was Stephanie, and what she needed was antibiotics and something to get her fever down. There was no way Trick was going to wait another several hours until morning and risk a doctor, staying there was their safest option.

Since a clinic was out, the only other thing he could do was find the nearest pharmacy and break in and steal what he needed. Well, not steal exactly, he'd leave the money for whatever he took behind, but he was still going to have to break in and take the necessary medications and bandages.

It wasn't a great plan, and he didn't feel good about breaking and entering, but he didn't see another choice.

If he did nothing Stephanie would die.

Simple as that.

And that wasn't going to happen on his watch.

"Hold on for me, honey," he murmured as he leaned down and touched a kiss to the tip of her nose. He also didn't feel good about leaving Stephanie alone and unprotected when she was in no condition to defend herself if necessary. "I'll be right back."

Although he'd thought she was mostly stuck in her feverish semi-conscious haze—like she had been the last several hours, he'd barely been able to get her awake enough to drink water—and wouldn't hear him, she immediately stirred.

Like they were impossibly heavy, her eyes opened so very slowly. "You c-can't leave," she whispered, her voice so soft and weak it was barely more than a hint of sound.

"Have to, honey. You need medicine to get better." Since he couldn't stroke her cheek to calm her because of her cuts, and he had the cold cloth on her forehead, he began to smooth her wild mane of curls because he had to touch her, needed that contact.

"You promised you wouldn't leave me," she murmured, a tinge of accusation in her tone.

Well, hell.

He had promised that.

And if it was any other reason than her life was literally depending on him bringing her something to get her fever down and start dealing with the infection, he wouldn't leave her alone for anything.

But this wasn't a choice, it was a necessity.

"I won't be long. Promise," he added as he reluctantly stopped smoothing her hair and stood.

Stephanie didn't say anything, just let her eyes fall closed. Trick wasn't sure if she had gone back into her restless sleep or if she was angry with him for leaving.

Since the idea of her being angry with him didn't sit right with him, tightening the knot of tension sitting heavily in his stomach, he tucked the blankets around her then picked up her good hand, squeezing lightly until she opened her eyes.

"I don't want to leave you, darlin', trust me, I don't. But this is something I have to do. I'm not going to sit here and watch you die. Don't ask me to do that. I promised you I would get you home, and I'm going to no matter what I have to do. Don't be angry with me for that, please, honey."

Something shifted in Stephanie's chocolate brown eyes. "Not angry ... scared. Without you here ..." she trailed off but didn't need to continue. It was the same way he felt. Without Stephanie close by he felt like something was missing.

Walking away from this woman was going to be hell.

He was ready to change everything he thought he wanted in his life to keep her, but he knew ... knew ... that when she got home and everything sunk in without her being distracted by her survival, she would hate him. Hoping for anything was just asking to get his heart broken. The best thing ... the only thing ... he could do for Stephanie was keep her alive and deliver her back to the people who could support her through the challenges she would soon be facing.

Walking away from her was the only option.

Stooping, he kissed the tip of her nose again. "I know, honey. I don't want to leave you either. But I won't let you die, you hear me? The world needs you in it. I need to know that you're in the world."

With that he turned, pocketed his weapon, and headed out the door, resisting every urge he had to go running back, drag Stephanie into his arms, and beg her to find a way not to hate him so that maybe they could make this bond between them grow into something that could last a lifetime.

~

January 25th
    5:42 A.M.

Come back.
    Come back.
    Please, come back.
    The words ran in a loop through her mind.
    Half the time Stephanie wasn't even sure what they meant.
    Who had to come back?

And why?

Other times, she knew it was Patrick that she needed. She couldn't explain the need if someone held a knife to one of her fingers again and threatened to cut it off, all she knew was that she needed him to be there with her.

He promised he wouldn't leave her.

Logically, she knew he didn't have a choice. She wasn't getting any better. The opposite. She was getting worse. Fever raged through her body like wildfire. It burned her from the inside out, slowly roasting her alive until her organs couldn't take the heat anymore and they just gave up on her.

The only time she got a break from the relentless fever that consumed her was when the chills came.

They weren't any better.

Instead of the fire, it was a blizzard dousing her in icy snow and sleet until the tremors wracking her body made her muscles cramp and ache to the point where she was ready to go back to the heat.

The vicious cycle just went on and on.

And on and on.

And on.

All she wanted to do was just close her eyes and rest.

Real rest.

Proper rest.

Peace.

That's what Stephanie wanted.

Just to close her eyes and drift off into a land that wasn't filled with pain, high temperatures, fevers, chills, and a craving for water that was too strong to ignore, so she kept reaching for the water bottle Patrick had left on the nightstand but getting little of it actually into her mouth and not sloshing down the sides of the bottle and onto the bedding.

It would be so easy to just let go.

Slip away ...

To a place where there was nothing but ... nothingness.

It sounded so beautiful.

Stephanie couldn't deny she was tempted. But something was stopping her. Something she didn't quite comprehend. It was just an understanding that if she left this earth then someone would miss her.

And she wasn't talking about her friends.

While, of course, they would miss her it wasn't the same as having family. Stupid as it was, Patrick felt like family.

He wasn't, and yet ...

Their lives had become so entwined that she could no longer quite tell where she ended and he began. But she did know, without a shadow of a doubt, that he would blame himself for her death. It would affect him ... deeply ... probably in ways she didn't even understand.

There was no way she could do that to him.

Dying wasn't an option.

Another chill hit and she cried out as her muscles spasmed. The shakes were so strong there was no way she could protect her maimed hand. It shook along with her, and the pain was so great that at least she was given a temporary reprieve.

Darkness overtook her and tossed her off the edge and into unconsciousness.

She had no idea how long she hovered there, floating in and out, hot one second, freezing the next, in agony through it all.

Maybe she was crying, her cheeks felt wet ... but then again maybe it was just sweat.

"Steph? Hold on, honey. I'm here. I'm here, darlin'."

Something cool—comfortingly so this time—wiped her brow, and then an arm slipped beneath her shoulders, lifting her. She wanted to cry out as the movement aggravated her headache, but she just didn't have the energy for it.

"Drink this, honey, then I need you to take some medicine for me."

Water touched her lips, and since she was so thirsty, she parted her lips and moaned in delight as the cool liquid slipped down her parched throat. It felt so good, and when the bottle was removed, she cried a protest.

"Swallow these for me, darlin'," a voice—one she knew instinctively belonged to Patrick even though she was too far gone to consciously think about it—urged.

A couple of small circles were placed on her tongue, and when more water was tipped into her mouth, she swallowed them without thought.

If Patrick wanted her to do it, then it was okay.

If Patrick was there then she was okay.

Once he took the water away from her again, she felt his other arm move under her knees and he scooped her up.

Even though a part of her was expecting it when her bare skin came in contact with the cold porcelain of the bathtub, her body reflexively tried to move away from it.

"No, honey, I'm sorry. I know this was torture last time, but I have to do it again to get your temperature down."

To back up his words, Patrick stripped out of his clothes and climbed into the tub with her, settling in behind her and caging her in between his legs. There was no way to prepare for the feel of the cold water pouring out of the faucet and directly onto her overheated body. Although, in theory, the cold water against her hot skin should feel good, it didn't seem to work that way. The cold water just added to her misery.

Resting her shaking body against Patrick's, she allowed the rumble in his chest as he spoke a string of soothing words to her, relaxing her. Stephanie couldn't work out what he was saying, her brain seemed to have reached a point where it could no longer decipher the world around it, but it didn't matter anyway.

He was there.

That was all that mattered.

"Patrick, stay with me, don't leave again," she mumbled. The fingers of her good hand searched out his and she clung to him. Any other time she would have been embarrassed, clinging to a man she barely knew, especially given how her ex had mocked her for being too emotional, but right now she didn't care. Patrick would make sure she was safe, he would take care of her, and he wouldn't leave her.

He promised he wouldn't.

Too exhausted to do anything else, Stephanie just let go, secure in the knowledge that so long as Patrick was with her nothing else could touch her.

Drifting off into more restless sleep, it wasn't until she woke sometime later that she realized the sleep had, in fact, not been restless.

It had been peaceful and restful, and she didn't feel so hot that she was being burned alive.

No longer wet, she knew she was in the bed and not the bath before she opened her eyes and turned her head to see Patrick curled up beside her. His eyes were closed, and for the first time since she'd met him, he looked peaceful, too.

Taking a moment to enjoy studying him without him knowing, Stephanie kept still and looked her fill. Thick, dark lashes fanned out against his tanned skin. He had a chiseled jaw and defined cheekbones, not too prominent but enough to highlight his eyes which were such a nice, warm brown. While he'd shown her glimpses of the easy-going, laidback man he was when he wasn't fighting for his life, she'd love to spend time with him when he could just relax and be himself.

She was doing the one thing she shouldn't.

Falling for him.

And not in a, she needed him to survive, kind of way.

Genuine feelings were developing. Despite the craziness of their time together, she didn't hold any of it against him. Quite simply she'd be dead if it wasn't for Patrick. His keeping quiet might have gotten her hurt, but it had kept her alive, and in the end that was the only thing that mattered. He'd done his best to take care of her, comfort her, care for her, and he hadn't left her behind even though it would have ensured his survival.

He was sweet, funny, kind, and it was obvious he cared about the people in his life. What was there not to like about him?

Was it wrong that she wanted to kiss him?

Without really thinking about it, Stephanie lifted her good hand and traced a trembling fingertip along Patrick's bottom lip.

Like the spell had been broken, his lashes fluttered, and a moment later, she was looking into those big brown eyes she could get lost in. When he saw her awake, Patrick smiled, reaching out to press the back of his hand to her forehead. "Temperature's going down, looks like your fever finally broke."

Only because of the antibiotics he'd gone to get her.

Once again, he had saved her life.

How could she ever repay him for everything he'd done for her?

"Thank you," she whispered, voice still weak.

He opened his mouth, and she got the feeling he was going to tell her it was nothing, but then his eyes softened and his whole expression warmed. "You're welcome. You should get more rest, you're still weak and not out of the woods yet."

Maybe not, but because of this man, she was closer than she should be.

"Will you hold me?"

"Nothing could stop me." With so much tenderness, he lifted her body until he could drape it over his own much the way he had when they'd both slept on the backseat of that car.

Strong arms banded around her, sturdy chest beneath her, warmth from his body seeped into her own and the reassuring feeling of his heart beating beneath her lulled her into sleep.

CHAPTER
Fourteen

January 26th
7:37 A.M.

Finally.

Finally, Stephanie was improving.

Trick had been feeding her Tylenol to both help with her pain and to bring down her fever and antibiotics every couple of hours, and it seemed to be doing its job. Slowly, her fever started creeping down. He'd kept up the cold baths, alternating between tucking her into the bed, letting her sleep, and then keeping her in the water every couple of hours.

There had been a moment when he first returned from stealing the lifesaving medications and found her barely coherent and only semi-conscious that he wasn't sure the medicine he'd stolen would be enough.

That anything would be enough.

He'd been ready to just take her to the hospital and hope for the best —it was worth it if it saved Stephanie's life even if it did put them both in a precarious situation—when her fever finally broke.

One moment she had been tossing and turning, sobbing although she didn't seem to be aware of it, as her body was thrown between raging heat and freezing cold, and then the next, she seemed to relax. It wasn't like she was magically better, but when he'd touched her forehead next, he'd been sure it was a little bit cooler.

Exhausted, he'd stretched out on the bed beside her and closed his eyes. It was only supposed to be a quick power nap, but he must have just passed out into oblivion because the next thing he registered was her soft finger brushing across his lip.

Relief had hit him hard when he'd awakened to find her watching him. While still haunted by pain, her gaze had been clearer, and her temperature seemed to have dropped even further. When she'd asked him to hold her there was no way he was going to say no to a chance to gather her close and wrap his arms around her.

Heaven.

That's what it felt like.

A little piece of heaven.

Holding a sleeping woman in his arms wasn't something he had ever done before. When you were only interested in a night of sex or maybe a couple of repeat performances, there was no need for snuggling.

But with Stephanie ...

He'd snuggle with her forever.

If only things could be different.

Knowing that the things he was starting to want were things that would forever remain outside his grasp almost made him want to pull away emotionally. All he had to do was keep her alive until his team got there. They didn't have to share, they didn't have to bond.

Sweet torture.

That's what it was.

And yet, even though Trick knew it was going to make it that much harder to walk away from her, he wouldn't give up these moments with her, talking, holding, and caring for her, for anything in the world.

A small moan caught his attention, and he turned to see Stephanie thrashing against the blankets covering her. The feverish flush was gone from her cheeks, and although he knew she still needed medical treatment, he was also sure that the worst was over. The infection was under control, her body needed rest, and he'd keep giving her the Tylenol and antibiotics until they were all gone, but he wasn't afraid he was going to lose her.

This time it wasn't fever she was fighting against, it was her memories.

Memories of the horrors she had endured. He could tell by the way her brow furrowed, the way her good hand clenched into a fist so tight her knuckles blanched.

What he wouldn't give to soothe away those fears.

Impotence raged inside him. There was nothing he could do other than wake her up, and that was only a temporary reprieve from the nightmare she would have to live when she was awake as much as when she was asleep.

Still stretched out on the bed even though he was sitting now, trying to figure out a plan on how to find the diamonds, he reached out and smoothed a hand over Stephanie's wild curls. Despite his reminders to himself that there was no future for the two of them, he couldn't seem to keep his distance.

Distance had always been the easiest thing in the world for him. To some extent, he still maintained a level of distance between himself and his team. They were his family in every way that mattered, but he didn't allow them all the way in. Humor and magic tricks were the way he maintained that distance. It was purely self-preservation, his own mom had stood by, preferring to keep her comfortable life than protect her only child, how could he ever expect to ever truly trust another person?

But Stephanie's unwavering devotion, her ability to hold in her cries of pain and horror while she was raped and tortured purely because she didn't want to make things harder for him had cemented her a place in his heart.

A place she would never even know she occupied.

As he stroked her hair, she slowly began to relax. Her fingers uncurled, releasing their death grip on the blankets, and the furrow smoothed off her forehead. Once she was sleeping peacefully again, he didn't stop stroking her hair.

Couldn't.

The need to touch her wasn't abating, it was growing with each second he spent by her side.

It was going to be hell walking away, but what else could he do?

Just because she didn't seem to hate him now, even seemed to seek comfort from his presence, it didn't mean she would feel the same way when she was back home and safe. Trick was convinced that when the reality of what had happened to her—of what he had allowed to happen —sunk in, she would hate him.

Seeing his sweet, brave Stephanie look at him with hatred in her eyes was more than he could bear.

If that made him a coward, then so be it.

Doubling down on his attempts to figure out where those diamonds were, Trick consoled himself with the knowledge that his team was on their way and that within the next twenty-four hours or so, he'd be putting Stephanie on a plane and sending her home. As much as he ached to know that it would be the last time he'd ever see her, and that these were the last few hours he'd spend with her, it was a relief to know she would be safe.

That was all that really mattered.

Not the fact that the more he thought about her walking out of his life, the more it made him want to do something stupid like ask her if maybe she would go out on a date with him once they were home.

It was stupid, she'd say no. Even if she did manage to find a way not to hate him, after losing her brother and her mom, and knowing what he did for a living, why would she invite the possibility of losing him too into her life?

No, there was no future for them, it was best not to try to hope for more and just be content with what was. Getting Stephanie home wouldn't even the scales in his favor, there was no way he could ever make up for allowing her to be so horrifically hurt, but at least it would be something.

"Patrick?" Stephanie's sleepy voice sent an arrow of something shooting straight through his heart.

Did she even realize she'd started calling him Patrick instead of Trick?

To her, it might not mean anything even if she knew that she was doing it. There was every chance it was just because they were getting to know each other better, and as the sense of familiarity grew, she wanted to use his real name and not his nickname.

To him, it meant something so much more.

Most of the guys he knew that were former or current military used their nicknames. Those names meant something to them, they were important, and they represented a huge part of who they were, not just what they did. But with most of those guys, the women they loved called them by their given names. It wasn't a rule or anything, but it happened more often than not, and hearing her call him Patrick made his heart flutter in an unfamiliar beat.

What was she doing to him?

"How you feeling, darlin'?"

After a slow blink, she gave him a small smile. "Better actually. Still feel too hot, and I don't think I'm up for another hike through the jungle any time soon, but I definitely feel better."

If she was making jokes with him then she was definitely doing better. Relief stirred something inside him, the growing feelings had taken root inside him in that dark, dank dungeon.

"What are you doing?" Stephanie asked as she carefully used her good hand to push herself into a sitting position, slumping against the bed's headboard.

"Trying to figure out where your brother hid the diamonds."

Her brow furrowed again, in confusion this time instead of fear. "I thought you knew where the diamonds were, and that's what you wouldn't tell them."

"I know your brother hid them, and he gave me some clues, but no one other than your brother knows where they are. If I can't find them, everyone involved in that op, the rest of my team, their loved ones, and all the family members of your brother's team, including you, will never be safe."

∽

January 26th
   10:04 A.M.

. . .

"Oh," Stephanie said as she used her good hand to haul herself up more so she was sitting properly beside Patrick rather than half lying. "I just assumed you knew where these diamonds the militia wanted were."

"I have a general idea, but your brother spoke in code. Not sure if it was because he was worried about being overheard or he knew someone had leaked his team's mission, and he wasn't sure who he could trust. Or if he was just dying and didn't even really think about it and was just speaking in gibberish, believing what he was saying made sense," Patrick said on a sigh.

A part of her wanted to snap that she'd gone through all that hell for nothing because he didn't even have the answers the militia wanted. Still, another part—the bigger part—recognized that Patrick had made the only choice he could to keep her alive regardless of what he knew.

Weariness was etched into his handsome face, and she felt it emanating from him in waves. The last thing she should do was add to his burdens by having a little meltdown, especially after everything he'd done for her. He'd kept her alive, he'd taken care of her when she was sick, he was risking his own life now by hiding out because she was too weak to do anything else rather than getting out of Liberia as quickly as he could which is what he'd do if he was on her own.

Not liking the wariness in his eyes, Stephanie knew she'd already given away a little of the frustration coursing inside her. That frustration wasn't really aimed at Patrick, it was at the militia who were using what she was sure were blood diamonds even if no one had outright said it, to fund terrorist activities. Who thought it was okay to kidnap people and hurt them so long as it furthered their own goals.

Filled with a need to ease Patrick's concerns that she somehow blamed him, she asked, "Did you try to find the diamonds?"

The relief she wanted to see in his eyes shone through and she relaxed. "Yeah, we looked before we brought your brother's body home. Even came back again. We couldn't find them." He hesitated for a moment. "Steph, you know—"

"I know," she assured him. And she did. If her brother had just told him where the diamonds were, maybe this could have all been avoided. Wondering what had been going through Chris' mind in those moments wasn't productive, her brother had been dying, might not have even known what he was saying. A thought occurred to her. "Maybe you can tell me what Chris said. I know I don't have any security clearance, but I already know about this whole mess now that I'm a part of it, and I know my brother better than anyone, maybe I can figure out what he was trying to say."

There was respect in his eyes, and she liked that he didn't see her as weak and pathetic even if she hadn't been struggling to live up to the standards she knew he would hold himself and his team to. "Honey, you're going to be getting out of here soon. While I was out getting you medicine, I was able to call my team. They're on their way. As soon as they get here, we're getting you to the plane and back home, then my team and I will try to track down these diamonds."

Home.

It was what she had been thinking about this entire time.

Dreaming about.

But now that she would soon be going there it suddenly didn't feel ... right.

Going home meant leaving Patrick behind and she wasn't ready for that yet. She needed more time with him. Just because she knew there was never going to be any sort of future between them, not even friendship, didn't mean she was ready to face that fact.

Couldn't she have just a little more time to live in fantasy land?

"What?" Trick asked, his calloused fingers caressing her forehead in what could only be described as a lover's touch. "I thought you'd be happy to be going home."

She was.

That wasn't the problem.

The problem was, Patrick wouldn't be coming with her. This was where they said goodbye, she'd never see him again, and Stephanie had no idea how to go forward without his presence, his support.

"Patrick, it's not ... what?" she asked when he got a funny, kind of goofy look on his face.

"You started calling me Patrick," he said like that explained everything. Only to her, it explained nothing. She did understand that to him it had some sort of significance.

"I can call you Trick again if you want?" she offered, wondering if he didn't like the closeness it inferred by her calling him by his given name, especially since she was doing it without his permission. He'd introduced himself as Trick, and she should have respected that, he didn't want her thinking of him as anything other than the Prey operative who would do everything he could to get her home safe.

"No." The word almost burst out of him, and she was a little taken aback by the vehemence behind it.

"Okay," she agreed slowly.

At her agreement, a look came over his face. It wasn't smug, per se, but it had a kind of ... male pride. Even though she still had no real idea of what was going on warmth settled inside her. Patrick at least liked her enough to want her to call him by his real name, and she couldn't help but feel like that meant something. Something bigger than she realized.

Opening her mouth to ask about it, Stephanie snapped it closed again when anything soft and warm was wiped off Patrick's face and his entire body went taut.

That something was wrong was evident.

While she had no idea how he did it—he wasn't really a superhero with x-ray vision and superhuman hearing—Patrick was highly trained, and if he had sensed something wasn't right, she one hundred percent believed him.

"Need you to go hide in the bathroom," Patrick said, holding his lips right above her ear so he could speak quietly enough no one else would hear him.

It was on the tip of her tongue to protest, to insist that the safest place in the world for her was right close to him, but he had already slipped into operator mode and she'd promised him she would obey all commands without comment. If he thought their best bet at surviving —and this was absolutely about survival—was for her to hide while he fought for both of them then she had to believe he was right. What did she know? She ran a gym, she knew nothing about fighting men like those in the militia.

With a shaky nod, Stephanie scooted over to the edge of the bed, planted her good hand on the mattress, and pushed to her feet. She had to lock her knees so they didn't buckle, but somehow, she remained standing and shuffled as fast as she could into the bathroom.

Even though she'd spent hours in the bath as Patrick tried to get her temperature down, the room looked unfamiliar.

Or maybe it was that it felt unfamiliar because Patrick wasn't there with her.

Stephanie knew she was way too dependent on him, but she didn't care. She liked him, he made her feel safe, he took care of her, and he seemed to like her, too. It didn't matter if she felt like she needed him to get through this ordeal because she knew deep down inside, in a place she had no idea existed before now, that she needed him for more than just a security blanket.

Climbing into the bath with the use of only one hand wasn't easy. Especially because she was still weak, dehydrated, and exhausted, but somehow, she managed to get inside. Once there, she lay down on her side, curled her knees up to her chest, tucked her injured hand beneath her neck, and wrapped her good arm around her legs.

At this moment, she felt so small, so helpless.

There was no way she could contribute to her own survival in this situation. For someone like her who had been raised to be as independent as possible while still having the safety net of a family who loved her, it felt awful.

Muffled thumps came from the other side of the closed bathroom door. She didn't remember closing it and wasn't sure if she'd done it on autopilot or if, once again, Patrick was there to watch out for her.

She ached to go to him, help him somehow, and she despised the fact that there was nothing she could do that would be helpful.

So she stayed, cried silent tears, trembled, tried to placate the knot of fear in her belly, and waited.

And waited.

And waited.

Finally, the door to the bathroom opened, and she prayed it was Patrick and that he wasn't dead and now the militia were coming for her.

CHAPTER

Fifteen

January 26th
10:18 A.M.

As he watched one of the three men who had broken into the hotel room head toward the bathroom door, Trick lost it.

His Stephanie was in there and she wasn't going to suffer again.

Not on his watch.

Shooting the men wasn't how he'd hoped this would go down. Gunshots would alert the staff and other guests at the hotel, and someone was bound to call the cops. Once the cops were involved, it would only be a matter of time before the militia got him and Stephanie back in their clutches. He had no idea how they'd found them at the hotel, but it didn't matter, all that mattered was killing them before Stephanie was hurt.

Ramming his elbow into the man trying to attack him from behind, Trick dropped his bodyweight, catching the man off-balance, and then drove his foot into the kneecap of the man attacking from in front.

Both men howled and released their grip on him, and he didn't hesitate to take advantage.

Grabbing his weapon from the waistband of his jeans, he'd hoped to eliminate the threat without using it, but it hardly seemed to matter. These guys weren't highly trained, they were making so much noise that he'd heard them before they could break down the door. Whoever was staying in the rooms beside this one would already know something was going on, so he may as well go for it and just kill all three of these men and get Stephanie out of there.

Before they could recover, he fired at the two men still in the bedroom with him, dropping both of them and then started for the bathroom.

Trick hadn't gone more than a step in its direction when the third man emerged.

He wasn't alone.

Pressed against his chest with a gun at her temple was Stephanie.

For the rest of his life the image of her clawing with her one good hand at the arm locked around her neck with a weapon so very close to her brain, an easy kill shot, would be seared into his mind. It would haunt him for as long as he lived, tormenting him, taunting him as a constant reminder of how many times he had failed this beautiful, brave, sweet woman.

Eyes wide with fear, she locked her gaze on him the second she saw him. It wasn't the fear he felt like a punch to the gut, it was her trust.

She believed he could get her out of this alive.

That she still trusted him to that extent after everything they had been through was a gift he most certainly did not deserve. But one he would treasure.

"Put the gun down," the soldier ordered.

It killed him that he didn't have another option but to do what the man ordered. If he tried firing a shot, with the way the soldier had positioned Stephanie's body, there was a chance he'd hit her instead.

Not a risk he could take.

For now, he would wait, comply, and strike as soon as an opportunity presented itself. There was only one soldier left and Trick liked those odds.

"Don't hurt her," he gritted out as he lowered his weapon and placed it on the floor by his feet.

Surprise flitted through the man's eyes. Clearly, he had expected more of a fight on Trick's part. But part of learning how to be an elite operator was knowing how to be patient.

Obviously pleased with the little bit of power he believed he'd gained, the man relaxed his hold on Stephanie, and reached for her injured hand. She whimpered when he grabbed her wrists and began to unwrap the bandages Trick had put on when she was in her fever-induced sleep.

"Maybe I should cut off the rest of her fingers," the man said with a smirk directed at both him and Stephanie. He wasn't one of the soldiers who had tortured them in the dungeon, and it seemed like he wasn't pleased he had missed out on the fun.

Hold it together, honey.

There was no way he would allow her to be mutilated again. If the man decided to try, Trick wouldn't hesitate to risk lunging at them and attacking. His girl wasn't going through that hell again.

No way.

Another whimper fell from Stephanie's lips as the soldier waved around her hand. While Trick wished she wasn't still trying to hold in her feelings for his benefit, she ended up doing something much more helpful than screaming.

At the sight of her maimed hand, Stephanie's already pale face drained of color, and he knew what was going to happen even before it did.

Nauseated by seeing her hand with the missing finger, Stephanie threw up.

All over herself and the soldier.

The man reflexively cursed and pulled away, releasing his hold on Stephanie, and putting enough distance between them that Trick could act.

Dropping to his knees, he scooped up his weapon, aimed it, and fired.

A kill shot.

The soldier dropped before he even realized what was happening.

Since there was no way the cops hadn't been called by someone who had heard the gunshots, Trick knew they didn't have much time.

Tucking his weapon back into the waistband of his jeans, he ran to Stephanie, who was still standing there shaking and staring at the body lying at her feet. Since she was in shock and he didn't have time to soothe her, Trick merely grabbed the hem of her now-soiled T-shirt and pulled it up and over her head. She made a small gasp of pain as he jostled her injured hand, but he didn't slow down.

Since he had known they might need to leave in a hurry, he had kept all the things he'd bought for them back in the bag. Now he unzipped it, yanked out another T-shirt and a pair of women's jeans, and returned to Stephanie's side.

There was no way to be gentle and quick, and since fast was paramount, he didn't allow himself to think about the pain he was causing Stephanie, and simply pulled the T-shirt down over her head and slipped her arms through the sleeves. Despite his best efforts, Stephanie's small moans of pain felt like darts stabbing into his skin.

Continuing on regardless, he knelt at her feet, lifted one leg and then the other, then stood, pulling up her jeans as he went. Stephanie didn't make a single move to either fight him or help him, and he hated that he couldn't spare a second to curl her into an embrace and just hold her. She'd been through so much, and held it together so well, but sooner or later she had to reach her limits.

Looked like maybe she had.

With the backpack on and one of the weapons in his hand, Trick wrapped his other arm around Stephanie's waist and lifted her. "Wrap your legs around my hips, honey," he instructed, and he was relieved when she complied. "Good arm around my neck." There was every chance the cops were already on their way or already there, and he needed to be able to defend them if he had to. There was no way he was going to rely on the hope that some honest cops would be the ones to show up. Not with Stephanie's life on the line.

Thankfully, he didn't encounter anyone as he ran them both out to the car. After setting Stephanie in the passenger seat and rounding the car, he jumped into the driver's seat, hotwired the car, and took off.

When he reached over to buckle her seatbelt, he found that she'd already done it and now had her bad hand cradled in her good one and was staring at it intently.

"You don't have to look at it yet, darlin', not if you're not ready," he told her as he drove out of the parking lot.

"I have to be ready at some point, may as well just do it. This is my reality now, I can't pretend it's not."

"But you don't have to rush yourself," he reminded her. After all the trauma she had been through, it was okay for her to take her time, but he suspected Stephanie was more the kind of woman who faced her troubles head-on.

Lifting her head, she looked at him through eyes that looked a little clearer now even if she was still shaking and much too pale. "You saved me again. Thank you. I don't know how I can ever repay you for everything you've done for me."

Whatever he'd done it hadn't been enough. She was hurt. Scared. Traumatized. Forever changed. "I don't want your thanks or for you to repay me," he muttered.

His fingers tightened around the steering wheel, and Stephanie must have noticed because she reached over and rested her good hand on his thigh. The heat of it seeped inside him and stilled his racing heart. Seeing Stephanie in danger ...

It about killed him.

The sooner he got her on a plane home the better.

"I know how I can pay you back," Stephanie said, completely ignoring what he'd just told her. "No one knows Chris better than me. I'm sure I can help you figure out where those diamonds are hidden."

January 26th
    10:41 A.M.

From the look Patrick shot her way, you'd think she had just told him she wanted to build a ladder that reached all the way up into the heavens.

All Stephanie wanted to do was help.

Find a way to make all of this make sense.

She'd lost a lot, but maybe if she could help Patrick and his team find the diamonds, dismantle the militia group, and make sure they couldn't go after anyone else on Patrick's team or any of the other family members of her brother's team, then she would be able to find a way to heal.

Right now that felt impossible.

No longer could she hide from the atrocities that had been done to her. Being forced to look at her maimed hand had proven that. This had happened, she'd been kidnapped, tortured, raped, and almost killed several times. How was she going to survive once the weight of it settled upon her? Stephanie had no idea, but she couldn't give up, she needed this to have happened for a reason. A purpose. Something outside herself.

"Honey, it's too dangerous for you here, you need to go home."

Even though Patrick almost always spoke to her in that same calm, soothing tone, for some reason this time it irked her.

He was talking to her like she was a victim.

Okay, so she was a victim, but he'd been kidnapped and held in that dungeon, too. He could have died just as easily as she could have, and when the militia were done with them his body would have been joining hers in some shallow grave in the Liberian jungle. They were both victims, yet she knew no one was going to talk to him in that overly controlled voice that he was using on her.

"I want to do this," she said, aware she sounded somewhat petulant and a whole lot stubborn. It wasn't like she was asking to don body armor and go into battle against the militia, but she was sure if he told her exactly what her brother had said, she could help him figure out where those diamonds were.

If that got her a little extra time with Patrick, that was just a bonus. Stephanie was all too aware that once they parted ways that was it. It was over. She'd never see him again.

"We've been fighting for our lives, you've been sick, you haven't had time to process." One of his hands came off the steering wheel and picked up her good hand, lacing their fingers together. "You've been through so much and I can't let you put yourself in danger for a second longer than is absolutely necessary."

His words echoed inside her head.

She knew all of that.

Had lived it.

But it was the first time someone had said it out loud to her, and that seemed to give her trauma power, strengthening it.

Tears burned the backs of her eyes, but she refused to let them fall. "I haven't fallen apart yet."

"You threw up at the sight of your hand and went into shock," Patrick reminded her.

"It saved our lives," she shot back.

"It's not a criticism, Steph."

"Felt like it," she muttered.

Pulling over to the side of the road with a jerk, Patrick unbuckled both their seatbelts and then yanked her over and set her on his lap. Surprise had her mouth hanging open and her good hand braced against his rock-hard pecs.

"Stephanie Fuller, you are without a doubt the strongest, bravest, kindest, toughest woman I have ever met. I am in awe of you. You will never know how much I appreciate what you did for me in that dungeon, refusing to beg me to tell them what they wanted. I don't care that you freaked at the sight of your hand, it does not detract one little bit from how amazing you are. You have held up better than I could have hoped for. Better than almost anyone else would in your situation. Better even than some trained operators would have. You are the very definition of a survivor. You're a superhero."

His impassioned speech, which held not a trace of the coddling tone he'd been using earlier, made her smile.

More than that, it made her cry.

Somehow, it managed to break through the barriers she had erected when her ex told her she was too emotional and needy.

Sobs burst out of her in a mess, and she buried her face against Patrick's neck as she wept. Not all her tears were for the horrors she'd lived through in West Africa. She cried for her brother who had died such a horrible death, and up until his last breath, had still been trying to make the world a better place. She cried for her mother who loved both her children but couldn't live in a world without one of them. She cried for Patrick who she knew had suffered just as much as she had in that dungeon, even if he hadn't been physically tortured.

And she cried for herself.

For the woman who had lost part of who she was when her ex had thrown her away when she needed him the most. For the woman who had lost even more in a dark, dirty, dank dungeon.

A woman who could never be the same again.

But a woman who was still standing.

Who wasn't pretending that anything was going to be easy, that anything was ever going to be like it was before, but who also wanted to find a way to go on. Just because it seemed impossible didn't mean that it was, and if she could do something that mattered, something that was bigger than herself, bigger than her suffering, then she knew that would help her believe that she had the strength to rebuild her life from scratch.

As she cried, Patrick held her close, his lips pressed against her crown, touching kisses to her head between murmuring soothing consolations she couldn't hear because of her sobs. His hand stroked the length of her spine in a continuous motion, up and down, up and down, as the warmth and security of his presence soothed something inside her.

Falling for this man was a recipe for disaster.

It was already a foregone conclusion that he was walking out of her life as soon as he knew she was safe.

Yet she couldn't seem to stop herself.

It didn't matter how many times she reminded herself that the end was coming—and quickly—she fell a little more with each soft touch and kind word.

"Thanks for letting me cry all over you, I needed that," she admitted as she lifted her head and offered Patrick a tremulous smile.

Movement outside the car caught her attention, and Stephanie blinked to clear her tear-drenched eyes.

Five big men dressed all in black were approaching their car.

Panic hit, stealing any relief and peace she'd gotten from finally allowing the dam to break and her emotions to come flooding out. The militia had found them again. How they kept doing it she had no idea, but it didn't seem to matter where they were, the truth was, there was just no safe place for her and Patrick in Liberia.

With her on his lap, there was no way Patrick could drive the vehicle which meant they were about to be captured and returned to that underground torture chamber. Pain and then death were all their futures would hold. She wouldn't be saying goodbye to Patrick as they got off a plane back home or if he put her on one and stayed behind. Instead, she'd be saying goodbye before watching him get executed or before her own execution.

This was all her fault.

She shouldn't have allowed herself the release of crying. She should have just kept her emotions locked down inside where they couldn't hurt her or anyone else.

"Patrick, men are coming," she squeaked, curling her good hand into his T-shirt and trying to use it as leverage to move back to her seat. Maybe if she was quick enough, he could stomp his foot on the gas and get them out before the five men converged on their car.

Instead of hurrying her into her seat so he could do something, Patrick merely hooked an arm around her waist and kept her right where she was.

Thinking he was going to shoot the men before they could abduct them, she buried her face once again against his neck, only this time she scrunched her eyes closed and worked on stamping down her fear. There was no way she could claim she could stick around long enough to help Patrick decipher her brother's last words if she couldn't handle what it took to stay alive in this dangerous place.

There were no gunshots.

There was no anything.

The next thing she heard was the car door being opened.

"About time."

CHAPTER
Sixteen

January 26th
11:00 A.M.

"About time you guys showed up," Trick told his team as Panther opened the driver's door.

"If you wanted us to show up quicker, then maybe you should have sent out an SOS sooner," Panther muttered, making Trick grin.

Damn, he'd missed these guys. He wasn't used to working missions alone, they were always together, there as a team. Of course, there had been times when they split up, but they never just up and went off to another country on their own.

While he was glad his team was there, Stephanie was so tense in his arms that it felt like one wrong move would shatter her into a million pieces.

Realizing she was unaware that this was his team and likely believed the men she had seen approaching the vehicle were more militia soldiers sent to abduct them, he swept his hand up her back and cupped the back of her head. "It's okay, darlin', these are the good guys," he whispered against her ear.

"Good guys?" Her head darted up and she took in Panther standing in the open door, Tank and Rock behind him. Slowly, she turned her head to see Axe and Scorpion standing at the now-open passenger door.

Instead of relaxing at the news that they weren't on their own anymore, if anything, she seemed to grow tenser, shrinking in on herself and pressing closer against his body. Just because he knew these guys, considered them his brothers, would die for any of them or their families, and would trust them not just with his life but with Stephanie's, too, to her they were strangers.

Big, scary-looking strangers.

In her mind, there was probably no difference between the men who had tortured her so mercilessly and his team. All of them had been big and carried weapons, giving off that air of trained confidence.

"It's okay, honey," he repeated, lightly squeezing the nape of her neck to draw her attention back to him. "These guys aren't going to hurt you."

While he felt her muscles relax marginally, he could still feel the tension flowing off her. On the heels of being attacked in the bathroom of their hotel room, it was no wonder she was on edge and not particularly keen to be around anyone she didn't already know and trust.

Trick couldn't deny it gave him a little boost to know he was firmly in Stephanie's trust category.

"Let me introduce you," he said, hoping that if she had some names to go with the faces, they wouldn't seem so intimidating. "This guy here is Panther. He has an eight-year-old son at home, the cutest kid you'll ever meet, smart too, just like his daddy. Standing behind him is Tank, he recently became engaged to a woman he kidnapped." He snickered.

Stephanie's round eyes somehow grew rounder, but he felt her relax a little more. "A woman he kidnapped?"

"Your buddy Trick here is lying," Tank muttered. "It was a job, and I was protecting her. She just didn't know that."

"See, kidnapped," he teased, and Stephanie managed a small smile. "Standing beside the big guy is Rock. Rock messed up with the woman he loved, but for some reason completely unknown to me, she found it in her heart to forgive him. Next step in Rock's master plan is to convince Ariel to marry him."

Rock rolled his eyes at him, but he knew that the man was pleased as punch that Ariel had allowed him into her life again after he'd hurt her so badly in the past. Trick knew how much guilt his friend carried around for the awful things he'd said and done, and while he didn't mean to make light of either Rock or Ariel's suffering, he used humor to remind himself and others how badly they needed light in their lives.

"On the other side of our humble vehicle we have Axe, he's our team leader and the only one of us who's married." Now wasn't the time to go into the whole Beth and Axe situation, and since he would very soon have to let Stephanie go for good, she didn't really need to be dragged into that mess. "And the other one is Scorpion. He went undercover to save a woman who didn't need saving. One he didn't even like. Oh yeah, they're now together. Guys, this is Stephanie Fuller."

When he'd stolen a phone—well, not technically stolen since he had left behind enough money to pay for it—while out getting Stephanie medication, he'd only told the guys the bare bones of what had happened. All he'd told them was where he was and that he wasn't alone, that he had a woman, another victim, with him.

At her name, he saw all the guys straighten a little. It was likely they had already figured out this had something to do with the mission involving the SEAL team and the diamonds when they learned he was in Liberia. But hearing Stephanie's last name had obviously piqued all their interests.

There would be time later to fill them in on all the details, once Stephanie was safely tucked away on a plane heading back home.

"How did they find us?" Stephanie asked softly, her gaze still nervous as it bounced from side to side.

Even though they needed to get moving because they were making a spectacle of themselves that wouldn't go unnoticed in this area that was clearly under militia control, the need to reassure Stephanie was too strong for him to ignore.

"When I went to get you medicine, I also got myself a phone. I called my team and left it on so they could track us through the GPS," he told her.

Although she gave a small nod, she still didn't seem to be able to relax. He got it. Every time these last few days she was surrounded by a group of men she was hurt, raped, or had a gun held on her.

"You ready to get out of here?" he asked, unwilling to move her until she gave him the okay.

Just like that, he saw the stubborn glint back in her eyes. His girl was a tough one, just like he'd told her, and he saw she was yet to give up on her belief that she could help him figure out what her brother had said so they could find the diamonds.

"Out of the car? Yes. Out of Liberia? No," Stephanie said, and as he shifted her so he could climb out of the car and gather her into his arms, he saw all five of his teammates looking at him with clear questions in their eyes.

"Stephanie thinks she can help us figure out where her brother hid the diamonds," he told his team as he carried her toward their waiting vehicle and slid into the middle row of seats. Even though he could—should—sit her beside him on the seat Trick found that he couldn't. Their time together was drawing to a close, but he wasn't ready to relinquish her just yet.

"I don't think I can, Patrick, I know I can," Stephanie corrected.

Hearing her call him by his first name had all five sets of eyes snapping toward him. There was a mixture of surprise, shock, and amusement on his friends' faces. Just because Stephanie had no idea what it meant when a woman called them by their real names, every single guy on his team did.

Only this time, it didn't mean anything.

Couldn't mean anything.

Even if he wanted it to.

"I want you safe," he told her firmly. Safe meant far away from Liberia and the men who wanted to hurt her.

Looking pointedly around the car and the five other men, she looked back to him. "I think I am pretty safe."

"You know what I mean."

"My brother has been dead for almost a year. I think if you—or anyone else—was going to figure out where those diamonds are they would have done it by now. Besides, the guys on his team, me and our mom, were the closest to him. They're all dead, Patrick. All of them, including our mom. I'm it. I'm all you've got. They aren't going to give up, they need those diamonds. And how do you know I'm any safer at home? Someone knew I was in Mexico and told the militia. Someone knew how to find you, too. I'm not safe at home."

Her words pierced his chest like a series of arrows.

Trick hated that she was right.

What if he sent her back home and she was abducted again? He could ask Eagle—the founder and CEO of Prey Security—to assign someone to watch over her, but he couldn't seem to stomach the thought of anyone other than himself watching her back.

It was stupid. Every single Prey operative was as trained as he was. Eagle himself wouldn't hesitate to take Stephanie into his home if that was what Trick asked for, but it wasn't the same. They wouldn't care about her the same way he would. To them, it would be a job. Prey was a family, and if Stephanie meant something to him, then she was a part of that family, but to him keeping Stephanie alive wasn't a job, it wasn't an obligation, it wasn't a responsibility, it was vital, tied into his own survival.

Imploring chocolate eyes pleaded with him. "Please, Patrick, don't send me away. This is where I feel safe. With you. I can help you with this. I know I can. Please."

~

January 26th
11:13 A.M.

What was she going to do if he said no?

Stephanie honestly had no idea.

If Patrick and his team forced her onto a plane back home, she could do nothing about it. But the idea of going home alone where she knew she wouldn't be safe and where she couldn't do anything to help terrified her.

Having a gun held to her temple had solidified to her just how desperate the militia was to get their diamonds back. They weren't going to stop. If they could kidnap her once, they could do it again.

The only place she felt safe was with Patrick.

The only way she knew to move forward was by finding meaning in the meaningless.

But how did she explain all of that to him without sounding needy and crazy?

There was no way she would be able to cope with Patrick treating her the same way her ex had, throwing her away after one relatively minor meltdown. He said he thought she was strong and brave, yet when presented with an opportunity to prove it, she got the feeling he wanted to back down and take his words back. Because that's what it felt like he would be doing if he shoved her onto that plane without even giving her a chance to see if she could make sense of what her brother had said.

Raking his hands down his face, Patrick then planted them on her shoulders. "I don't like the idea of you being in more danger."

"I don't like the idea of you being in more danger," she shot back. Whatever she felt for him, it was strong, and the last thing she wanted was for anything to happen to him. But if these last few months had taught her anything, it was that life could change in the blink of an eye. Nothing was certain. Nothing was guaranteed.

"She's got you there, brother," Scorpion said with an amused smirk.

Although she was downright terrified of these five men, even knowing they were the good guys and Patrick's friends, she gave the man a grateful smile, thankful she might have at least one ally.

"What you said in the car right before your team showed up, did you mean it?" she asked.

"One hundred percent," Patrick replied without hesitation.

"Then I ... need you to prove it." It kind of felt like emotional black-mail even though that wasn't how she'd meant it. Her ex had messed with her head more than she realized, and she had lost faith in herself. Patrick's words had bolstered her confidence, but if she felt like they were empty words and not really what he believed, then any gains in confidence she'd made would be eradicated. With everything else to deal with, she didn't need to doubt herself.

A pained sigh fell from Patrick's lips, but she got the feeling it had less to do with her and more to do with the fact that he just honestly didn't like the idea of her staying there a second longer than she had to. "It's up to the guys," he finally said.

These men might scare her because they were all so big and intimidating, and it didn't seem to matter how many times she reminded herself that Patrick trusted them implicitly, but she forced herself to shift on Patrick's lap so she could see them all.

The one called Axe was driving, Tank sat in the passenger seat, Scorpion and Panther were behind them in the backseat, and Rock was beside Patrick in the middle seat. She was still on Patrick's lap even though there was just enough space for her to squeeze in between him and Rock. Stephanie was grateful for her ability to memorize faces and the names that went with them after a single meeting. It helped a lot in her business and even more so today.

These men were a unit, she was the outsider. They knew nothing about her except that she had been abducted along with their team member and friend. There was no reason for them to believe she could be of any use to them.

"I'm cool with her helping," Scorpion said immediately. That was twice now he'd been nice to her, and she felt a small surge of confidence.

"I think we could use the help," Panther agreed.

Two down but still three to go.

The man beside her—Rock—studied her for a long moment. She felt his probing stare deeply and watched as it traveled across the wounds on her face, down her chest as though it could see beneath her T-shirt to the bruises still littering her torso, before settling on her hand. Stephanie fought the urge to squirm. If she wanted to prove to these men she had value, she couldn't let on how much they intimidated her.

"I think she can handle it," Rock pronounced, surprising her since she was sure he had been going to say she didn't have what it took.

"Our women are tougher than we give them credit for. I think she's earned her place," Tank said, turning in his seat to look at her.

Even though she didn't point out that she wasn't Patrick's woman, nor had he asked or even intimated that he wanted her to be, she was grateful for more support. Four of the guys had okayed her helping them, that only left Axe.

There was something extra intimidating about the man. He wasn't any bigger than the others, and yet ... there was a darkness that seemed to cling to him like a second skin. Since Patrick hadn't told her much about the men on his team, she had no idea what it was about, nor did she intend to ask.

"I think that none of us, or the people we love, are safe until those diamonds are removed from the equation," Axe spoke slowly, never taking his eyes off the road as he drove. "I think the only one who might be able to do that is Stephanie. So far, we haven't been able to figure it out ourselves, so why not give her a chance? The last thing I want is for this to wind up touching Beth. She's been through more than enough."

That was it. Five out of the five guys had agreed to give her a chance. That just meant the one man she needed to support her the most had to tell her what she needed to hear. Stephanie didn't know or care why Patrick's opinion of her was so important, she only knew it was.

"One condition," Patrick said when she turned hopeful eyes on him.

"Done."

"You don't even know what it is," he reminded her, although amusement danced in his dark eyes.

"I don't care. I want to help, I don't want to do anything stupid, I don't want to put you all at risk, I just ... need to do this. So, whatever it is, I agree," Stephanie told him.

"Rock is a medic. You're going to let him give you a proper assessment, and whatever he tells you he needs to do, you'll let him. You're dehydrated, still have infections, and are weak. We're going to go somewhere you can rest, where we can get some IV fluids and antibiotics into you. Rock is going to need to clean your hand. It's not going to be pretty."

"I can take it," she assured him. She'd survived everything else, and she would endure this, too.

"You won't pretend you're not in pain while he does it," Patrick added.

"But—"

"You already agreed to my conditions," he said, cutting her off.

"You said one condition, that was like five," she muttered, making at least one of the guys in the vehicle snort in amusement.

"Take it or leave it, darlin'," Patrick said in a tone that told her he knew he had her backed into a corner. Since he was also trying to make sure she got a little medical attention, she could hardly argue with him about it, and he knew it.

"You know this is the first time you've been a jerk to me since you woke up," she grumbled, even though she wasn't really all that mad. For the first time in days, she actually felt like she and Patrick were going to make it out of this mess alive, it wasn't just the two of them anymore.

"Trust me, Trick is always a jerk," Scorpion said, grinning at his teammate.

"Those magic tricks are the most annoying thing ever," Panther agreed.

Patrick didn't seem to mind the guys teasing him, he just rolled his eyes at them and then fixed his gaze on her. "Today, you rest. Tomorrow, we'll see if we can figure out what your brother was trying to say."

"Tomorrow," she echoed, that high from a moment ago fading fast.

Even though she had known it was coming, the expiration date had just been stamped on her relationship with Patrick. Stephanie knew without a shadow of a doubt that tomorrow or the next day when she helped them find those diamonds, it would be time to say goodbye to Patrick once and for all.

CHAPTER

Seventeen

January 27th
6:23 A.M.

"I've never seen you like this before."

Trick looked over his shoulder at Panther, who was leaning against the door jamb, studying him.

Truth was, he'd never felt like this before.

Women had always just been for fun. He hadn't wanted to let them get too close, hadn't thought he cared about finding one woman who could provide for all his needs, not just his sexual ones but all the ones he hadn't even realized he had. Hadn't thought he had it in him to provide a woman with what she needed.

Sure, he was okay at calming victims and knew what to say and how to say it to put people at ease. He loved the brother-sister relationships he had with Beth, Tillie, Ariel, and Jessica, but he wasn't interested in finding a forever person for himself.

Still wasn't, unless it was this woman.

"I don't know how she did it," he said honestly.

"I've heard that when you meet the right person, your other half, that's how it happens," Panther said.

"You weren't in love with Andy's mom?" Trick asked. It was rare for Panther to bring up anything to do with his ex. The woman had bailed on her husband and son when Andy was only a year old, and while it had never seemed like Panther was all that broken up about it, Trick had always wondered whether he was hiding a broken heart and that's why he never dated.

"At the time I thought I was, but looking back I know I wasn't. But I've seen enough true love in Axe and Beth, Tank and Tillie, Rock and Ariel, and recently in Scorpion and Jessica to know what it looks like. You've fallen for her."

"Hard not to. She's amazing. I'm in awe of her. I ... can't get enough of her. But it doesn't change the fact that I sat there and let her be raped and tortured. There's no way she could ever want me the same way I crave her."

After Stephanie had won over his team and they'd okayed the idea of her staying on to help see if she could figure out her brother's last words rather than get right on a plane home, her exhausted body had given out and she'd fallen asleep. On the drive to the small place his team had secured, he had filled them in on all the details of what had happened to him and Stephanie. Safe to say, she now had a whole team of overprotective big brothers who were as in awe of her and her strength as he was.

"I don't know about that, brother," Panther said. "Don't do anything you might wind up regretting, yeah?"

Before he could comment, Stephanie shifted on the bed, blinking open sleepy eyes. Damn, she was adorable all sleep rumbled. He could totally get addicted to waking up in the mornings to see her all soft and sweet like this.

"Is it morning?" Stephanie asked.

"Yeah, darlin', it's morning." It felt like the most natural thing in the world to reach out and smooth her wild mass of curls off her cheek. Tenderness flowed through him, he just wanted to grab this woman and drag her into his lap, wrap his arms around her, and keep her there, right where he knew he could protect her.

Sadness filled her eyes, and he wondered if she was realizing how close they were getting to having to say goodbye to one another. For the last week or so they had been all each other had. They'd been one another's everything, and now they were about to go cold turkey.

"Good news, honey. Rock says he's going to take the IV out so you can take a proper shower before we head out in a couple of hours."

"A hot shower does sound nice," Stephanie agreed. "And I do need to do something about this mess." She waved her bandaged hand at her hair, then stared at it. While she hadn't wept or screamed or done much of anything while Rock had thoroughly cleaned the wound, she had gripped his hand in her good one and squeezed tightly enough he was surprised she hadn't broken his bones.

"You hungry, Steph?" Panther asked.

"Mmm, yeah, I think I actually am," she said, offering his friend a smile.

"The guys made a huge stack of bacon, eggs, and toast. You should see how much this guy eats," Panther told her.

Turning her smile on him, it felt like being bathed in sunlight. "Yeah, he told me he has a huge appetite. I am yet to witness it though."

"Let's get you fed so Rock can remove this thing, and then you can take your shower." When he reached for her, looping the IV bags around his shoulders so he could take them with her, then scooping her up, she made no protest about being carried. Didn't tell him that she could walk on her own or seem embarrassed for him to be carrying her around in front of his friends, men she didn't know and was obviously still skittish around. Trick hoped that was because she felt comfortable enough with him to crave his presence like he craved hers.

The tiny house had only one bedroom, and of course, they'd all agreed that Stephanie needed the bed. He'd slept on it along with her, but only after she'd asked him to. Just because she hadn't had time to process the ordeal she'd lived through, it didn't mean she wasn't a rape victim, and he was careful about not doing anything to freak her out.

In the living room kitchen combo, the other guys were sitting around the table where there were indeed copious amounts of food.

Stephanie's eyes were round when she saw it. "How can the seven of us eat this much?"

"You're in for a shock, girl," Rock told her as he took the IV bags and hung them on a kitchen cabinet beside the chair Trick deposited Stephanie in.

While all the guys, himself included, piled their plates high with food, Stephanie took a single piece of toast and a slice of bacon. Even though he wanted to urge her to eat more, she needed to start rebuilding her strength, Trick also understood that it was going to take time for her system to be able to return to normal, so he let it be.

"So ..." Stephanie said once they all started eating. "Are you ready to tell me what my brother said?"

There was no putting it off any longer. He could see how much it hurt Stephanie to think about her brother's final moments, but there was a determination there he couldn't not respect and admire. She wanted to help, she wanted to make sure others didn't suffer like she had, his girl was completely and utterly amazing. No other way to describe her.

"It sounded like gibberish," he reminded her. Just because Stephanie wanted to help, it didn't mean she could. There was every chance Chris hadn't even known what he was saying, he'd been quickly losing blood and had died mere minutes later.

"I'm prepared to not be able to actually help, I just need to try."

"The SEAL team moved in, took out the first group of men, and were able to secure the diamonds, but then all hell broke loose," he told her gently. "The intel they'd been given was way off, and they were overrun by the militia. They held them off for a while, but unfortunately, we arrived too late to save any of them. I was the one who talked to your brother, who was with him when he died."

Tears glistened in her eyes. "Thank you. For being there for him, I always hated the idea that he might have died alone."

"There was nothing I could do to help him, and he knew it. All he said to me was, "Way-apa-apa Ma-U-I". I had no idea what that meant, still don't. We ran the word through all the dialects spoken in Liberia and compared it to every city and town on the map across the country, not just in the area where his team was ambushed, but we couldn't find anything that might have matched."

Stephanie was quiet for a moment, chewing on her toast, seemingly unaware that the six of them were watching her like a hawk, hoping for any clue, however small, she might be able to give them.

Her brow did that adorable crinkle thing it made when she was concentrating, and with the cuts on her cheeks clean and beginning to scab and a little of her color back, she looked so much better than she had yesterday morning when she had a gun pressed to her temple.

"Waianapanapa State Park, in Maui. The only big vacation we ever took was when I was a kid. I was ten, Chris was sixteen. My mom saved for months to take us to Hawaii. I tried to pronounce the name of the place we were going, but I got it wrong. Chris called me a baby. He was a great big brother, but he was still my brother and he teased me mercilessly about my childish mispronunciation."

"What does Hawaii have to do with the diamonds?" Tank asked.

Stephanie shrugged helplessly. "I have no idea."

"He can't have been talking about the physical location," Scorpion said.

"So, it had to be something to do with what you did while you were there," Rock added.

"What did you do on your vacation, honey?" he asked her.

"Typical vacation stuff," Stephanie replied. "We hiked, swam, Chris in particular loved the freshwater caves."

"The militia used to be based in Buchanan," Axe said. "They were near the beach, there are caves in the area."

Cheeks pinking in excitement, Stephanie reached for his hand. "Did I do it? Did I help you figure out where the diamonds are hidden?"

Pride for his girl unfurled inside him. "Yeah, honey, I think you did."

～

January 27th
    2:26 P.M.

This was it.

The final few hours she and Patrick would spend together and it wouldn't even be just the two of them.

Although Stephanie couldn't deny that she felt a deep sense of satisfaction knowing she had hopefully helped Bravo Team find the diamonds, the pang of sadness seemed to far outweigh it.

"You okay?" Patrick asked, nudging her shoulder.

What was there to say to that? Physically, she was beat up and almost at her limit. Psychologically, she hadn't even allowed herself the freedom to think about anything because she was too afraid of falling apart. Call her crazy, call her being in denial or shock, call her trying to run and hide from her trauma, but all of it seemed to pale in comparison to knowing that in just a few short hours, this man was going to walk out of her life.

Now wasn't the time to tell him all that though.

Maybe there never would be a right time.

Even if there was, it wasn't now.

Not when Patrick and his team were preparing to search the caves for the diamonds. It could be dangerous, not the caves so much, she was sure men like this could take on the raging ocean in the middle of a storm, let alone caves that tourists frequented. But the militia had found them once already, there was every chance they could find them again.

She didn't want Patrick—or his team, who were slowly winning her over and gaining her trust mostly because they were all trying so hard not to make her feel intimidated or threatened—to get hurt.

Ever.

"Just nervous, I guess," she answered, not entirely dishonestly. Stephanie was nervous about everything. The diamonds, the militia, leaving Patrick, going home, having no choice but to face her ordeal, fear that she wasn't strong enough to weather the storm of emotions she knew was coming.

"If you want, we can drive you to the airport, get you on the plane, and then come back and look for the diamonds," Patrick offered.

They'd gone over that already, and she had insisted there was no way she would feel safe sitting alone on a plane or allow one of the men to stay with her. They needed to watch each other's backs, she didn't want anyone getting hurt.

Whether or not she was safe had never really entered her mind before she was kidnapped. She had just kind of assumed she was. Naïve really, given that she knew what kind of world they lived in, but didn't all normal people carry around an unfounded sense of security?

"No, I'm good. I'll be perfectly safe waiting for you guys here at the car," she assured him, somehow even managing to paint on a smile so he didn't worry.

"Come here." Patrick wrapped an arm around her shoulders and pulled her into an embrace.

It was absolutely pure instinct that had her sinking down into his chest, allowing him to be strong for her for just a moment. One moment of soaking up his warmth and the security his hold brought her. Right here, held so tenderly, this was the safest place in the world. Because in Patrick's arms she didn't just feel physically safe but emotionally safe as well.

"Thank you," she whispered, touching her lips to his chest right above his heart. Patrick might never know how deeply she craved him, how badly she didn't want him to leave her when they got home, or how much he meant to her, but it wouldn't change anything. When he left, he would take a piece of her heart along with him.

She would have sworn she felt a shudder ripple through him and his arms tighten around her, but then he stooped, kissed her forehead, and took a step away from her.

"We'll be back as soon as we can," he reminded her.

"I know."

"We really don't mind dropping you at the plane," Tank told her.

It was sweet that he also wanted to reassure her, but she could handle this. Fact was, she had to learn to handle being on her own. Her friends would support her, but they knew nothing about what she had lived through. Their safe little bubbles hadn't been popped and she was going to have to find her way forward alone.

"I'll be okay," she promised. Since she had to start somewhere on her healing journey, it may as well be now. The first step to figuring out how to survive was finding a way not to be terrified of being alone.

"You will be," Rock agreed, and for some reason him saying it, when he didn't have all the reasons Patrick did to lie to her to try to make her

feel better, did actually make her feel better. If someone like Rock
thought she could be okay then maybe she really could be.

One day anyway.

"Stay in the car," Patrick reminded her as he gripped her hips and
gently lifted her up and into the driver's seat. She had the keys to the car
and instructions from the guys that if anything happened to them, she
was to drive to the airport—they'd programmed the GPS with directions—and then call Prey, the number was in the phone they'd
given her.

Could she actually follow through on that and leave them behind?

Stephanie wasn't sure yet, but she was praying she didn't have to
find out.

Patrick half closed her door but then opened it again and leaned
down. Expecting another forehead kiss, Stephanie was shocked when,
instead, his lips brushed across her own. The kiss was brief, barely
lasting a split second, and yet every single cell in her body seemed to
quiver at the light touch.

What would it be like if he kissed her for real?

It hurt—an actual physical ache somewhere deep in her soul—to
know that she would never find out the answer to that question.

After he closed her door, Stephanie watched Patrick and his team
walk away until they disappeared into the trees where they'd hidden
the car.

There was no reason to believe anyone would stumble upon her, no
reason to believe that the militia had any idea where they were or that
they would be able to find them again.

Yet none of that seemed to matter.

Anxiety churned in her gut, soured it, and made her nauseous all
over again.

It sucked always feeling so sick. The constant stream of adrenalin in
her system was keeping her going when she would have already long ago
reached her limits, but it also kept her shaky and unsteady. It was too
much, she couldn't keep going on like this, but how long would it take
until her body and her mind believed that she was safe?

Never.

That was the answer that immediately popped into her mind, and she hated that it was probably true. Her sense of security had been well and truly picked up, shaken, and then burst like a soda bottle when you unscrewed the cap.

It was gone forever.

Could never fully come back.

Every time she thought her life couldn't get any worse it somehow did, and she was terrified of what was going to happen next. Maybe that was why she was twitchy and on edge. She was just sitting there waiting for the next bad thing to happen to her.

Like life really did just get enjoyment out of beating up on her, no sooner had she thought it than the passenger door of the car was ripped open so violently it almost looked like it was going to be pulled right off its hinges.

Terror pulsing through her veins, Stephanie turned to find the man from her nightmares standing there grinning at her.

The man who had cut at her face, who had raped her, who had cut off her finger, who would have continued to hurt her until he realized it wasn't going to get him what he wanted, and then he would have ended her life and never felt an ounce of remorse.

This man had no soul. There was no other way to explain someone with no empathy, morals, or conscience. He was a soulless monster, and he was reaching for her.

"You miss me?" he asked, then laughed like he'd said the funniest thing ever.

There was no mistaking his intent as he grabbed one of her legs and yanked her sideways so she was angled awkwardly toward him. Greedy hands reached for the waistband of her jeans, and as he unzipped them something snapped inside her.

Patrick was protective of her, the only condition he'd given her when he agreed to let her wait for him and his team in the car was that she be armed. He'd wanted to leave her a weapon, but she wasn't used to guns, and she felt uncomfortable using one if she had to so Scorpion had suggested something else.

A knife.

Without conscious thought, her fingers curled around the handle, then she plunged it into the man trying to yank her pants over her hips.

Once wasn't enough.

Pain, fear, and anger all throbbed together inside her like a physical being needing to get out. Stephanie pulled the knife back and thrust it into her tormentor again.

And again.

And again.

She couldn't stop.

It would never be enough.

CHAPTER
Eighteen

January 27th
    3:18 P.M.

The caves were beautiful.

This would be an amazing place for a vacation, watching the sunset on the beach and swimming through the caves, but given the reason they were there, Trick wasn't able to fully appreciate the beauty of it.

All he wanted to do was try to find the diamonds and get back to Stephanie.

Just because she thought her brother was talking about their family vacation to Hawaii when they were kids, it didn't mean Chris had been trying to say that the diamonds were hidden in the caves here in Liberia. For all he knew, the man was just out of it and reminiscing about happy times with his family because he knew he was dying.

But they had to try. No one he loved and cared about was safe until those diamonds were found. Not that taking the diamonds out of the equation made the militia no longer dangerous, but they would no longer have a reason to come specifically after the people connected to the botched SEAL mission.

His girl wasn't going through anything else.

The day was calm, and so was the ocean, making it easier to search the cave. Almost a year had gone by since Chris Fuller and his SEAL team were killed, and the chances that the diamonds were still there and would be easily findable were not all that high. Someone could have stumbled upon them. It wasn't like they would announce to the world they had found stolen diamonds when the amount of money they could get from them would make it much more worth their while than turning them in.

Even with the six of them there, it would likely take them hours to find the diamonds, if at all. If they couldn't, then sooner or later, they were going to have to give up, go back to the vehicle, get Stephanie to the plane and back home, then maybe come back and search with a second Prey team as well.

Whatever it took to get this wrapped up so he didn't have to worry about his loved ones.

"Look over there at the rocks," Panther suddenly said, drawing everyone's attention. "What does it look like?"

Rocks.

That was the first thing that came to his mind. Trick knew that they could be on a wild goose chase. Chris Fuller had been dying, there was no way he ever could have foreseen that his sister would be dragged into the mess, so his words weren't necessarily clues.

"Looks like an S to me," Scorpion replied.

"Yeah, I could see that," Rock agreed.

"S for Stephanie?" Tank asked, although none of them could answer that question because none of them really knew what the SEAL team's intention had been or what had been going through Chris' head when he was dying.

"Maybe." Trick shrugged. This was feeling more and more like they were running in circles chasing their tails and weren't going to come up with anything.

"Guys, we've got eyes on us," Axe called out. He was a little away from the rest of them keeping watch.

"How many?" Tank asked.

"At least three, probably more," Axe replied.

"We check under the S and get back to Stephanie," Trick said. As badly as he wanted those diamonds, he wanted her safe more. If the militia had somehow found them again, he didn't want her alone and unprotected.

There were no disagreements, and the five of them headed toward the S Panther had spotted. It was an odd rock formation, and it really did look like the letter S. When they reached it, they began searching around for any signs that the diamonds might be nearby.

Trick felt like they were clutching at straws, but he wasn't going to let the best lead they'd had in months pass by without at least checking it out. If the diamonds weren't there, they didn't lose anything by looking.

Diving down into the water, he kept going, swimming with firm strokes, holding his breath with no problem. He'd always loved the water and almost chosen the Navy and being a SEAL over joining the Army and trying for Delta Force.

Just as he was about to turn around and swim back up to the surface, something brushed against his arm. At first, he thought it was a piece of seaweed or maybe an animal, but then he saw it was black. Long, too, like a drawstring to a bag or something.

Grabbing hold of it, he pulled on it but found it was weighted down.

His lungs were screaming at him for oxygen, but he wasn't going anywhere until he figured out if this was what they were looking for.

Feeling like he was hunting for millennia-old sunken treasure, Trick followed the black string until he found the bag it was attached to. Grabbing hold of it with both hands, he was able to bring it with him as he kicked his legs to propel himself back up to the surface.

Once his head broke the surface, he dragged in a couple of breaths and then immediately moved to open the bag in his hands.

It was the diamonds.

How about that. Stephanie's idea had actually helped, and they'd found in an hour or so what the military and Prey had been unable to locate for months.

His girl was going to be thrilled when she learned that she'd been the one to help them find the diamonds. Trick knew it was important to her to help and suspected it had to do with her ability to find meaning from what had happened to her so she could process her ordeal.

"Is it them?" Panther asked.

"Sure is." He held the bag out so the others could see.

The rising mood of the team, despite the fact they suspected they were being watched, was dampened when Axe yelled out, "They're heading toward the vehicle."

Axe's words sent a chill down his spine.

Stephanie.

Unaware he'd said her name aloud, Tank placed a reassuring hand on his shoulder. "We'll get to her in time. We won't let them hurt her."

Passing the diamonds off to Rock, Trick started swimming for the shore. Axe had already started toward the beach, and the others quickly followed behind him. Their plan had been to not engage with the militia should they encounter them unless they had to in order to defend themselves.

Trick would set the world alight if that was what it took to protect Stephanie.

It seemed to take hours, although logically, he knew it wasn't more than minutes for his feet to hit the sandy shore. Axe had already disappeared into the trees, and Trick took off at full speed to follow.

Stephanie would be okay.

She had to be.

Most likely he or Stephanie, or both of them, had been tagged by the militia when they'd been taken. Maybe he should have thought of that and had his team check them over when they got there, but honestly, he had been too preoccupied with needing to make sure that Stephanie got the treatment she needed to think of anything else.

A failure on his part.

One he would never forgive himself for if Stephanie was hurt because of him.

Now he was glad that she was close by and not alone at the airport because if they had both been tagged, there was no way he would have been able to get to her in time.

The muffled sounds of grunts and muted screams had his head

about to explode. What was going on, and why had he agreed to leave Stephanie alone?

He should have stayed with her, or at least insisted that one of his team should. They were in a dangerous country, she was being hunted, and she was injured and still weak. He never should have left her alone.

Ever.

The last thing he expected to see when he finally came upon the car was a dead body lying half in and half out of the passenger seat, and a bleeding Axe trying to wrestle the knife out of Stephanie's hands. From the vacant look in her eyes and the way she hadn't responded to Axe's voice even though she knew who he was, told him that whatever had happened had finally been enough to make her snap.

～

January 27th
    3:57 P.M.

Eliminate.
    Eliminate.
    Eliminate.
    Destroy.
    Destroy.
    Destroy.
    Make it stop.
    Make it stop.
    Make it stop.
The words kept running through Stephanie's head. She wasn't even sure she knew what they meant anymore, only that they were important.
    More than important.
    They were survival.
    Without them she would die.
    A horrible, painful, drawn-out death.

Somehow, she knew that even as she struggled to process anything else going on around her.

Wet.

Something was making her wet, and small slivers of pain in her hand vaguely captured her attention, but it wasn't enough to make her stop.

She wasn't stopping.

For anything.

No way was she going to allow anyone to hurt her again. She was going to protect herself by whatever means necessary.

Arms grabbed at her, and she spun, flinging out her knife at this new threat.

It was weird. She couldn't really see anything but her own fear, a living, breathing red entity that consumed her vision. She couldn't really hear either, other than a whooshing in her ears, which she guessed was more than likely the sound of her own pulse.

The only thing driving her was a kind of animal instinct for survival.

Then she felt it.

Warmth, peace, security. A different set of arms closed around her, and she felt her body be moved until she was all but cocooned in a soft little bubble that eased the fear pounding through her insides.

A soothing sound began to hum in her, slowly overtaking the whooshing until it disappeared altogether.

"Shh, honey, it's okay. You're okay. You did so good, darlin', so good. I'm so proud of you, so in awe of you. You're okay now, honey. You're okay. Come back to me now, okay, Steph? I need you to come back to me."

Patrick.

Patrick was here.

She was okay.

He'd keep her safe.

"P-Patrick." Her voice startled her, coming out so much weaker and shakier than she had expected.

It was like coming out of a trance. Her vision cleared, and while other colors crept back into her world, red remained dominant. Her clothes were streaked with red, it was all over her exposed skin and her bandage as well.

In her right hand, she clutched a knife so tightly she could see how white her knuckles were.

Lying half in and half out of the passenger seat of the car was a body that was very clearly dead.

Had she done that?

"I'm right here, honey," Patrick crooned in her ear. "I need you to do something for me. Is that okay?"

Unable to take her eyes off the body, she managed a single nod.

"I need you to let Rock take the knife. Can you give it to him, honey?"

Although she nodded, Stephanie couldn't help tensing the second Rock stepped closer. His smile was encouraging, his eyes empathetic, and he moved slowly, cautiously, toward her, obviously doing his best not to cause her any distress.

Even when he reached her, and his hands reached out to gently cover hers, she found she couldn't make her fingers uncurl.

"It's okay, honey. We're here now. You did great. You did exactly what you had to do to protect yourself. Now I need you to give the knife to Rock."

Somehow, she managed to force her fingers to uncurl, one at a time, until Rock was able to ease it out of her hand and into his own.

"We have to get going now, darlin', okay? The guys are going to get into the car and they're going to give me a blanket to wrap around you. I don't care about getting the blood on me, but you're shaking, and I'm worried you're going into shock."

She was shaking?

Thinking was beyond her right now, so she made no protest, no comment at all when Patrick gathered her up and moved from the driver's seat, where he must have moved to pull her onto his lap, to the back seat. The body of the man she had … killed … hit the ground with a muted thump as the other five men jumped into the vehicle.

The roar of the engine springing to life sounded too loud for her ears, and she wanted to apologize for the metallic stench of blood that filled the car. For the blood that had not only soaked into the passenger seat, but was also streaked all over the windows, the ceiling, and the entire front of the car.

Did she really do all of that?

Stephanie wasn't a violent person. Actually, she couldn't even kill bugs because the idea of hurting another living being let alone ending its life made her feel sick.

Now she'd taken a human life.

Instead of the horror she thought she should be feeling, Stephanie felt oddly ... empty.

"Shock, honey, it's just shock," Patrick murmured against her ear, his body warm as it wrapped around hers.

Kind of glazed and fuzzy, she looked around the car. None of the men were talking, and she wasn't sure if it was because they were afraid that anything they said or did would set her off again.

Not unfounded.

She had lost it.

Killed a man.

Something had snapped inside her.

Stephanie had not been in control of anything she had done in the car. All she remembered was the car door opening and the man who had tormented her standing there. When he reached for her, her mind had splintered and done what it needed to. Or maybe it had just been consumed by a need for revenge because she wasn't sorry the man was dead even if she was in shock.

When her gaze settled on the backseat and Axe and Rock sitting there, she was startled to see that Axe had removed his shirt and there was a jagged wound on his shoulder.

It looked like a knife wound.

Had she done that?

Vaguely, she remembered arms wrapping around her. Arms that didn't belong to Patrick—she would know him anywhere and had immediately snapped out of her trance when she sensed his presence— had grabbed her just before Patrick had been there.

Axe.

It must have been Axe.

She'd hurt him.

Regret washed over her, and without thinking, Stephanie shoved at Patrick's shoulders, and before he could grab for her, she was climbing over the seat to get into the back, running a fingertip along Axe's chest just under the bloody wound.

"Did I do that?" she asked, turning tear-drenched eyes on Axe.

"You were in shock, honey," Patrick said quickly. "You didn't realize it was Axe."

"I hurt you," she said softly, continuing to stroke around the wound as though she could somehow wipe it away.

"Hey." Axe reached out, tucked a finger under her chin, and nudged until her gaze shifted from the wound to meet his. "You did amazing. You hear me? None of us could be prouder of you. You did exactly what you should have done. You defended yourself against a threat."

"You weren't a threat though," she said.

"No. But you didn't know that. You were acting on instinct. Someone else grabbed you and you did what you needed to do," Axe told her.

He was being so nice about it, but Stephanie felt awful. Killing that horrible man who had hurt her, and who would have killed both her and Patrick if given a chance, meant nothing. She was glad he was dead, relieved, but she hadn't wanted to hurt Axe.

It wasn't a conscious decision, she just launched herself at Axe and wrapped her arms around his neck. "I'm sorry."

She could tell she'd caught him by surprise, and it took a moment for his arms to come up and return her hug. "I'd tell you again that you did the right thing, but I don't think you'll believe me, so I'll just say all is forgiven."

"Thank you." Whether he thought she had to apologize or not she needed to hear him tell her that he forgave her for stabbing him. Just because she'd lost it and hadn't really been in control of her actions, she had still hurt someone who didn't deserve it, and she didn't like that.

"Once I get done patching up Axe, I'm going to need to look at your hand," Rock told her as she pulled back, a little embarrassed to have thrown herself at Axe like that.

"My hand?" Looking down at her hand, she saw there were a couple of reasonably deep wounds across her palm. She must have cut herself when she was stabbing her attacker to death. Stephanie hadn't felt the blade slicing through her skin and she didn't feel the wounds now.

There was too much adrenalin flooding through her system.

The sound of gunshots startled a small shriek from her, and the back window exploded behind her, sending glass shards showering down around her, Axe, and Rock.

"Stephanie!" Patrick shouted her name, and she felt his terror mixing with her own.

"I got your girl," Axe said, and the next thing Stephanie knew, she was being shoved down onto the floor of the car, a large body covering her own and keeping her in place as more gunshots rained down upon their vehicle.

CHAPTER

Nineteen

January 27th
    4:24 P.M.

Trick was going to jump out of his skin.

Someone was shooting at their vehicle, and he didn't have his girl in his arms.

Just because he trusted his team with his life—more importantly with Stephanie's life—didn't mean he didn't want her right by him. It was the only way he could convince himself that she was safe. Seeing her, touching her, that was what he needed, but it wasn't what he could have right now.

Axe had Stephanie pressed into the floor of the car, using his body as a shield, and he knew there wasn't anything that his friend wouldn't do to keep her safe. He would protect her as though she was Beth because they all knew that Stephanie was important to him.

More than important.

Somehow, in the midst of surviving hell and running for their lives, she had earned herself a permanent place in his heart and it was killing him that he would have to walk away from her.

Wishing things were different couldn't change anything, but he could make sure Stephanie lived, got back home, was safe and protected once she got there, and someone looking out for her psychological health as well.

That started with eliminating this threat.

Damn, he was so sick of having Stephanie's life in danger. Couldn't they catch a break? It broke his heart that she had been forced to kill to protect herself, but at the same time, he was so very proud of her.

She was a superhero, no doubt about it.

While Axe kept Stephanie out of the line of fire, and Tank drove like a madman to get them to the airport and the plane that would finally take them home, he, Rock, Scorpion, and Panther moved to the windows and began to lay down fire.

There were four vehicles out there that he could spot, which meant there were anywhere between eight and almost thirty men chasing them if their vehicles could hold the same number of people as theirs.

Not great odds but not awful either.

Thanks to his team, they had significant firepower on their side, and they had the diamonds. Once they got them out of the country, they cut off a significant portion of the militia's finances. Not enough to wipe them out permanently, but he was sure Eagle would be talking to every contact he had about eliminating the terrorist group as a threat.

They were driving through a town on their way to the airfield, but it didn't slow their pursuers down. The other vehicles were trying to move out to box them in. Unlucky for them Bravo Team was way too trained to allow that to happen.

Tank's evasive driving techniques kept them ahead of the other vehicles, and the shots the rest of them were firing were slowly taking out the militia's vehicles. A well-placed shot that obviously took out the driver of the closest car sent it weaving wildly before it went off the road and slammed into a parked car.

That was one down, but there were still three to go, and that was assuming the militia hadn't called in reinforcements, which, of course, they likely had. Their best chance at getting away was going to be getting to the plane before they were overrun.

A grunt from beside him told him a stray bullet had hit its mark.

"Panther's hit," he told the others.

"Just a nick," Panther quickly added.

"Floor the gas," Axe said from the backseat.

"Going as fast as I can without crashing," Tank said tightly from the driver's seat.

"Got another of them," Rock said with satisfaction as the second car following them crashed.

"Call the pilot and tell them we're coming in hot," Axe ordered.

Since the rest of them were shooting, and protecting Stephanie was Axe's job, Tank was left to handle driving and calling at the same time.

A bullet whizzed by so close to his face that Trick could feel its heat. Anger fueling him, he fired another round of bullets at the next car, and it, too, went spinning wildly out of control as it went off the road.

That only left one, but one was all it took. A hit to their tires or a shot to the engine and their car would be toast. Once that happened, not only would it be him and Stephanie who would be taken back to that hellhole, but his whole team. Just thinking about the pain Beth, Tillie, Ariel, Jessica, and Andy would suffer if their loved ones didn't make it home was almost more than he could bear.

Worse was knowing he would have failed Stephanie, and she would never go home.

Unacceptable.

His girl was going home. Even if she could never really be his girl, he was making sure she had the life she deserved. Happiness, joy, belonging, a person who could have her back and make her feel safe enough that she never had to worry again about being demonstrative with her emotions. Someone who relished the amazing, strong, brave woman that she was, and saw her for the superhero she was too damaged by her ex's harsh words to believe herself to be.

That was what he wanted for her even if it couldn't be him.

Shifting so he could lean out the window, Trick trusted his team to lay down covering fire so he could get a good shot off at the final car. Opposite him another man leaned out the window as other shooters fired from inside the vehicle. Taking aim, Trick fired, hit the man with one shot then aimed at the driver.

Another shot, and finally, the world around them turned silent.

It ended up being Stephanie who broke the silence. "Is it over?" her muffled voice asked from where she was still pinned down beneath Axe's much bigger body.

"Yeah, honey. For now," he added because as much as he didn't want her to worry, he also needed her to know that they weren't out of the woods yet.

Slowly, Axe lifted his body off Stephanie's and helped her up, she immediately touched a kiss to his cheek. "Thanks for protecting me," she murmured then scrambled over the back of the seat and all but threw herself into his arms.

Trick couldn't deny there was a surge of alpha male satisfaction in knowing that he was what Stephanie craved when she needed to feel safe, but there was also a deep sense of sadness that he couldn't give her this for much longer.

Since time was quickly running out for them, he held her tight against him, locked in an embrace he wished could last forever.

Forever.

The word had never really held any meaning to him until this woman came into his life. They might have met in the darkness, but she had brought light to his world. She'd shown him what it felt like to have someone put you first for no benefit to themselves, simply because they wanted to. Stephanie had given him the one thing he needed most and hadn't even realized how desperately he needed it.

It killed him—quite literally killed a piece of himself—to know he couldn't do the same.

He couldn't give her what she needed.

So, he was going to have to do what she had done for him and put her first, walk away no matter how much he didn't want to.

The rest of the ride passed quietly. Once they got on the plane, Rock would have his hands full. Between the cuts on Stephanie's palms from the knife, the wound she had inflicted on Axe, and Panther getting shot, the medic would be busy. Then there was the fact he was almost positive Stephanie had been tagged, they'd need to deal with that before she got home.

Whether he was part of her future or not, he had to know that she was safe.

It was the only way he'd be able to walk away.

Finally, they pulled up beside one of Prey's private jets. Trick thought they were going to make it, but just as they all climbed out of the vehicle, half a dozen other vehicles came screaming down the road toward them.

They had to get on the plane. If they stayed and tried to fight the soldiers off, they'd never make it, there were just too many of them. Unless they had anti-aircraft missiles on them, once the plane took off there was nothing the militia would be able to do about it.

Snatching Stephanie up and into his arms, he pressed her face to his shoulder and shouted, "Hang onto me."

Like she'd done before, Stephanie wrapped her arms and legs around his shoulders and hips, and Trick started returning fire at the men shooting at him and his team. Leaving nothing behind in the vehicle, his team grabbed their packs, and the six of them covered each other as they ran for the plane.

Already Trick could hear the jet's engine spring to life, the pilot ready to take off as soon as they were all on board. With Stephanie in his arms, they were the first ones on the plane. Panther was next, followed by Axe. Rock came after them, and then finally, Scorpion and Tank joined them, closing the door behind them.

Wasting no time, the pilot started down the runway. Soldiers were still out there, still firing at the plane, but it was too late.

They were already moving, and less than a minute later, they were taking off.

It wasn't until the earth grew small beneath them that Trick finally relaxed and drew a real breath. They'd gotten away, they were all safe and mostly uninjured, but when the plane next touched the ground it would be time.

Time to walk away from the woman who now held his heart in her hands.

January 28th
   5:47 A.M.

And that was that.

Stephanie tried to hold back her tears as the plane touched down.

It was time to say goodbye to Patrick, and she wasn't anywhere close to being ready for that.

Why did it have to hurt so bad?

Given that they had only known each other for a grand total of one week, walking away from him should be easy. But in that one week she had lived a thousand lifetimes. She'd known what it was to stare death in the face, had suffered unimaginable agony, and had learned what it was like to selflessly put someone before herself.

Not that Stephanie had ever considered herself to be a selfish person, but she wasn't really selfless either. Although she was starting to accept that she hadn't done anything wrong by needing her ex to offer support and comfort when she was grieving, and that she wasn't gaining anything by hiding her emotions, she still, for some reason, felt like she had been selfish somehow.

Her ex's words echoed in her head, no doubt, but they'd been said at a time when she was vulnerable, and so she'd absorbed them, internalizing them and making them a part of herself.

Knowing how much Patrick appreciated her not begging him for mercy when she'd been tortured had reminded her that she did know how to hold her emotions in for someone else's benefit. That she could put someone before herself in a way she had never known she was capable of.

Patrick had been her everything this last week, and having to let him go and find a way to go on without him was nothing short of terrifying.

As though he felt the same way she did, his lips were pressed to the top of her head, and as the plane had begun its descent, his arms had tightened around her.

If he didn't want to let her go, then why was he?

Didn't he know she would give anything to stay right where she was?

You could ask him to stay.

The voice in her head had been taunting her the entire journey back home. As badly as Stephanie wanted to ask Patrick to stay with her, she was scared to. What if he wasn't attracted to her? How could he be? She was covered in wounds that would leave behind scars and missing a finger, add in the fact that she had been raped, and she was hardly a winning catch. What man would ever be interested in her after this?

Doubt was assaulting her from every angle. She wasn't pretty enough. She wasn't even sure she could have a real relationship after what she'd been through. She didn't have enough left in her to offer a man what he needed, let alone a man like Patrick who she respected, admired, and liked so very much.

Just because she was falling for Patrick, it didn't mean he was falling for her. To him, she could just be a burden and a job he was looking forward to handing off as soon as they walked off the plane.

Only that didn't feel right.

So why wasn't he asking if he could stay with her?

The plane stopped moving, and all the other guys stood, gathering their things. There was a somber feeling in the air, and she knew it was because of her. Stephanie just wasn't sure if it was because everyone couldn't wait to get rid of her or if none of them wanted to get rid of her.

She kind of felt like a stray cat that had shown up, you felt sorry for it, were filled with an urge to care for it, but at the same time you didn't exactly want it and hadn't invited it into your life.

One by one, the guys filed off the plane, all except Axe who came and stood before her, looking down at her with an expression she couldn't quite read. Finally, he stooped, touched a kiss to her forehead, and stood again.

"You got this, Stephanie. Believe in yourself." Then he turned and walked out leaving her alone with Patrick.

If she expected him to give some big, heartfelt speech it didn't happen. He stood with her in his arms—he'd barely let go of her since they entered the plane in a hail of bullets—and carried her down the stairs and over to a waiting ambulance.

He didn't say a single thing as he set her down on the stretcher with such gentleness that it made her eyes sting and her heart ache. A single squeeze of her good hand was all she got, and then he whispered his lips across hers, released her hand, and turned his back on her.

Stay!

Don't leave me!

The words screamed inside her head, but she couldn't seem to make them come out of her mouth. She was so afraid that if she asked him—begged him—to stay, he'd say no. That was something neither her poor battered body or her poor battered heart could take.

There had been so much loss this past year, first her brother, then her mom, then the loss of a relationship she had believed was going to last a lifetime. If she asked Patrick to stay and he turned her down Stephanie knew she wouldn't be able to recover from that.

So, she watched him walk over to join his team. His shoulders were hunched, and he walked as though he were in pain. Since she knew he didn't have any physical injuries—she had insisted that Rock look him over thoroughly from head to toe, and Patrick had acquiesced to make her feel better—she wondered if it was his heart aching, too.

Paramedics bustled around her, covering her with a blanket, checking her vitals, and starting an IV, but she paid them no attention. Her gaze was locked on Patrick as he and the rest of his team climbed into a vehicle and drove off.

He'd really done it.

Left her all alone.

It turned out it didn't matter whether she asked him to stay and he left, or if he left anyway, because either way, her heart had been shattered into a million pieces.

Not even when she had woken alone in that underground cell in Liberia had Stephanie ever felt as alone as when her stretcher was maneuvered into the back of the ambulance and the doors closed behind them.

She had no one.

No one.

Sure, there were friends she was sure would come if she called, but she didn't want just someone who would come if she called, she wanted someone who not just wanted to be with her but had to be with her. Part of her had believed that was Patrick. It wasn't until he actually left her that she realized she had believed all along that he wouldn't be able to walk away from her any more than she could walk away from him.

Because if their positions were reversed, there was no way she would have been able to leave him alone in an ambulance while she walked off with a whole team of people around her.

Patrick wasn't going home alone. He had his teammates and their families. She'd heard a little about Panther's little boy and the other guys' wives, fiancées, and girlfriends. There would be a whole family of people to support Patrick and make sure he was okay after what had happened, and she had no one. She was going to the hospital alone, and once she was discharged, she would go home alone.

To an empty house and an empty life.

She was no longer the same woman she'd been when she got on the plane to go to Mexico. That woman had died in a dungeon in Liberia surrounded by blood, with the sounds of her own screams echoing inside her head.

She didn't know who she was now, and didn't know how to believe in herself like Axe had told her to do.

All she knew was that, somehow, over the last week, she had handed her heart over to Patrick and he had taken it with him when he left.

He doesn't want your heart.

The reminder did little to help ease any of her pain. When her ex dumped her and she found out he'd been cheating, Stephanie had thought she understood what it was to be heartbroken. But what she had felt then and what she felt now were not even in the same stratosphere.

What she'd felt for her ex was nothing like what she felt for Patrick. In a week, Patrick had become a part of her, a part she had now lost and she didn't know how to go on without it. What would her feelings be like for Patrick if he hadn't walked away? If he had stayed, and they had helped each other heal from their ordeal, if he had asked her out, they'd dated, and fallen all the way in love.

Knowing what she felt for him already it almost terrified her to think about how strong those feelings would have developed over time.

Would have, but now wouldn't.

Because Patrick was gone.

And she was all alone.

CHAPTER Twenty

January 28th
6:37 P.M.

It felt wrong.

Everything felt wrong.

Leaving Stephanie alone in that ambulance while he walked away with a team of people by his side was wrong. Not calling one of her friends, even though she had insisted that she didn't want any of them with her right now was wrong. Not telling her that he had developed feelings for her was wrong. Not saying goodbye was wrong.

Not having her here in his arms was the most wrong of all.

It had only been just over twelve hours since the plane landed and he had left her in the care of paramedics, and Trick was pretty close to losing his mind. How was he going to survive the rest of his life without having her by his side?

Honestly, he wasn't sure how he could.

If this was even a tiny portion of what Axe felt when Beth was missing those eight long months, or Tank when he had to convince Tillie he was handing her over to a mob boss, or Rock when Ariel was missing for those nine hellish weeks, or Scorpion when he got out of the cult but knew Jessica was still there and in danger, Trick had no idea how his teammates had survived.

This was hell.

There was simply no other way to describe not having the person you needed safe in your arms.

Knowing they were scared and hurting made it so much worse.

Stephanie had looked at him with open betrayal in her eyes when he'd walked away from her. It was all he could do not to turn around and run back to her and beg her to promise him she wouldn't wind up hating him now that she was back home and the full horror of her situation was going to sink in.

Staying with her was going to cause more harm than good. Trick was convinced of it. It was the only way he could make himself walk away. The last thing he wanted to do was cause her more pain and suffering on top of everything he had allowed to happen to her.

At every turn, he'd let her down.

No more.

It had to stop.

He cared about her enough to put her needs above his own.

His hands itched to reach out and pick up his phone and send another text, but he'd already harassed enough.

Right?

Despite the worst timing imaginable, Prey had stepped up like it always did when one of them, or someone important to one of them, needed help.

Trick wasn't a complete monster. Despite Stephanie's insistence she didn't want to call any of her friends and ask them to come and stay with her at the hospital, Trick knew she couldn't be alone. That was the absolute last thing she needed after what she'd just been through.

So, he'd made sure she wouldn't be alone.

Calling in Prey's resident psychiatrist, Dr. Piper Hamilton-Eden, he'd asked the woman if it would be possible for her to go to the hospital to meet Stephanie when she arrived.

Not only was Piper an amazing psychiatrist, warm, caring, compassionate, and easy to talk to, she had lived through two traumas, one as a child and one a couple of years ago. Now happily married to Alpha Team's medic Arrow, the couple had welcomed their first child two weeks ago, a daughter they had named Dana after Piper's childhood friend who had been murdered.

Being a new mom, Trick had been prepared for Piper to tell him she couldn't go to the hospital but would organize something else, but that wasn't what the woman had done. She'd simply packed up her newborn, taken the baby with her, and headed straight to the hospital. Knowing firsthand what Stephanie was going through there was no way the woman wasn't going to do everything in her power to help.

And that right there was what Prey was all about. It was what it meant to be protected by Prey, to be part of the family, there wasn't anything they wouldn't do for one another, including taking a newborn to the hospital to be there for someone you didn't even know but that you knew mattered to one of them.

Expecting Arrow at least to give some pushback on the idea of Piper and his two-week-old daughter camping out in a hospital, Trick was shocked when Arrow readily agreed to help out by caring for Dana in between feeds so Piper could focus on Stephanie. Maybe it was because the memories of what Piper had gone through were still so fresh in his mind that he could put aside his family's needs to think of what he'd want someone to do for him if it was Piper in that hospital bed.

Prey was the family Trick had dreamed of when he was a kid, and Stephanie was everything he had never allowed himself to wish for because he hadn't known if he had it in him to love a woman like she deserved to be loved. But what he felt for her, after such a short time wiped away his fears. If he allowed himself to do so, he could fall in love with Stephanie far too easily.

That was it.

He had to check-in.

Piper would likely be happy to indulge his need to constantly check up on his woman.

How's my girl?

. . .

Watching those three little dots bouncing up and down ripped at what little patience he had left, and by the time—even if it was only seconds —her response came through he was about ready to crawl out of his skin.

> She's just waking up
>
> Eagle pulled strings, got me allowed in
>
> recovery so I didn't have to wait until
>
> she got assigned to a room to see her
>
> She's groggy, but surgery went well. Her hand
>
> has been cleaned and the wound closed
>
> Once she heals, she'll need physical therapy
>
> but her hand will be fully functional

Relief would have stolen his ability to stand if he wasn't already lying on his couch. Stephanie was okay, at least physically.

> Was she okay with you being there?

> She's still groggy. Had no idea who I was
>
> or why I was there
>
> I just told her a friend sent me
>
> I'll talk to her more in the morning right

now what she needs most is rest

You too, Trick

Get some rest

You need it

Doing anything other than lying here thinking of Stephanie and how badly he wanted to be there with her was out of the question right now. If Stephanie was suffering, then he had to be too. It was only fair.

Thanks for being there for her

Means the world to me

The thought of her being alone ...

Was one he couldn't even put into words.

She's not alone

I'm here, I'll make sure she's okay

But, Trick, she's going to want you

No, she's not

Is someone there with you?

I don't think you should be alone

any more than your girl should

. . .

Trick was about to reply that he was alone, that he'd sent his friends away to be with their families the second they reached the compound because the idea that he was surrounded by people while Stephanie was alone was making him nauseous.

Suffer.

He had to suffer just like he'd stood by and allowed her to suffer.

Before he could type out a text telling Piper he was fine by himself and that Stephanie was the priority, not him, there was a knock on his cabin door. A moment later, it opened, and Axe and Beth walked in.

Even though he hated it and knew he didn't deserve it, a piece of himself settled to see two people he cared about there in his home.

> I was but Axe and Beth showed up
>
> Can't promise I won't text a
>
> million more times tonight

> As many times as you need

"What are you guys doing here?" he asked, tossing his cell phone onto the couch beside him.

"Beth said you can't be alone tonight," Axe replied as the couple walked somewhat awkwardly beside one another to join him by the fireplace.

"I made brownies," Beth said tentatively, holding out a plate piled high with brownie squares. "Someone told me they're your favorite."

His heart both swelled and broke at her words. This was the Beth they all knew. She was so kind and sweet, always worrying about others, and yet she had no idea who they were and didn't remember how much they loved her. She had no idea that when she was still fresh out of the hell she'd lived through, he had spent hours with her in the kitchen teaching her how to bake. The recipe was still inside her head, but nothing else, not the memories of the fun they'd had together.

Seeing the longing on Axe's face every time he looked at the wife who didn't remember him reminded him that nothing in life was guaranteed. Axe thought he had it all, and then one moment it was just ... gone, and no matter how hard he tried, he couldn't get back the woman he loved even as she stood beside him.

Sometimes you only got one chance at happiness, and Trick was starting to wonder if he had taken his chance and thrown it away when he walked away from Stephanie.

~

February 4th
    10:34 A.M.

None of this made any sense to her at all.

Stephanie had been all prepared to be alone in the hospital, yet in reality, she hadn't spent a single second without someone in her room. Why these people she didn't know seemed to have decided to make it their mission in life to ensure that she was never alone she didn't have a clue. She knew who they were, but only because they had introduced themselves to her, she just didn't know what had initiated this keep Stephanie company plan.

Was it Trick?

Had he asked them to come?

As badly as she wanted to ask one of them, Stephanie wasn't sure her heart could take it if the answer was no.

Piper was the first one she had met. The woman had been there when she woke up from surgery, cradling a newborn in her arms and telling her that even though it didn't feel like it right now everything was going to be okay.

Of course, she hadn't believed that.

How could she?

How could everything be okay when the one thing she needed to make it through this ordeal wasn't there?

For some reason, she'd been unable to make herself respond, so Stephanie had simply stared at the woman, not altogether sure she wasn't a drug-induced hallucination. Only when she woke up next, the woman was still there, sitting in a chair in the corner reading a book. Other than asking her if she needed anything, Piper hadn't done anything other than be there.

Although Stephanie kept expecting her to launch into a speech about how you grew from the darkness, and how everything happened for a reason, and that one day she would look back on this whole ordeal and see it in a new light, it never happened.

Piper was just there, and it turned out that was exactly what she needed.

Stephanie wasn't ready to talk about what she'd been through with anyone other than Patrick who had lived through it with her, but she did need to know that someone was there.

On the second day, another woman had come breezing into the room, all spunky energy that belied her tiny size. The woman had introduced herself as Tillie, and she had immediately placed the name as being Tank's fiancée. Later that same day, a quiet woman with the most gorgeous golden-brown eyes had appeared. She'd introduced herself as Ariel, who she knew was Rock's girlfriend. The following morning, a blonde who oozed confidence was standing at the window, sipping a cup of coffee and staring out at the world. The woman had introduced herself as Jessica, Scorpion's girlfriend.

All the women connected to the men on Patrick's team had come to visit her in the hospital. What did that mean?

Did it mean anything at all, or was she just clutching at straws?

And, who was Piper, and how did she fit into all of this?

She had to be someone connected to Prey, but who? Why was she making time to be there for someone she didn't know when she had a tiny baby who needed her?

Stephanie was so confused.

What made matters worse was that she was going to be released in a few days. The infections that had almost taken her life in Liberia were under control, the bruises covering most of her torso were now a sickly yellowy-green color. The cuts on her right hand from the knife she'd used to kill the man who had abused her were healing, as was her maimed hand. She was mostly at the point where she could do things for herself and didn't need a nurse's assistance.

Which meant she could go home.

Every hour she'd spent locked in that dungeon in Liberia she had dreamed about how amazing it would be to go home, but now that it was a day or two away at most, the idea terrified her.

In the hospital she wasn't alone. Doctors and nurses were always coming and going, and one of the women was always there. She couldn't—didn't—expect them to follow her home, which meant the second she was discharged Stephanie was officially on her own.

Maybe it wasn't such a good thing that the women had decided to adopt her while she was in the hospital. It was only delaying the inevitable and making it harder than it had to be. She'd been prepared to be alone the second Patrick walked away from her at the ambulance, but now she'd gotten used to these women always being there, watching her quietly, not pushing themselves on her but making sure she knew they were there.

How was she going to cope when she had no one?

"W-who are you?" she blurted out to Piper who was with her this morning. They must have worked out a schedule because there was always one of them there. Always. No exceptions. Didn't matter if she woke in the middle of the night gasping and shaking from a nightmare, they were there. Around the clock, and she appreciated it so much she could never put it into words.

The smile Piper gave her was genuine. "I work for Prey. I'm their on-staff psychiatrist."

So, the woman was a shrink. Stephanie wasn't sure what to think of that. The hospital had tried to set her up with a counselor several times, but she just couldn't do it. Those people didn't understand, how could they? Their safe little world had never been shattered into smithereens like hers had.

"Why are you here?" There. She'd done it. Asked the question she had been dying to know the answer to from the moment she woke up and realized that a group of women connected to Prey had dragged her into something she didn't quite understand.

Standing, Piper set her book down and pulled the room's only chair up beside the bed. "Because Trick asked me to be here for you. Because I know what you're going through, and I can't imagine how I would have felt if I'd had to lie in a hospital bed all alone and try to make sense of it all."

"How could you know what I'm going through?" The words came out with a desperation she hadn't intended. It was meant to be an accusation, she didn't want to be appeased, didn't want to be told someone got what it had been like to be tortured and humiliated when they didn't have the faintest idea. But just because she didn't believe this woman or any other counselor could understand, it didn't mean she didn't desperately hope that they could.

"Because I was abducted as a child, raped, and watched my best friend get murdered. Then a couple of years ago, I was taken, beaten, raped, all because someone decided to blame me for their problems." Tentatively, Piper reached out and covered Stephanie's good hand with her own. There was no anger at Stephanie's accusation, no tentativeness in the way she spoke of her own ordeal, just warmth and empathy. "I want you to know you're not alone. Not ever. Whatever happens with Trick, if he ever gets his head on straight or not, you are part of Prey's family now, which means you are never alone."

"Snack time, Mommy," Jessica said as she entered the room carrying the baby in her arms, Piper's husband Arrow following along behind.

"Morning, Steph," he greeted her with a warm smile, and today she didn't flinch at his large, intimidating presence. "You need to get Scorpion to knock you up, Jess, so you stop stealing people's babies. Practically snatched her out of my arms," he told his wife as he kissed her full on the lips.

"Eww, no," Jessica replied, handing over the infant to her mother. "Not yet, I don't want any more responsibility in my life. Besides, I like having Mason's attention all to myself. And I did not snatch your baby, mister, I just can't resist her, she is the cutest and the absolute bestest baby in the whole world. Aren't you, cutie-pie?" She clucked at the baby as Piper settled her into the crook of her arm. "So, what's going on here this morning?"

"Stephanie and I were just talking," Piper replied. "I was just informing her that she's now part of Prey's family."

"Absolutely she is." Jessica offered her a warm smile that Stephanie found she couldn't not return.

"Foregone conclusion," Arrow added. The first time he'd come into the room while she was awake, Stephanie had almost freaked out. Her head knew she was safe and Arrow was not a threat to her, especially when he'd introduced himself as Piper's husband and baby Dana's daddy, but her body hadn't gotten the memo. It just saw a big man and freaked out, associating all of them with her captors. She felt bad about that now because Arrow was a good man who clearly loved his wife and daughter with everything he had to give them.

"I was also telling her that I understand what she's going through," Piper continued. As though she knew her words would hurt her husband with the reminder of her own ordeal, she reached out and stroked his arm before unsnapping her bra and beginning to feed her daughter. "I'm not the only one either," Piper added with a glance at Jessica who readily nodded.

"Girl, I'm going to call up the others and tell them to get down here because you need to know that while you might be the newest member of the club, you're not the only one there. We get it, all of us. We've been where you are, and that's why we absolutely intend to make sure you know we got your back until that idiot Trick gets his head on straight."

That was the second time in as many minutes that someone had called Trick an idiot and implied that, sooner or later, he was going to come to her. Stephanie couldn't allow herself to believe that could be true because if she hoped, and it didn't happen, it would crush her.

But this, friendship with these women who seemed to get her, maybe that was something she could try.

CHAPTER
Twenty~One

No one was texting him back.

Trick was about a second away from losing his mind.

All afternoon, he'd been texting the girls for updates on Stephanie, but not a single one of them had replied.

Something was wrong, he was sure of it, and it was driving him crazy.

Should he go to the hospital? Check on her himself?

It went against everything he believed to go there. If he went and saw her, Trick wasn't sure he would be able to walk away from her again. But staying wasn't an option, he'd be doing more harm than good for both of them. The last thing he wanted to do was bring her any more pain and he couldn't shake the fear that inserting himself into her life was going to cause her more pain.

Pulling out his phone, he started sending out texts. Not just to Piper but to his friends' women as well. It seemed that all of them had decided they wanted to be there for Stephanie. It both warmed his heart to know that his girl was surrounded by people who had lived through their own traumatic ordeals and, therefore, could support her in the ways she needed to be supported, but it also made him wonder how this was going to work long term.

He was no saint, there was no way he could have Stephanie that close to him and not wind up caving to temptation and going to her. Not that he would ever rip away her support system and ask Tillie, Ariel, and Jessica to leave her alone when she so badly needed friends who got her, that would just be cruel, and he had no intention of deliberately hurting her if he could avoid it.

> Piper, answer me

> Is Stephanie okay?

After waiting a full minute and getting no reply he tried the next number.

> Jess, are you with Stephanie?

> Is she okay?

Nothing.

> Tillie, have you seen Stephanie today?

> I need to know if she's okay

Again, there was no reply, and his blood pressure jumped another dozen points.

> Ariel, if you're with Steph tell me

> I have to know if she's okay

before I lose my mind

If no one was going to tell him what was happening, he would have to go down there and find out himself.

It had been a week since they returned from Liberia, and as far as he had been aware, Stephanie was healing well. All signs of infection were gone, her strength was returning, and they were simply waiting until she was able to do things for herself, since both of her hands had been injured, before discharging her.

Had that changed?

Had something happened?

A horrible thought occurred to him. Had Stephanie hurt herself?

Just because she was strong didn't mean she was invincible. No one was. And the trauma she had suffered was severe. Beatings, maiming, rape, and killing to protect herself, it was a lot to deal with in such a short space of time.

Was it too much to deal with?

Heart in his throat, he launched off his couch where he had pretty much lived this last week and scanned the room in search of his keys. If no one was going to tell him what was going on, he had no choice but to go to the hospital to get answers.

No way was he letting his girl give up. Even if he couldn't have her, he had to know that she was out there somewhere, living her best life.

As he located his keys, the door to his cabin swung open and all five of his teammates and Beth filed into the room. Their expressions were serious, and he didn't like the vibe he was getting from any of them.

They were here to give bad news.

Trick froze, unable to do more than drag in a single shaky breath. "What happened to her?" he asked, voice strained as he fought against the terror coursing through his body.

Tank's eyebrows drew together. "What happened to who?"

Who did he think? "Stephanie. Is she okay?"

Understanding dawned on their faces, and Rock offered him a reassuring smile. "She's okay. Nothing happened to her, that's not why we're here."

"Then why are you here?" he asked, thoroughly confused and not altogether positive they were telling him the truth.

"We're staging an intervention of sorts," Panther replied.

"And the girls say to stop texting them, they're busy with your girl," Scorpion told him, and finally, he was able to draw a proper breath.

The girls weren't not answering him because something had happened to Stephanie.

Mad he could take. In fact, he kind of liked that Stephanie had found a new group of people to love and support her and be on her side. It warmed his heart and soothed a little of the fear he'd been carrying around since they returned home. His girl wasn't alone, that was all that mattered to him. While he ached to be the one who was there for her, by her side, holding her as she traversed her way through the aftermath of her ordeal, the important thing was that she wasn't doing it alone.

"So what's the intervention for?" he asked as he went back to the couch and dropped down onto it. There was nothing he needed an intervention for. He was doing what he felt was best for someone who meant the world to him. Trick didn't necessarily expect his friends to get that. How could they? They hadn't been there in that room while he'd been chained to the wall and unable to do a single thing to prevent Stephanie from suffering unimaginable horrors.

"The girls think you need to hurry up and get your head on straight," Scorpion informed him as the guys and Beth took seats in his living room.

"What makes them think it's not on straight?"

"You're here, and Stephanie is in the hospital," Rock answered simply.

"The girls don't get it. They can't." It wasn't meant as an insult, Trick loved every single one of those women like a sister, there wasn't anything he wouldn't do for them, but they simply didn't understand.

"Then help us get it," Panther said. "We want to understand. We know you like her, a lot, so why aren't you there with her?"

"Are you worried she doesn't feel the same way?" Tank asked when Trick didn't say anything.

"No. I know she has feelings for me," he said softly. It had been written all over her face when she'd watched him walk away from her, it had been evident in the way she clung to him the entire plane ride home. What they had been through together had created a bond that could have grown into something more if he hadn't thrown it all away when he walked away.

"Then what?" Axe asked, a hint of frustration in his tone. It was obvious that Axe couldn't comprehend walking away from the woman who had captured your heart. Despite Beth's attempt to hold him at arm's length, Axe hadn't budged. He gave her space, but he always made sure she knew he was right there. All she had to do was reach out and touch him.

Frustration buzzed inside him as well. Did they really need him to spell it out for them? Were they that stupid they couldn't get why he couldn't be there for his woman when every single cell in his body cried out for her?

"What?" he growled. "I'll tell you what. I stood there like a useless hunk of flesh while an innocent woman was beaten, cut, maimed, and raped. I did nothing to help her, nothing to stop it. Nothing. And through it all she wouldn't beg me to make it stop, wouldn't even scream or cry out in pain, all because she actually seemed to understand that it was as hard for me as it was for her. How can she possibly heal with me there?"

They all sat there, frozen, staring at him in shock at his outburst. Outbursts had been part of who he was as a child carrying around so much anger, but his team rarely saw him lose control like that.

In the end, it was Beth who scooted closer to him on the couch, and tentatively reached out a trembling hand to place on his shoulder. "I don't think you're scared about Stephanie blaming you," she whispered in that soft way of hers. Even though Beth never raised her voice, when she spoke, there was something about her that made you listen. "I think that you blame yourself, so you're punishing yourself. It's easier to push her away and pretend that you don't deserve her than to allow her to offer you the same comfort you would give her." As she spoke, Beth's gaze darted to Axe, and he had a feeling she was actually speaking to both of them not just to him.

Trick blamed himself, absolutely. But was Beth right? Was he staying away because he wanted to punish himself? And in doing so was he really punishing both himself and Stephanie?

∾

February 6th
   1:22 P.M.

It was here.

Release day.

As soon as the nurse returned to the room with the discharge papers, Stephanie would be walking out of the hospital.

Crazy as it sounded, she was almost as scared as she was happy to be getting out. Being there was like being in limbo. It was like she was back from Liberia but wasn't home. Even though she knew it wasn't possible to stay in the hospital forever, nor did she want to, there was an element of safety that being there gave her.

An element she would soon have to give up.

Already, her friends had gone to her house to prepare it for her arrival and make sure it was well stocked with food, fruits and veggies, and plenty of comfort food. They'd ensured there were fresh sheets on the bed and clean towels in the bathroom. They'd made sure there was toilet paper, and laundry powder, and detergent for the dishwasher, all the practical little things so she didn't have to worry about them.

Her place had also been fitted out with what she suspected was an absolutely top-of-the-line security system, too.

Protesting the system had quickly become pointless. It had only taken her a few minutes of listening to her new friends' absolute determination to make sure that she felt safe in her home to make her realize she may as well just give in because it was already a foregone conclusion.

Not that she was really complaining. The system would help her to feel safe.

Well, safer at least.

Nothing was ever going to make her feel completely safe ever again.

But at least this would help, and she was willing to take any bit of help she could get.

After talking the other day with Piper and the girls, Stephanie couldn't imagine how she would get through this without them. It helped so much knowing they actually understood what she was going through. They had encouraged her to reach out to her other friends, and she had, and been overwhelmed by their response. Everyone was being so nice to her, so supportive, and as much as she appreciated it something was still missing.

Someone was still missing.

Determinedly she shoved away all thoughts of Patrick. He had made his position clear. He wasn't willing to give what might be between them a chance. Unlike her new friends, she didn't believe he was going to get his head on straight and come to her, so she had to find a way to be okay with that.

"You ready to get out of here?" Tillie asked as they waited for the nurse to return.

"Yep." Stephanie tried to inject enthusiasm into her voice, but judging from the expression on Tillie's face she had failed big time.

"You know," Tillie said slowly. "When I got shot, I sent Gabriel away when I woke up. I was angry, scared, and confused, and he had lied to me. I didn't know how to be in the same room as him and not want to simultaneously yell at him for hurting me and climb into his lap and beg him to hold me and never let me go."

They'd talked in depth about the horrors these women had lived through, and honestly, Stephanie thought every single one of them was a superhero. These women were brave, strong, tough, and fiercely loyal. They loved with huge open hearts and didn't hesitate to support one another. She was beginning to understand in a very real way that Prey was one big family, and she had apparently been accepted into the fold. That these women hadn't held back in talking about the traumas had helped her so much. It made her not feel so alone.

"Patrick never betrayed me though," she reminded Tillie. She totally got though why her friend had felt like she needed space to sort through her emotions after everything she and Tank had gone through. But their situations weren't exactly the same.

"Didn't he?" Tillie asked. "You know that, and I know that, but does he know that? Or does he think that he let you down in the worst possible way?"

Stephanie's brow scrunched. She hadn't thought of that. She thought she had convinced Patrick that she didn't blame him for anything that had happened. But maybe his own guilt wouldn't allow him to believe it. There was nothing else she could say or do to convince him, especially if he wasn't even prepared to give her a chance.

Before she could comment, the nurse breezed into the room with the discharge papers, and fifteen minutes later, she was walking outside for the first time in over a week. The fresh air on her skin felt delightful even if it was freezing cold with a hint of snow. The overcast day was nothing special, just another winter day, but to her it felt like a new beginning of sorts. As terrified as she was, this was her life now. This new person that she was discovering beneath the layers of pain and trauma was the new Stephanie, a woman who, if nothing else, was a survivor.

Just because she had no idea how she would navigate her new world didn't mean she wasn't going to figure it out.

Time would help, the support of her friends would, too. Maybe with each passing day her future would become a little clearer. Stephanie wasn't excited about this journey she found herself facing, but whether she wanted to or not she had to travel it. The only other option was giving up and letting herself die, and she knew she couldn't do that. If she did, it would make everything she had endured for nothing.

"Happy to be out?" Tillie asked.

"Happy, sad, scared, you name it, I'm probably feeling it right now," she admitted. It wasn't easy to talk about her feelings, not after everything her ex had put her through, but Tillie and the others had been so open with her that she felt she owed it to them to be the same. They had bared their souls, their deepest secrets, their darkest pain, all for her. What kind of coward would she be if she hid hers from them?

"It will get better. I know it doesn't seem like it, but it really will. It will never go away, but learning to live with it will become easier," Tillie assured her. "Gabriel is parked down the street. Do you want to walk, or do you want me to text and ask him to come get us here?"

"Let's walk," she replied. The fresh air would do her good, and she had a feeling once she reached home it was going to take her a while to gather enough confidence to make her way outside again. The scars she carried weren't ones she could hide, and she wasn't ready for the world to see her like this. It was different at the hospital, everyone was dealing with something, but out there in the real world, where people would look at her, pity her, wonder about what had happened to her and if she deserved it ... that she wasn't ready to face yet.

Side by side, she and Tillie walked from the hospital's front doors down the street to where Tank was parked and waiting for them. She appreciated so much that these new friends of hers had made sure she had company around the clock while she was in the hospital, and she appreciated even more that they wanted to keep that going once she was home.

But Stephanie knew she had to learn to stand on her own two feet.

Facts were no one could stay with her every second for the rest of her life. If she didn't learn how to be okay by herself now, she was only creating a safety net that sooner or later was going to disappear.

May as well just get it over and done with.

Besides, the only safety net she really wanted she couldn't have. It made her feel guilty that these women weren't enough to soothe her fears, not completely, not in the way Patrick was. As much as it hurt that he had walked away from her, she couldn't really be all that angry with him. After all, he had lived the ordeal along with her, he was suffering, too.

Just because he was trained to go through things like what had happened to them in Liberia, it didn't mean he wasn't still a human being. He had feelings and emotions, and she knew he had to be struggling to come to terms with it all just like she was.

That was the worst part, knowing they were both suffering and that what they needed was each other. She wanted to soothe and comfort Patrick every bit as much as she longed to have him soothe and comfort her.

The loud honk of a horn drew her attention a split second before Tillie screamed her name.

Snapping her head to the side, she saw that she had been lost in thought, stepped out onto the road without looking, and a car was barreling down upon her with no time to jump out of its path.

CHAPTER

Twenty-Two

February 6th
   2:02 P.M.

He wasn't going to get to her in time.

That horrifying realization almost took Trick to his knees.

Coward that he was, he'd come to the hospital but been unable to make himself go to Stephanie's room. Just because he had, as the girls put it, finally gotten his head on straight, it didn't mean it wasn't already too late. He was all too aware that he could have blown any chance he could have had with her.

But just because he couldn't go inside, it didn't mean he could leave.

Especially knowing that if he waited near Tank's car, he'd get a glimpse of his girl.

The moment he saw her he'd felt ... peace. That was the only way to describe it. Something inside him had settled and he'd known it wasn't too late. All he had to do was explain to her why he'd been stupid enough to try not to even give them a chance, and he knew he could make her understand.

Just like he'd known it would, the second he saw her he was unable to stay away. Something was drawing him toward her, and he had already been out of his car before realizing what he was doing.

That was the only reason he at least had a shot at reaching her.

It wasn't an accident.

The car was aiming right for her. She'd stepped out onto the street to cross, but even if she hadn't, the driver would have got her.

Tires screeched.

Tillie screamed Stephanie's name.

Trick made a sound that he could only describe as a wounded howl of pain because the woman he was falling in love with was a split second away from being mowed down.

Since he wasn't sure he could make it in time, Trick did the only thing he could. He threw himself at her. His body collided with hers, and he took her to the ground just as the car whizzed past mere millimeters from their tangled limbs.

Although he'd angled his body as they'd fallen so he took the brunt of the fall, he heard Stephanie's grunt of pain. As much as he hated knowing he'd caused her pain it could have been so much worse.

The squeal of tires followed by a gunshot and then a crash told him everything he needed to know. Tank had taken care of the threat. He'd seen the same thing he had, that it wasn't an accident, the driver had been aiming at her, and it was an intentional hit and run that would be passed off as an accident.

"You okay, honey? Are you hurt?" he asked, gripping Stephanie to him tighter than was strictly necessary, but his heart hammered in his chest, and he could hardly breathe.

"Patrick?" she stammered.

One second, he was holding her in his arms, reveling in the feel of her alive and in one piece, and the next she was shoving at his chest and trying to scramble away from him.

Letting her go wasn't easy, but he was the one who had created this distance between them, so he had no choice but to acquiesce.

"H-hurt? I ... no. I don't th-think s-so. I s-stepped into the s-street," Stephanie stammered, her face five shades past pale. "I'm s-sorry."

"That car was aiming right for you," Tillie said, wrapping her arms around Stephanie as she turned terrified eyes to him.

Soothing either of their feelings wasn't going to be productive. "Yeah, it was."

"But ... what ... who?" Stephanie asked, the shakes settling in.

"Tank?" he called out.

"Yeah, it's her," Tank replied.

"It's who?" Stephanie asked, looking over her shoulder to where Tank was dragging a woman around their age out of a car. "Wait ... is that ... Misha? She was Duncan's wife. Duncan was on Chris' team. I didn't meet them often, but a couple of times he convinced me to tag along to a team barbecue."

This wasn't something that should be shared outside the circle of those with the appropriate security clearance, but Stephanie had almost died because of this, she deserved to know that it was over now, that she was safe. Tillie didn't need to hear it, but he guessed he had about as much chance of convincing her to leave her friend as he did asking her to grow wings.

"It is, honey. Duncan and Misha were dirty. Working with the Liberian militia. Duncan was the reason the SEAL team was ambushed, he just never expected to be double-crossed and killed along with his teammates."

Brows furrowed, she tore her gaze from Misha who was being cuffed and put in the back of Tank's car. "Misha knew I was going to Mexico. She checks in on all of Chris' teammates' families."

"She knew where my team and I lived, too. She came with cookies to thank us for trying to save her husband and his team not long after they were killed," he explained. They'd discovered all of this just over the last couple of days, but it had helped to make sense of things, and with Duncan dead, he'd known that once Misha was apprehended there would be no threat left hanging over Stephanie's head, and he could relax a little.

"It was because of her we were taken," Stephanie said softly, her trembling increasing.

His hands ached to reach for her, but he knew she wasn't ready for that yet. He might not be the enemy, but he wasn't an ally either. He'd hurt her in leaving and had to prove that he would never walk away again.

Clenching his hands into fists, he nodded his agreement. "Yeah, it's Misha's fault. But she can't hurt you again, darlin'. I promise. Steph, can I take you home?"

At his question, she went completely still. "Tillie and Tank were taking me."

"Tank has Misha in the back of his car, he needs to stay here till the cops come." Not exactly true, he could easily move the woman to his vehicle and wait for the cops, but he wasn't above using anything at his disposal to convince Stephanie to spend time with him. Really, they should all stay and give statements, but his girl needed to get home, the cops could question her later.

"Umm ..." She drew it out, obviously conflicted. Trick could tell a part of her wanted to say yes because, whether she realized it or not, her body had drifted toward his as though pulled by the same force that drew him toward her. Abruptly she straightened, her gaze zeroing in on his hands. "Your hands are shaking."

"Of course they are. I almost lost you. I don't think I'll ever forget the fear I felt knowing I might not get to you in time."

Her mouth parted in a silent O, and then she blinked, gave her head a shake and turned to Tillie. "Do you mind if I go home with Patrick?"

The knot in his chest eased a bit to hear her call him Patrick and not Trick. He hoped that meant there was still hope, still a chance.

"Don't mind at all, so long as you're okay," Tillie replied.

Sure she wasn't ready for him to touch her yet, Trick led the way to his car, so very aware of Stephanie trailing along behind him.

Once they were both in the car and buckled in, and he had pulled out into the traffic he found he didn't know what to say. All he wanted to do was stare at her. Even with the shock she'd just suffered, she looked good, the wounds on her face were healing, and she looked stronger than she had in Liberia now that she'd been eating and drinking properly.

"So, are you ... okay?" he asked tentatively.

For a moment, Stephanie looked at him like he was crazy, then a dam inside her seemed to crack and then break wide open because her expression turned desperate. "You left me. You left me. You left me," she repeated her voice growing louder each time until she was shouting it.

Pain lanced his chest. "I know, honey, I'm so sorry."

"Why?" she asked brokenly, with so much vulnerability his heart shattered.

"Because I didn't want to hurt you."

"I don't understand. I'm trying to. I really am. Because I know it wasn't my ordeal, it was our ordeal, and you're hurting, too. I thought I understood that when we got home you were leaving, but I didn't. When you left me, it hurt so much, I wanted so badly to beg you to stay."

"Why didn't you?"

"In case you said no," she said softly.

"Say no?" he repeated incredulously. "Why on earth would I say no?"

Lifting her hand, she brushed it across one of the healing wounds on her cheek. "Because of this. Because I'm damaged now. Because I was raped and I don't know if I can be with a man, because I'm ugly, because—"

"Stop," he shouted, unable to listen to her talk about herself like that a second longer. "You are perfect, and beautiful, and so compassionate it makes you even more beautiful. You're my superhero. What you did for me in that cell ... I can't ever repay that. No one has ever put me first like that before. Only you, my sweet, brave, beautiful girl, only you."

"So why did you leave?" she asked on what was dangerously close to a sob. If she broke down in tears now it would destroy him.

"Because I couldn't bear to see you hate me," he admitted.

"Hate you? How could I ever hate you?"

"Because it's my fault you were hurt," he roared, slamming his fists into the steering wheel.

"I told you I didn't blame you."

"I blame me."

"You stayed away out of guilt?"

"Yeah, darlin'. It was hell. I needed you, knew you needed me, but I don't deserve you, honey."

"I get to decide what I deserve," she said on a huff. "I thought ... I thought it was me. That you didn't come because a man like you wouldn't want a woman like me."

"Never heard anything so ridiculous in my life. You're way out of my league, darlin'. But I guess I finally got my head on straight."

"What does that mean exactly?"

"It means if you'll have me, I'm yours. Forever."

~

February 6th
2:36 P.M.

"Oh ..." Stephanie breathed. Not the answer she had been expecting at all.

What had she expected?

Possibly an admission that he liked her. An apology for leaving she had hoped. But she hadn't expected him to tell her that he was hers for the rest of their lives.

Patrick had to mean something else ... but what?

"I don't understand." She rubbed at her temples with both hands. Her doctors and nurses had encouraged her to use her bad hand as much as she was able to, and although she didn't like looking at it—it was a horrible visual reminder of her ordeal—her finger wasn't going to regrow itself so she had to get used to it.

"What's not to understand, honey?" The smile he gave her was amused, but there was lingering doubt and uncertainty in his eyes that she couldn't ignore. Patrick might have been putting on a good front, but it was just that: a front. Underneath, he was every bit as unsure about her as she was about him.

She knew what she felt, what she wanted. She wanted the two of them to spend time together, she wanted them to help one another heal, but she also wanted to get to know this man and see what could be.

But it was too soon for talk of forever.

Wasn't it?

"We hardly know each other. There is no possible way for you to know that you want to be with me for the rest of your life," she said.

"Isn't there?"

"Of course not. It's ridiculous."

"It's instalove."

That dragged a surprised laugh out of her. "Instalove?"

"Yeah, in those romance novels Ariel and Tillie are always reading."

"Sounds like you've been reading them if you know about instalove," Stephanie teased. For the first time since Patrick had walked away, she felt like she could breathe normally. He was here and somehow that meant everything was going to be okay.

Patrick shrugged. "What can I say? The best way to keep a woman happy in bed is to know exactly what she wants. Couldn't think of a better way to find that out than reading books mostly written by women for women. I thought I didn't want forever, or maybe I felt like I wasn't good enough for it, but that all changed when I met you. No one has ever put my needs before their own. Not once. My team, we watch each other's backs, but you ..." He huffed out a breath, and she got the feeling he was attempting to rein in his emotions. "You just put me first because you wanted to, because you cared, because you understood me. That was when I knew. You were mine."

"Yours?" she echoed, feeling like she was in a dream. A wonderful, magical dream she never wanted to end.

"You know, it's actually pretty alpha of me to know what I want and go after it. You. You're what I want. What I learned this last week is that I can't live without you."

"But to already say forever?" As much as she wanted this to be real, she couldn't help a molecule of doubt.

"People date for years and still divorce," he reminded her. "I know in my heart that you're it for me, but if you're unsure I'll wait, convince you that you can't live without me."

"I can't live without you," she murmured.

A slow smile curled up his lips. "So you're mine? Forever?"

Did she really want to hold back on principle? And if she did, what was the appropriate amount of time before you could declare your undying love? A month? A year? Did it really matter?

She knew.

Had known since he so tenderly took care of her, and she felt his guilt and regret rolling off him in waves.

Patrick Kramer was hers.

"Forever," she agreed. "You're mine forever. And I'm yours."

"Damn, I wish I wasn't driving right now because if I wasn't, I would be kissing you like I never intended to stop," he said as he grabbed her hand and pulled it to his lips, kissing the inside of her wrist over and over again as though he couldn't get enough of it.

The kisses were soft, sweet, tender, and full of the love he felt for her, and they ignited a throbbing between her legs.

Obviously interpreting her lack of response as her having a bad reaction to his words, Patrick tried to backpedal. "We don't have to kiss, darlin', not till you're ready. We go at your pace, I promise, I won't rush you. I don't care if all we do is hold hands, or sit beside each other, I just need to be with you."

And that right there was why she knew.

"I care," she said softly.

"Care about what, honey?"

"I care if all we do is hold hands or sit beside each other. I need you, too. All of you."

"There's no rush, darlin'. You've been through so much, you need to give yourself time to heal."

"You said it yourself. Sometimes you just know. What that man did to me, it wasn't my choice, but with you it absolutely is. He took something from me I didn't think I could get back. I didn't think I could ever look at sex the same way again, and I can't. But with you it wouldn't be sex, it would simply be us, me and you, making love."

Patrick groaned, and she knew he was trying to cling to control. "Are you sure, honey? Because I didn't come to you for sex."

"I'm sure." Weird thing was she was absolutely positive. Every inch of her body, heart, and soul craved Patrick.

His grip on her hand tightened, and neither spoke for the rest of the drive, too preoccupied with the energy humming through the vehicle. Patrick seemed to know where he was going, and ten minutes later, they were pulling up at her sweet little house.

It felt good to be back there, mostly because she wasn't alone, she had the person she wanted the most in the world there by her side. Patrick turned off the engine, rounded the car, and lifted her into his arms, carrying her up the front path and inside.

Inside smelled like fresh flowers and homemade cookies, and she saw both sitting on her kitchen counters. Tears stung her eyes, these new friends of hers thought of everything. They'd taken such good care of her, and she could never repay their kindness, not in a million years.

"Are you sure?" Patrick asked her again as he headed upstairs.

"If you back out now, I might have to take care of my needs myself," she retorted, making him laugh. Stephanie would be lying if she said she wasn't nervous because she was. There was a chance that just because she believed this was what she wanted, her mind might have other ideas and throw up roadblocks. But the thing was, if that was what happened then she already knew Patrick would deal with it and not make her feel bad.

"If you change your mind, I'll stop," he said as he reached her room and laid her on the bed.

Stephanie smiled up at him. "I know."

"I'm going to make love to every inch of your delectable body," he murmured.

His touch was soft, gentle, and reverent as he stroked the pad of a fingertip lightly over the healing wounds on her cheeks. Following his finger were his lips as he kissed each cut, soothing away a little of the horror of how they had been inflicted.

Leaving the hospital, she had dressed for comfort not style, and beneath her zippered hoodie, she wasn't wearing a bra. As he eased down the zipper Patrick sucked in a breath as he bared her naked chest.

"Mmm, so pretty," he said softly as he swirled a fingertip over first one of her nipples and then the other. The gentle touch had them pebbling, and the throbbing between her legs intensified.

While she knew he had seen her naked every second of those days they spent locked in that underground prison, this was different. So very different. It felt like the first time, even as she knew it wasn't.

Like he'd done with her face, his lips followed everywhere his fingers touched. He pressed the lightest of kisses to each of her nipples, and then he stroked and kissed every one of the lingering greenish-yellow bruises.

Each touch seemed to soothe something inside her. It couldn't take away what had been done, couldn't change it, but it could help it heal. Healing would be a long and bumpy journey, full of ups and downs, but Stephanie was certain that together she and Patrick could traverse it and come out the other side.

"So soft," Patrick whispered against her skin as he trailed a line of kisses down her stomach, stopping at the waistband of her leggings. "Cat leggings," he chuckled as he hooked his fingers into the waistband with one hand while his other slipped behind her back and lifted her so he could pull the leggings and her panties over her hips. "I remember you telling me they're your favorite animal when you almost became breakfast for a leopard."

"Always wanted a cat, but we couldn't afford a pet growing up." Then as an adult, she'd been too busy with college and building her business to take on the responsibility of a pet. Maybe now would be a good time though, while she spent the next few weeks and months recovering.

"We can get a cat if you want one," Patrick said as he tossed her leggings and panties aside, leaving her spread out naked before him.

There was no embarrassment since they had been naked together before, and from the way his appreciative gaze roamed her body as though she were a buffet, and he didn't know where he wanted to begin, she couldn't even think that her cuts and bruises made her less attractive to him. With Patrick, she would always feel beautiful, and because he thought she was beautiful that would always be enough.

Climbing onto the bed with her, he picked up her bandaged hand and touched a kiss right above where her nicely healing stump was. Tears pricked at her eyes, but she smiled up at him, with soft kisses and featherlight touches, he was healing her in a way he didn't even know.

When he settled between her spread legs there was no fear, only wonder as he leaned in and pressed a kiss against her center.

"So beautiful," he whispered, his breath warm against her wet flesh and she shuddered as delightful little tremors shot through her body.

This time, his fingers followed his lips, and he began to trace circles around her entrance. His touch was slow and lazy like he had all the time in the world to enjoy her. But for her, each touch just wound her tighter, drove her higher, and she wanted to beg him for more.

Somehow, she restrained herself, positive that Patrick needed this to heal every bit as much as she did.

Still, when the tip of his finger finally slipped inside her, she sucked in a breath. Then when his lips found her needy, throbbing little bud and closed around it, she knew she was drifting up to heaven.

His tongue swirled against her bundle of nerves, and inside her his finger stroked in a steady rhythm, going deeper each time. It was wonderful. The most perfect thing ever.

A gasp fell from her lips when he added a second finger, every muscle in her body felt so tight, begging for a release. Still Patrick took his time, stroking, licking, sucking, making her feel the most wonderful things.

As his teeth scraped across her bud, Stephanie exploded, coming hard on his fingers and his lips. It felt ... there weren't even words to describe those amazing feelings, feelings she clung to, not ready to let them go yet.

When she finally floated back down to earth, she found Patrick watching her with a tender smile, but when she reached out to him, intending to strip him of his clothes, he grabbed her wrist and kissed each of her fingertips.

"Uh uh, darlin'. That was only round one. I intend to make you come a whole lot more before I let you touch me. I'm going to make you come with just my mouth, then with just my fingers, then I might watch while you touch yourself so I can memorize just how you like it."

With anyone other than Patrick, she would be mortified to touch herself with them watching, but this was Patrick, and he had declared himself hers forever, and somehow that meant there was no embarrassment between them.

Only love.

Only warmth.

Only safety and strength.

Only perfection.

CHAPTER

Twenty-Three

February 7th
  8:14 A.M.

"Is it my turn yet?" Stephanie whined.

Well, it was more of a breathy moan as he thrust his fingers deep inside her, making her suck in an uneven breath as her hips flew off the bed seeking more.

"Pretty sure I've given you a turn, pretty girl," he teased as he pressed the pad of his thumb hard against her bundle of nerves making her gasp. Actually, they'd had sex twice the day before, but both times he'd had her coming down from a high before he'd plunged inside her. It wasn't that he didn't want her hands on him, or her mouth for that matter, it was that this was all about her. There was no better feeling in the world than knowing he was taking care of his girl in every area that mattered.

"I want ..." Her words fell away when he turned his fingers inside her so he could brush them against the spot he knew would drive her wild. Trick had learned exactly what his girl liked, he touched, he'd tasted, he watched as she touched herself, and he'd memorized all of it.

He knew how much pressure it took to push her over the edge, he knew every nuance of her expression and body language, knew how long he could keep her hovering on the edge before tumbling off it. Knew each breathy moan, each gasp, each hitch of her breath as she was worked higher and higher.

Knew it all and was utterly obsessed.

Never before had he been inclined to spend more than a couple of days at most with a woman, but this woman truly was his forever. He could never get tired of her, she was addicting, she was perfection, and she was all his.

"What do you want, darlin'?" he asked as he increased the pace of his thrusts and the pressure of his thumb simultaneously. As much as he loved tasting her, having her come all over his tongue, he loved this, too. Balancing on one elbow above her, being able to watch her, all beautiful and flushed in the throes of pleasure as he touched her, brought him pleasure.

"More ... you ..." she panted, so close to coming he could feel it.

"Here you go, my sweet, beautiful girl." Pressing hard against her bud, he felt her entire body tremble, then her internal muscles clamped around his fingers as her orgasm hit. Throughout it, he kept touching, kept stroking, wanting to make it as good for her as he could.

When he felt nothing more than the occasional ripple of pleasure he slid on a condom, lined himself up, and thrust into her in one smooth move.

Heavy-lidded eyes looked up at him, and her plump pink lips were curved into a lazy smile as he set a steady pace. Practice meant he knew just how to position himself so he could build another orgasm inside her. Coming at the same time as Stephanie was absolutely his favorite thing in the world.

Her good hand lifted to press her palm to his chest, right above his heart, but he grabbed it, pulled it away, and reached for her other hand and pressed that to his chest. Trick wanted her to know that what he loved most about her was her bravery and strength, her maimed hand was a reminder of both. Yes, it was also a reminder of her pain, her suffering, but he wanted them both to focus on the fact that they had survived, and that out of that darkness had grown the most beautiful of things.

Their love.

Reaching for her good hand, he brought it with his to where their bodies were joined. Linking their fingers together, he brought both their thumbs to her bud and began to circle it just the way she liked.

"Mmm, Patrick, that's ... perfect," she mumbled through a haze of mounting pleasure.

Pleasure was building inside him, too, he could feel it but held it back, no way was he coming until they were riding that wave together.

"You're perfect, honey. Complete and utter perfection."

Her cheeks turned the prettiest shade of pink, and he couldn't hold off any longer. Pressing both their thumbs harder against her bundle of nerves, Trick thrust faster into her, and a moment later they reached the peak.

"Patrick," his name fell from her lips as her body trembled and then clamped around him for the second time in minutes.

Watching bliss fill her face, he let himself go, coming harder than he ever had before.

"I didn't know it could be that good," Stephanie mumbled against his lips when he leaned down to kiss her.

"It's love, darlin'." It was the first time he'd said the L word out loud. He'd said he wanted her forever, but something—fear, he guessed —had held him back from actually telling her that he loved her, and not in a silly instalove analogy. "I love you, Stephanie, do you know that?" he asked as he smoothed a curl off her damp cheek and tucked it behind her ear.

The most beautiful smile lit up her entire face. "I love you, too, Patrick. Do you know that?"

"Yeah, honey. I know. I feel it." In a place deep inside. He'd never been loved before, not by his parents, not by the women who kept his bed warm, only ever by this woman and it was the most amazing feeling in the world.

From here on out his job was to protect this woman, take care of her, and make sure nothing ever hurt her again. And to that end, he hadn't done all of that yet this morning.

"Come on, let me clean you up and then feed you. I've already eaten this morning so it's only fair we get some food into you."

Stephanie laughed as he pulled out of her and swatted at his shoulder even as she blushed. "Waking me up with your head between my legs and your mouth on me is not eating. We both need some breakfast."

"Best meal of the day, I can assure you. Can't wait for seconds," he teased as he scooped her up and carried her into the bathroom. Last night they'd made good use of the shower, and he couldn't wait to run her a bubble bath later, but right now he really did need to feed her. Her body was still healing, and to do that it needed fuel.

After wiping her down with a warm washcloth, he pulled on a pair of sweatpants, and Stephanie put on a pair of leggings and one of his hoodies. Damn, he liked the sight of her in his clothes, it made him feel all possessive, and it was hard to keep his hands off her and not strip her naked again and have his way with her.

"Food, you need food," he muttered as he grabbed her hand and pulled her along down the stairs with him.

Before they made it to the kitchen, Stephanie's doorbell rang, and he diverted them toward the door. He was expecting the guys and their women later as they brought a surprise for Stephanie, but not this early.

Early morning visits were never a good thing.

Ever.

Solemn faces met him as he answered the door. The girls weren't there, but cradled in Axe's arms was the tiny gray bundle he'd asked them to bring.

"What's wr—" Stephanie broke off as she saw what Axe was holding. "Is that a kitten?"

"Your kitten," he corrected as Axe handed over the little gray fuzzball.

"You got it for me?" she asked in wonder as the kitten let out a small mew and immediately snuggled into her.

"Taking a page out of Mouse's book. A story for another day," he added as her expression turned confused. "You always wanted a pet, now you have one." The smile on her face as she looked from the kitten in her arms to him was everything he had hoped it to be, and he just wished this moment wasn't about to be ruined by whatever news the guys had brought with them.

"What's wrong?" he asked as he ushered his girl and her kitten over to the couch.

The guys followed him inside, locking up behind him, and once they were all seated, Stephanie looked around at them. "Should I go?"

"Stay," Axe said before Trick could reply. "This is about Beth, about what happened to her, it's about our Bravo Team family, and you're a part of that now. The others already know."

"Know what?" Trick asked again. Whatever it was was bad, he could tell that, but he needed to know how bad.

"The blood we found in the farmhouse, the tests came back," Axe explained.

It felt like a lifetime ago that he and his team had raided the farmhouse, hoping to find Sarah and bring her back with them where she would be safe from Leonid Baranov. Instead, all they'd found was the woman's blood smeared all over the kitchen.

"The blood didn't belong to Sarah," Axe announced.

"Huh? Then whose is it?" Had Sarah managed to kill whoever had been sent to kidnap her and then fled, not knowing where to go to be safe?

"DNA tests say that the blood belongs to a relative of Sarah's," Axe told him. "A female relative. A daughter. We think that whoever kidnapped Sarah from the farmhouse killed her daughter in front of her to gain her compliance."

That opened up a whole new world of questions they didn't have answers to. Who was the father of Sarah's child? Was it Leonid Baranov? Someone else? Where was Sarah now? Was she still alive? Why kill her daughter when Baranov could easily have taken the child along with him, and either used her himself or sold her to another sick monster?

Pulling Stephanie into his arms, Trick held her tightly as he worried about the biggest question of all. What did it all mean for Beth, Axe, and the rest of Bravo Team?

Can Panther make room in his and his son's life for a single mother and her traumatized daughter in the fifth book in the action packed and emotionally charged Prey Security: Bravo Team series!

Buried Scars (Prey Security: Bravo Team #5

Also by Jane Blythe

Detective Parker Bell Series

Count to Ten Series

Broken Gems Series

CRUSHED RUBY

FRACTURED DIAMOND

SHATTERED AMETHYST

SPLINTERED EMERALD

SALVAGING MARIGOLD

River's End Rescues Series

COCKY SAVIOR

SOME REGRETS ARE FOREVER

SOME FEARS CAN CONTROL YOU

SOME LIES WILL HAUNT YOU

SOME QUESTIONS HAVE NO ANSWERS

SOME TRUTH CAN BE DISTORTED

SOME TRUST CAN BE REBUILT

SOME MISTAKES ARE UNFORGIVABLE

Candella Sisters' Heroes Series

LITTLE DOLLS

LITTLE HEARTS

LITTLE BALLERINA

Storybook Murders Series

NURSERY RHYME KILLER

FAIRYTALE KILLER

FABLE KILLER

Saving SEALs Series

SAVING RYDER

SAVING ERIC

SAVING OWEN

SAVING LOGAN

SAVING GRAYSON

SAVING CHARLIE

Prey Security Series

PROTECTING EAGLE

PROTECTING RAVEN

PROTECTING FALCON

PROTECTING SPARROW

PROTECTING HAWK

PROTECTING DOVE

Prey Security: Alpha Team Series

DEADLY RISK

LETHAL RISK

EXTREME RISK

FATAL RISK

COVERT RISK

SAVAGE RISK

Prey Security: Artemis Team Series

IVORY'S FIGHT

PEARL'S FIGHT

LACEY'S FIGHT

OPAL'S FIGHT

Prey Security: Bravo Team Series

VICIOUS SCARS

RUTHLESS SCARS

BRUTAL SCARS

CRUEL SCARS

BURIED SCARS

Prey Security: Athena Team Series

FIGHTING FOR SCARLETT

Christmas Romantic Suspense Series

CHRISTMAS HOSTAGE

CHRISTMAS CAPTIVE

CHRISTMAS VICTIM

YULETIDE PROTECTOR

YULETIDE GUARD

YULETIDE HERO

HOLIDAY GRIEF

Conquering Fear Series (Co-written with Amanda Siegrist)

DROWNING IN YOU

OUT OF THE DARKNESS

CLOSING IN

About the Author

USA Today bestselling author Jane Blythe writes action-packed romantic suspense and military romance featuring protective heroes and heroines who are survivors. One of Jane's most popular series includes Prey Security, part of Susan Stoker's OPERATION ALPHA world! Writing in that world alongside authors such as Janie Crouch and Riley Edwards has been a blast, and she looks forward to bringing more books to this genre, both within and outside of Stoker's world. When Jane isn't binge-reading she's counting down to Christmas and adding to her 200+ teddy bear collection!

To connect and keep up to date please visit any of the following

Made in the USA
Monee, IL
14 April 2024

56929342R00142